4/30/15
#9.95

Oxford School Shakespeare

Coriolanus

Edited by

Roma Gill, OBE
M.A. *Cantab.*, B. Litt. *Oxon*

OXFORD
UNIVERSITY PRESS

PR
2805
.A2
G55
2012

OXFORD
UNIVERSITY PRESS

Great Clarendon Street, Oxford OX2 6DP

Oxford University Press is a department of the University of Oxford.
It furthers the University's objective of excellence in research,
scholarship, and education by publishing worldwide in

Oxford   New York

Auckland   Cape Town   Dar es Salaam   Hong Kong   Karachi
Kuala Lumpur   Madrid   Melbourne   Mexico City   Nairobi
New Delhi   Shanghai   Taipei   Toronto

With offices in

Argentina   Austria   Brazil   Chile   Czech Republic   France   Greece
Guatemala   Hungary   Italy   Japan   Poland   Portugal   Singapore
South Korea   Switzerland   Thailand   Turkey   Ukraine   Vietnam

Oxford is a registered trade mark of Oxford University Press
in the UK and in certain other countries

British Library Cataloguing in Publication Data

Data available

ISBN: 978-0-19-839037-4

10 9 8 7 6 5 4 3 2 1

Printed in Great Britain by Bell and Bain Ltd., Glasgow

MIX
Paper from
responsible sources
FSC
www.fsc.org   FSC® C007785

Cover artwork by Katherine Asher
Illustrations by Martin Cottam

For Ron
Oxford School Shakespeare
edited by Roma Gill

Macbeth
Much Ado About Nothing
Henry V
Romeo and Juliet
A Midsummer Night's Dream
Twelfth Night
Hamlet
The Merchant of Venice
Othello
Julius Caesar
The Tempest
The Taming of the Shrew
King Lear
As You Like It
Antony and Cleopatra
Measure for Measure
Henry IV Part I
The Winter's Tale
Coriolanus
Love's Labour's Lost
Richard II

Contents

The Times

Have you heard the news today? There's been a fresh outbreak of fighting, and the peace treaty (the one that was made the other day) has been broken. Drought is widespread, and grain is in short supply—although there are rumours that those in power have been stockpiling it for themselves. Politicians make speeches, but they don't understand what the ordinary people want. The gulf between rich and poor, 'haves' and 'have nots', is getting wider—and so is the generation gap: young and old don't have the same values any more.

This is the world today, that was the world yesterday—and the world of ancient Rome more than two thousand years ago. Nothing changes. History can teach its lessons, but history has no final solutions. The same issues must be confronted by every age in its own time, and settled, for a time, in its own way. But the processes of history can offer, always, some illumination.

The action of *Coriolanus* takes place around 500 BC. The last of the kings who have ruled over Rome ever since its foundation in *c.* 753 BC has been expelled, and Rome is now a republic—an *aristocratic* republic. All power is in the hands of the wealthy patricians, noble families descended from the original inhabitants of Rome, who have formed a national council or senate. The place of the king is taken by two consuls, patrician magistrates elected annually by members of the senate. Ordinary citizens, the plebeians, have very little power to begin with but soon find leaders and spokesmen in plebeian magistrates—the tribunes—appointed for their protection. Inevitably there are conflicts and struggles between the two classes, patricians and plebeians, the privileged and the unprivileged. These are interrupted only by national struggles against neighbours like the Volsces which are at first defensive but will become increasingly aggressive until, before the beginning of the first millennium AD, Rome becomes mistress of all Italy and conqueror of vast overseas territories. By this time, however, the internal fighting of her citizens will have developed into civil war and destroyed the republic.

In this fighting Shakespeare found an immediate link between the world of Coriolanus and his own seventeenth-century England

where, in 1607, the peasantry of the Midlands counties had joine
in riotous assemblies to protest against their patrician overlord
The following year, when he was writing his play, a cruel wint
brought further poor harvests. Hoarding and price-fixing force
the prices of corn ever higher, until the farm labourers i
Shakespeare's home town of Stratford-upon-Avon were driven t
complain that 'they were as good be slain in the market-place a
starve'.[1] Oppression by usurers with escalating lending rates wa
the first cause of the citizens' dissatisfaction in Shakespeare
source, 'The Life of Coriolanus' in Plutarch's *Lives of the Greel
and Romans*, but the dramatist chose instead to focus on
secondary cause—the corn shortages. In the first scene c
Coriolanus the Roman citizens, 'resolved rather to die than t
famish', give eloquent voice to their English counterparts, and t
the troubles of the poor and needy of all times, everywhere: 'Wha
authority surfeits on would relieve us. If they would yield us but th
superfluity while it were wholesome . . . '

The eternal relevance of the play invites its directors t
experiment with different period settings, but Shakespeare's actor
would have worn their own contemporary clothing. In this bool
the artist has drawn actors on Jacobean stages in Jacobean dress
and historical figures in imaginary settings wearing early Romar
costume. On the cover of the book Coriolanus appears to be
dressed in some military uniform of the nineteenth century, but the
white shifts of supplicants worn by the other characters—
Volumnia, Virgilia, and Young Martius—are timeless.

---

[1] J. M. M. Martin, *Midlands History*, 7 (1982), p. 30.

The People

Caius Martius A Roman warrior whose 'natural wit and great heart did marvellously stir up his courage to do and attempt notable acts' (Plutarch), but whose intolerance makes him incapable of living amicably with his fellow men—although he has close relationships with his mother and his wife. The name 'Martius' means 'pertaining to the god Mars', and the addition 'Coriolanus' was bestowed on him after his exploits in the battle against Corioles (*Act 1*, Scenes 4–10).

Volumnia The mother of Caius Martius, a widow who delights in her son's martial prowess and attempts to groom him for a career in politics.

Menenius Agrippa An elder statesman, described by Plutarch as one 'of the pleasantest old men and the most acceptable to the people'.

Cominius A Roman patrician, consul and high-ranking general.

Sicinius Velutus and **Junius Brutus** The tribunes of the people. Magistrates of plebeian birth, these were charged with the protection of the people against other magistrates and given the power of veto for this purpose. They could summon assemblies of the people to discuss public affairs and propose changes of the law, and their persons were inviolable.

Aufidius The Volscian rival of Caius Martius.

The Action

Act 3

Act 4

Act 5

Coriolanus: commentary

Act 1

There is much to be accomplished in this first act which, in modern editions, is divided into eleven scenes:

1 Rome: the citizens in revolt; Martius warns of Volscian threats
2 Corioles: Aufidius warns of threats from the Romans
3 Rome: at home with Volumnia
4 Martius outside Corioles
5 Romans in retreat
6 Romans victorious
7 Cominius and his troops retire
8 Corioles is secured
9 Martius encounters Aufidius
10 Martius named 'Coriolanus'
11 Antium: Aufidius wants revenge

} the war against the Volsces

Scene 1   In a city where the rich get richer and the poor die of starvation, the stage is suddenly filled with angry men—*hungry* men, wielding whatever weapons they can lay their hands on. The scene is set in ancient Rome (*c.* 490 BC), but the situation is only too familiar. The conflict is between rich and poor, those who have and those who have not. For one man the solution is simple: kill Caius Martius, 'chief enemy to the people', and 'we'll have corn at our own price'. There is a single dissentient voice—but there are no ears to listen. In a very few lines, Shakespeare has startled the audience into attention, demonstrated the power of mob hysteria, introduced different opinions of Caius Martius, the play's leading character, and opened up most of the major issues in the play.

The noisy arguments of the citizens are momentarily silence by the approach of Menenius Agrippa, 'one that hath always love the people'. He speaks to them easily, but he does not share th racy prose of their speech: his status as a patrician is revealed by h pentameter verse. At first his arguments make little headway, bu he seduces the mob into silence when he begins the fable of th belly. The belligerent First Citizen is suspicious—'you must nc think to fob off our disgrace with a tale'—but even he consent with some measure of impatience, to fit his speech to Meneniu blank verse and indulge the old man's humour in this well-know story. The heat seems to be going out of the situation when Caiu Martius arrives, although his full-throated vituperation seem calculated to stir up rather than pacify their resentment.

From Martius we learn that these are not the only dissatisfie citizens in Rome: others, in 'several places of the city', are cryin against the Senate with complaints of hunger and demands fo corn. They also seek representation in the governing body, and th granting of this has provoked Martius' present wrath. His politica philosophy sees it as the thin edge of a wedge which, in time, wil 'Win upon power', taking the opportunity to gain even greate force and find more cause for political unrest. Further debate i silenced, however, by the Messenger's announcement, confirmed by the Senators, that the Volsces are preparing for anothe onslaught, led by Tullus Aufidius, Martius' great rival.

War is welcome! Fighting an enemy provided an outlet fo energies which might otherwise be turned to crime anc insurrection, and such was a popular Roman solution fo domestic problems of unemployment and population control Many in Shakespeare's first audiences would have given thei approval! The citizens, who will of course become the commor soldiers, are less assured than the patricians—the officer classes. Ir Shakespeare's own stage direction, they 'steal away', incurring the scorn of Martius—although his epithet 'rats' has already been used by Menenius (line 159).

Martius leaves the scene with the patrician party and the stage is left to the two tribunes whose appointment Martius has so vehemently opposed. Their hatred of him is undisguised, and the scene ends—as it began—in opposition to the play's protagonist.

Scene 2 The Volsces preparing to attack Rome have learned of the Roman counter-offensive: both sides have their spies. Tullus Aufidius, like Martius, is in possession of more military intelligence than the Senators, and he is well informed also about the famine in Rome, the mutinous citizens, and the ambivalence of Roman feelings towards the man who is his great rival and enemy.

Scene 3   After the noisy public scenes of strife and strategy, we reach an oasis of domestic calm. The scene is of Shakespeare's own invention, although the details of Martius' upbringing were all supplied by Plutarch's narrative, which describes how Martius took a wife at his mother's desire, 'and yet never left his mother's house therefore'. Now we begin to understand the Citizen's observation that Martius' achievement has been all 'to please his mother and to be partly proud' (*1*, 1, 35).

Volumnia compelled her son to become the man he is. When he was still 'tender-bodied'—'a stripling', according to Plutarch—she sent him to find fame and honour in the wars; and delighted in his achievement (which she seems to measure in the number of wounds he has sustained). The feminine gentleness of Virgilia, her daughter-in-law, almost faints at the very mention of blood but conceals, nevertheless, a firm resolution that will not yield to the persuasions of her older companions. Valeria completes the female trilogy—mother, wife, and virgin. In this scene she appears to be contemporary with Volumnia, domestic in her interests, and somehow possessed of confidential information; later in the play her much-praised chastity (*5*, 3, 64–7) suggests that Shakespeare perhaps thought of her as a 'vestal virgin', an aristocratic priestess of Diana. Her chatter is expressed in a rapid prose, although Virgilia's speech retains something of a formal verse rhythm.

The conversation of these ladies, seemingly trivial enough, gives valuable information to audience and readers about the psychology of Martius: his upbringing, his conduct and strategy in the wars are described proudly by Volumnia and, unwittingly, by Valeria in her account of the child's pursuit of the butterfly. In the closing lines of the scene, Valeria gives essential information about the division of the Roman army under two commands to fight the Volsces in the battlefield and outside their main city of Corioles: 'They nothing doubt prevailing'.

Scenes 4–10   The 'butterfly' episode of the previous scene (lines 62–7) is re-enacted in the military manoeuvres of the next seven scenes whose action, apart from the single combat between Martius and Aufidius (Scene 9), is based on Plutarch's narrative.

Scene 4   In the Roman camp Martius quickly establishes his leadership over his co-commander, but the sudden surge of Volscian soldiers through the gates of Corioles takes the Romans by surprise, driving them away from the city and through one of the side doors of the stage—

Scene 5   —in order to enter again through the opposite door, followed by an irate Martius. His anger makes him almost incoherent, but it has the desired effect: the soldiers obviously support him as he beat back the next Volscian onslaught—though they will not go so far as to follow him inside the gates of Corioles and show no compassion when he is shut inside at the mercy of the enemy. Lartius is quick to believe that all hope is lost, and pronounces a clumsy (and premature) obituary eulogy—which is no sooner spoken than Martius shows himself, 'bleeding', on the city walls (the stage balcony). Rallied by Lartius, the Roman soldiers fight their way into the city where—

Scene 6   —military discipline is forgotten in an outbreak of looting which further incenses the still-bleeding Martius. While Lartius urges him to take rest, Martius is excited by the bloodshed: his own loss of blood is indeed 'physical' (medicinal) to him. His desire to show himself, thus wounded, to Aufidius will contrast, later, with his refusal to show himself with his scars to the citizens of Rome.

Scene 7   Unlike Martius, Cominius in retreat consoles and encourages his soldiers. The confusions of war bring contradictory reports, but the appearance of Martius, 'as he were flay'd', is reassuring. The relief is welcomed with near-hysterical delight, but Martius is eager to renew the fight (Cominius would have recommended 'a gentle bath') and rallies the troops with words of encouragement, urging patriotism and honour. Now these soldiers are enthusiastic, lifting Martius shoulder-high as though they would use *him* as their weapon: 'O, me alone! Make you a sword of me?'

Scene 8   Shakespeare's stage direction tells all: Corioles is secured, and Lartius with his army will now join Cominius. The scene is only necessary to allow time for Martius, the actor as well as the character, to prepare for his single combat with Aufidius in a scene devised by Shakespeare.

Scene 9   Plutarch observed that 'because of the many encounters between Martius and Aufidius, besides the common quarrel between them, there was bred a marvellous private hate one against the other'.

The duel is interrupted when certain Volsces come to the rescue of Aufidius.

Scene 10   The wounded Martius cannot endure to hear Cominius' long-winded commendations: he has done no more than his best—and even this is not good enough: 'He that has but effected his good will Hath overta'en mine act'. Rewards, as well as praises, he rejects, but the addition 'Coriolanus' flushes his face with pleasure. In his happiness he remembers the misery of a poor captive, once his host in Corioles—but the man cannot be saved: his name is forgotten. Suddenly Martius becomes conscious that he is tired, and his wounds are aching.

Scene 11   Aufidius takes the defeat personally, and is ashamed of his rescue by the Volscians. Suddenly revenge becomes more important than honour and, with a self-consciously crude expression that condemns his own act, he resolves to 'potch at [Martius] some way' so that 'wrath or craft may get him'.

Act 2

Triumph changes to disaster within three scenes as Coriolanus ventures into politics:

    1   Coriolanus returns triumphant from the battle

    2   Cominius presents Coriolanus to the Senators

    3   Coriolanus is elected—and denied

Scene 1   A proleptic—anticipatory—irony now becomes the characteristic mode of the play: every expression, whether of hope or fear, is denied emotional impact by the pre-knowledge of the audience/reader, observing with informed detachment.

    Waiting for news from the battlefront, Menenius provides comedy in his war of words with the two tribunes who tolerantly allow him to insult them as 'a brace of unmeriting, proud, violent, testy magistrates, alias fools' whilst characterizing himself as 'a humorous patrician'. The Roman ladies bring news that the audience already knows: the fighting is over and the conquering

hero is returning. He bears another garland—and several ne
wounds for Volumnia and Menenius to gloat over!

Trumpets herald the procession leading Martius to a victor
ovation—and elaborate stage directions indicate the presentatio
Shakespeare desires. Martius, who went to war as Cominiu
lieutenant, now returns 'Coriolanus', supported on either side b
Cominius and Lartius. The procession (which in Rome would hav
started outside the city walls) halts for a moment before proceedin
(line 203) towards the Capitol.

The warrior hero, suddenly, and surprisingly, kneels down a
the feet of his mother—then rises, perhaps embarrassed by he
teasing and her praises, with a tender greeting for his wife. Hi
reference to widows and childless mothers strikes a discordant not
in the mood of celebration, but the moment soon passes, overtaker
by the joy of Menenius which cannot resist the opportunity fo
gibing at the tribunes, the 'old crab-trees here at home' who wil
never be persuaded to change their opinions of Martius. For the
present these are silent, and the patrician party goes on its way wit
the rejoicings of Volumnia. Her wishes have been fulfilled—all bu
one . . .

Doubtless the tribunes hear and understand. Thei
observations as the scene comes to an end anticipate the
subsequent action: Martius, albeit reluctantly, will 'stand fo
consul' but his 'soaring insolence' will quickly incense the people
against him. And this is exactly what the tribunes want.

Scene 2   Two worldly-wise civil servants are exchanging views on Martius
when the procession enters. Menenius opens the business (which
appears already to have been set on foot) and stage-manages the
proceedings. Cominius is invited to speak the formal ovation, and
the tribunes must listen—although they show themselves sullen
and touchy, ready for any occasion to take or give offence.
Coriolanus is embarrassed, and leaves the stage before Cominius
can begin the encomium which, clearly, he has prepared well in
advance. With studied wit and enlivening imagery ('act the woman
. . . prov'd best man', 'pupil age Man-enter'd', 'weeds before A
vessel under sail') the speech builds up to a dramatic climax with
its description of the fighting in Corioles, where Martius was (as
the audience saw) 'a thing of blood, whose every motion Was tim'd
with dying cries'. The Senators are impressed, and Martius is
recalled to their favour—but the tribunes are biding their time!

There is yet one condition remaining to be satisfied and
Menenius delicately leads his protégé to the sensitive matter of

speaking to the people in the market-place. Martius has a neurotic abhorrence of this public demonstration of his wounds, although he knows it to be necessary and customary, and pleads to be excused. But Menenius is relentless—and the tribunes know how to lay their plans.

Scene 3   The citizens rehearse the roles they are to play in the election of the new consul and discuss their candidate. Martius, still reluctant and needing the urging of Menenius, presents himself in the gown of humility and the first citizens try to elicit the proper responses from this taciturn figure. But Martius clutches his garment round him, refusing to display those scars which the people are eager to see. Asked individually, they cannot withhold their 'voices', but the votes are accepted with such contempt that they are immediately regretted—'An 'twere to give again . . .' The next group is less easily won but Martius overcomes their criticism and, still without showing his scars, persuades their 'voices' from them. Despising himself for begging the election he feels to be deserved but resisting the temptation to abandon the endeavour, he forces himself to give a better—though cynically over-dramatic—performance in his next ordeal.

The third encounter is the last: Martius has 'stood [his] limitation' and the tribunes must give their acceptance of him. The final stage is the 'approbation' (=formal confirmation) in the Senate house. Coriolanus may at last change his clothes and make his escape.

But the citizens return to the tribunes for an analysis of Martius' performance and then, with words provided by Sicinius and Brutus (which absolve the tribunes themselves from any blame), hasten to the Capitol to deny their election.

Act 3

A second chance, and a trial—but no reconciliation:

1 Coriolanus speaks his mind
2 Rehearsal for the trial
3 Coriolanus is exiled

Scene 1   Coriolanus, having exchanged his 'vesture of humility' for the regalia of his new status as 'lord consul' (line 6), moves in procession towards the market-place for the people's final approbation—which we know will never come. His mind, however, is on Aufidius: the Volscian peace has been short-lived (the fighting has accomplished nothing) and Aufidius nurses his old hatred at home in Antium.

    The procession is suddenly halted by the tribunes who bar the way to the market-place. Coriolanus is quick to understand: this is 'a purpos'd thing, and grows by plot To curb the will of the nobility'. Despite the efforts of Menenius and Cominius to restrain him, Martius persists with a tirade against 'the mutable, rank-scented meinie' which is more than enough, in the eyes of tribunes, to convict him of high treason. The patricians also incur his criticism: they are 'reckless', neglecting to consider what danger may arise when authority is divided and the plebeians oppose their power to that of the nobility. This is too much for the tribunes, and they demand the arrest of Martius. Immediately the crowds surge on to the stage. A brawl is threatening, and whilst Menenius tries in vain to pacify both sides, Sicinius adds more fuel to the citizens' wrath.

    Big questions are asked in this scene, the political heart of the play. 'What is the city but the people?' Where should authority be invested? What is the role and responsibility of the individual?

    When another scuffle begins the patricians succeed in driving away the tribunes, aediles, and citizens so that Coriolanus can be escorted from the scene. Even Menenius is exasperated by his behaviour—'What the vengeance, Could he not speak 'em fair?' The tribunes and the 'rabble' return again, and Menenius attempts to conciliate them, agreeing with Sicinius in his 'disease' imagery but denying its extent: Martius is 'a limb that has but a disease' and the cure will be easy. Facing the mob with no weapon other than his rhetoric, Menenius stems the tide of rage, urging Martius' blood shed for his country, the supporters who would take action on his behalf, and even the hero's education—'bred i'th' wars Since a could draw a sword . . .' A brief respite is achieved.

Scene 2   Coriolanus is unrepentant and undeterred, only surprised that his mother does not share his attitude. Volumnia hears him out, and then adds her counsel to that of Menenius and the Senators. All agree that the plebeians—the 'herd'—must be satisfied. Volumnia now shows a different face to her son, and her suggestions of 'policy' strike at the very root of his existence, his honour. For Volumnia, the end will justify the means—and she proceeds to instruct Martius in the gestures and language of a supplicant. She is determined that he shall perform the role she has designed—'He must, and will'—but Martius is reluctant. Dissimulation is abhorrent to him and, as he parodies his mother's instructions, a sudden revulsion makes him reject her teaching: 'I will not do't, Lest I surcease to honour mine own truth, And by my body's action teach my mind A most inherent baseness'.

Volumnia turns the screw yet again with her feigned indifference and veiled threat, 'I mock at death With as big a heart as thou', and her son capitulates. He will play the role she has designed for him and bring home the prize she desires. Confronted by her own hypocrisy, Volumnia turns away dismissively: 'Do your will'. With 'mildly' as his watchword, Coriolanus goes to the market-place.

Scene 3   The tribunes have set up their own scene: they have their accusations ready, the citizens have been schooled in the parts they must play, and the action will go according to their simple plot. They will 'Put him [Martius] to choler straight' and, being angered, he will speak 'What's in his heart'—which will be enough to destroy him.

Coriolanus is surrounded by patricians and senators to protect him from the people. Menenius stands close, providing interpretation and gloss for the blunt answers and a curb when Martius rises to the tribunes' bait. But the word 'traitor' is dynamite, and Martius explodes—to the great satisfaction of the tribunes! The obedient citizens clamour for instant execution but Sicinius commutes the sentence to banishment. Cominius attempts to offer a plea of mitigation, but the tribunes will not hear and the mob howls for the penalty. Martius spurns them away and, with warnings, curses, and a grand theatrical gesture ('I banish you') sweeps away in high disdain. The rejoicing citizens follow, 'to see him out at gates'.

Act 4

Changing sides! Coriolanus joins Aufidius:

1 Coriolanus leaves Rome

2 Volumnia berates the tribunes

3 News from Rome: Nicanor talks to Adrian

4 Coriolanus enters Antium

5 Coriolanus meets Aufidius

6 Rome is peaceful

7 Aufidius is jealous

Scene 1   Shakespeare develops this scene from a few lines in Plutarch describing how Martius had taken 'his leave of his mother and wife, finding them weeping and shrieking out for sorrow, and had also comforted them to be content with his chance'. Now he is calm and accepts the situation with the stoic fortitude that his mother (he says) has always recommended. Whereas Plutarch says that Martius had already decided upon revenge, Shakespeare's character seems not even to take the matter seriously, as though expecting the Romans to call him back—'I shall be lov'd when I am lack'd'. Alone, having refused Cominius' companionship, Martius goes out from the city to be 'a lonely dragon' in his fen, only to be caught with 'cautelous baits and practice'. The lines are, proleptically, ironic—as is his promise that his friends shall hear from him, 'and never of me aught But what is like me formerly'.

Scene 2   Rome is quiet: the citizens can be sent home, and the tribunes must keep a low profile because the nobility are now 'vex'd' and leaning to the side of Martius. Volumnia, seconded by Virgilia, launches an attack worthy of her son on those whom she sees as being responsible for this 'brave deed'. Menenius, still the peace-maker, can only shake his head: 'Fie, fie, fie'.

Scene 3   Tension relaxes in this short scene, which has no counterpart in Plutarch's narrative. Nicanor, informing against Rome, accounts for the passage of some time since Coriolanus left the city. The nobility—senators and patricians—have turned against the citizens and now Rome lies open to the enemy army of the Volsces.

Scene 4   Coriolanus is at the lowest ebb of his fortunes. As he enters Antium, his face 'muffled' to avoid detection, he ponders on the changes in human relationships: nothing is certain—sworn friends fall to 'bitterest enmity' for the most trivial reason, and worst enemies, just as easily, 'shall grow dear friends'. Nothing is stable—including his own affections. This short speech provides the closest insight into his thinking that Martius allows, and it represents—or takes the place of—the many days of thought described by Plutarch which resulted in a determination to be revenged on the Romans: 'Whereupon he thought it his best way first to stir up the Volsces against them'.

Scene 5   Comedy frames the meeting in Antium of Martius and Aufidius. Shabby, cold and hungry, Coriolanus is changed out of all recognition as he mingles with the servants, and Aufidius, although he acknowledges a 'command' in the stranger's face, cannot identify Martius until the name is spoken. With unconcealed bitterness, Martius tells of the ingratitude of his 'thankless country' whose citizens have hounded him into exile, and of the 'mere spite' that drives him now in urging Aufidius to take this opportunity for revenge. Former rivalry is put aside as Aufidius extends a lover's welcome to the man of his 'nightly' dreams, recalling how he has dreamed of fighting Martius when they were 'down together . . . fisting each other's throats'. Now he addresses Martius as 'most absolute sir', offering a half share in his commission for an assault on Rome.

     The Servingmen discuss this 'strange alteration' and debate the respective merits of the former rivals. Learning that war is imminent, they rejoice at the prospect of activity in 'a stirring world again'.

Scene 6   Meanwhile in Rome the tribunes are basking in self-congratulation—until the news comes that the Volsces have invaded Roman territories. The first report is seconded with the rumour, soon confirmed, that Martius has allied himself with Aufidius. Ironies follow fast upon each other, as every hope and belief meets immediately with its contradiction. Cominius and Menenius are quick to attribute all blame to the tribunes and their 'apron-men' who have brought a 'trembling' upon Rome that is 'quite incapable of help'. The citizens quail before their abuse and, speaking now as individuals, attempt to excuse themselves: 'though we willingly consented to his banishment, yet it was against our will'. The tribunes, alienated from their followers, bring the scene to a close.

Scene 7   Already the alliance is under strain. Aufidius resents his new colleague's popularity, although he is at a loss to explain his reasons. His analysis of Martius' character is generous but, as he realizes, and as the confused syntax shows, inadequate as an explanation of his feelings. The final threat, however, is unambiguous.

Act 5

Another triumph for Martius—and the final disaster:

1 The Roman appeals to Martius

2 Menenius is rejected

3 Volumnia pleads and succeeds

4 News comes to Rome

5 The ladies return

6 Aufidius is revenged—and Coriolanus is killed

Scene 1   The tribunes in desperation turn to Menenius and eventually, after much flattery, he sets off for the enemy camp. But Cominius has no hope: his own appeal has already been rejected by a new Martius who refused to recognize even his friends in Rome—he 'cannot stay to pick them in a pile Of noisome, musty chaff'.

Scene 2   Menenius fails to impress the Volscian guards by his boasts of intimacy with their new leader, but the approach of Coriolanus and Aufidius gives him fresh confidence—which, with the play's characteristic irony, is soon dashed. Coriolanus, somewhat uneasily, calls Aufidius to bear witness to his cold resolution before leaving the old man to face the mockery of the guards.

Scene 3   Coriolanus, still wanting the approval of Aufidius, vows to listen to no more embassies from Rome, but the vow is no sooner made than it is broken. The final trial is yet to come, and, as the Roman ladies approach his exalted chair of state, his emotions spill out in words that only the audience must hear. Having resolved to resist 'affection', to deny 'Great nature', and to 'stand As if a man were author of himself', Martius is immediately overthrown by his own instinct. Once again (as in *Act 2*, Scene 1) the conqueror kneels at his mother's feet. As she raises him up, Volumnia kneels herself—along with Virgilia, Young Martius, and Valeria, whom Martius greets with unusual fervour (Shakespeare disregards Plutarch's explanation that Valeria was the instigator of this female embassy).

Although warned that any requests must be refused, Volumnia is determined to speak out—in words taken, with very little alteration, from North's translation of Plutarch: Shakespeare knew how to respect his source! She first pleads *pietas*—family values—the strong Roman obligation of loyalty to family and country: 'thou shalt no sooner March to assault thy country than to tread—Trust to't, thou shalt not—on thy mother's womb That brought thee to this world'. Virgilia adds her strength to the threat, and even Young Martius speaks out against his father. Coriolanus is moved. He rises to his feet—but he does not go away.

Volumnia renews her attack, now urging the honour that could be achieved by a diplomatic solution, then threatening the disgrace in which his name would be held. Rising to a rhetorical climax, she pleads that Martius, having shown the power of a god, should also imitate the graces of the gods and show their mercy—and then, exhausted, she relaxes into a semi-comic depiction of herself as a mother hen, clucking to her favourite chick. When there is still no response, Volumnia has one final weapon: the ladies kneel, briefly, then Volumnia withdraws herself and them, disowning her son and hinting of a time for future speech, when Rome is on fire and she (presumably) is facing death.

The silence when she stops speaking—perhaps the longest silence in the history of theatre—is more eloquent than words. Nature has triumphed, and Coriolanus is defeated. He knows the outcome now, and accepts with tragic dignity: 'But let it come'. He has hope that something may be salvaged—but Aufidius leaves nothing in doubt.

Scene 4   Menenius' predictions are confounded when a tide of joy sweeps through the city.

Scene 5   In a final procession the ladies are escorted through the city—passing from one side of the stage to the other—by rejoicing senators. But none of them will speak.

Scene 6   A reception is prepared for Martius. Aufidius confides h
disappointment to certain Volsces—perhaps the same who rescue
him from his duel with Martius in *Act 1*, Scene 9—who join the
accusations to his. The sound of drums and trumpets heralds th
approach of the conqueror as Martius returns in triumph
confident of the welcome that his negotiated treaty will receive. Bu
Aufidius denounces him as a traitor who has surrendered the
conquest to his wife and mother for 'certain drops of salt'. Martiu
rises to the challenge magnificently, but now the Volscian citizens
no less changeable than those of Rome, howl for their revenge—
and the noble lords, like the Roman patricians, are powerless t
restrain them. Martius is killed by Aufidius' conspirators, and thei
leader mounts the dead body in triumph. His rage quickly subside
under the reprimands of the lords, and Aufidius joins in th
decreed mourning, honouring Coriolanus by becoming one of th
bearers who carry the body from the stage.

The Man

'A brave fellow, but vengeance proud' (2, 2, 5)

No hero comes in for more abuse and criticism than Coriolanus. Every character in the play has an opinion of him, and every voice is loud to make it heard. Coriolanus is 'a very dog to the commonalty', 'a foe to th' public weal', 'a disease that must be cut away', 'a boy of tears' and—for all that—a 'rare example' whose 'nature is too noble for the world'. Friends and foes alike try to explain him, to excuse and to blame him, but there is nobody who can *understand* him. Even his mother, who brought him up and has a charter to extol him, hesitates in bewilderment at certain crucial points in her son's career to destruction. When she attempts to save him from the results of his own behaviour, urging him to mitigate his anger and contempt for the plebeians, she meets with absolute refusal:

> Would you have me
> False to my nature? Rather say I play
> The man I am.   (3, 2, 14–16)

Coriolanus is very sure of himself—of who he is and of what he is doing. Not for him the moments of self-doubt, self-questioning, that win the audience's sympathy for even the most villainous of Shakespeare's characters, and allow access to the innermost workings of the most devious mind. The heart and mind of Coriolanus are rarely laid bare in soliloquy, and his words are, for the most part, spoken 'out front', where they can be heard and understood by all on stage, and not 'aside', in confidence to the audience. In consequence, he remains a perpetual enigma, open to all investigation but yielding to no single interpretation.

Plutarch, the biographer of this semi-mythical hero with few friends and no social skills, was inclined to ascribe his subject's failings to a lack of education, presenting him as

> . . . a good proof to confirm some men's opinions that a rare
> and excellent wit, untaught, doth bring forth many good

and evil things together, like a fat soil bringeth forth herbs and weeds that lieth unmanured. For this Martius' natural wit and great heart did marvellously stir up his courage to do and attempt notable acts. But on the other side, for lack of education, he was so choleric and impatient that he would yield to no living creature; which made him churlish, uncivil, and altogether unfit for any man's conversation.

This explanation diminishes Coriolanus, rationalizing him and plucking the heart out of his mystery so that he becomes a monster of *virtus*, a scourge for the society that created him. From this he is redeemed by Shakespeare, whose recreating genius had the marvellous ambivalence praised by John Keats as 'Negative Capability', which was 'capable of being in uncertainties, mysteries, doubts, without any irritable reaching after fact and reason'.[1] Shakespeare *presents*—he does not *judge*: that is the privilege of directors and actors, of audiences and readers. *Your* privilege, in fact.

---

[1] 'Negative Capability', defined in a letter to George and Thomas Keats, 21 December 1817, in *Letters of John Keats*, ed. H. E. Rollins (1958), vol. 1.

Shakespeare's Verse

Easily the best way to understand and appreciate Shakespeare's verse is to read it aloud! Don't be captivated by the dominant rhythm, but decide which are the most important words in each line and use the regular metre to drive them forward to the listeners.

Shakespeare's plays are written mainly in blank verse, the form preferred by most dramatists in the sixteenth and early seventeenth centuries. It is a very flexible medium, capable—like the human speaking voice—of a wide range of tones. Basically the lines, called 'iambic pentameters', are unrhymed and have ten syllables with alternating stresses (just like normal English speech) which divide them into five 'feet'. The rhythm of the pentameter is initiated for *Coriolanus* in the first scene of the play when Menenius attempts to pacify the mutinous citizens. These have been talking to each other in prose—conventionally the proper medium for humble or comic characters—and Menenius' verse emphasizes the status of the character:

> **Menenius**
> I téll you, friénds, most cháritáble cáre
> Have thé patrícians óf you. Fór your wánts,
> Your súffering ín this déarth, you máy as wéll
> Strike át the héaven wíth your stáves as líft them
> Against the Róman státe, whose cóurse will ón
> The wáy it tákes, crackíng ten thóusand cúrbs
> Of móre strong línk asúnder thán can éver
> Appéar in yóur impédimént. For the déarth,
> The góds, not thé patrícians, máke it, ánd
> Your knées to thém, not árms, must hélp. Aláck,
> You áre transpórted bý calámitý
> Thithér where móre atténds you; ánd you slánder
> The hélms o'th' státe, who cáre for yóu like fáthers,
> When yóu curse thém as énemiés.

At the beginning of his career Shakespeare wrote regular, 'end-stopped' lines in which the unit of meaning was contained within the pentameter. Now he is fully in control of every aspect of

his medium, and in *Coriolanus* the verse is flexible, tough, an
sinewy. The sense runs freely between the lines, checked only by
mid-line pause (a 'caesura') to give added emphasis, allowing th
characters to talk, to argue and persuade, and even to shout abus
at each other. The length of the lines, now, may be longer o
shorter than the basic ten syllables of Shakespeare's earl
pentameters, but the rhythm is never lost, even when a line :
shared between two speakers. Pressure of emotions, or merely th
ease of relaxed conversation, may call for the elision of syllable
(o'th', i'th', you'st) just as in the quarrels or chattiness of everyda
life:

> **First Citizen**
>   Your bélly's ánswer—whát?
> The kíngly, crówned héad, the vígilant éye,
> The cóunsellor héart, the árm our sóldiér,
> Our stéed the lég, the tóngue our trúmpetér,
> With óther múniménts and pétty hélps
> In thís our fábric, íf that théy—
>   **Menenius**
>   What thén?
> 'Fore mé, this féllow spéaks! What thén, what thén?
>   **First Citizen**
> Should bý the córmorant bélly bé restráin'd,
> Who ís the sínk o'th'bódy—
>   **Menenius**
>   Wéll, what thén?
>   **First Citizen**
> The fórmer ágents, íf they díd compláin,
> What cóuld the bélly ánswer?
>   **Menenius**
>   Í will téll you,
> If yóu'll bestów a smáll—of whát you háve little—
> Patiénce a whíle, you'st héar the bélly's ánswer.

Source, Date, and Text

The main source of *Coriolanus* was Plutarch's *Parallel Lives of the Greeks and Romans*, which was written in Greek in the first century AD, translated into French (by Jacques Amyot) in 1559, and then into English (by Sir Thomas North) in 1575. North's translation gave Shakespeare the characters and plot outlines for four of his plays—*Julius Caesar, Antony and Cleopatra, Coriolanus*, and *Timon of Athens*—and Shakespeare so respected North's vigorous colloquial prose that he often retained its phraseology and idioms, making only slight adjustments for the purpose of rhythm and emphasis (see 'Plutarch', p. 143). The fable of the belly which is told by Menenius in *Act 1*, Scene 1 has its counterpart in Plutarch but owes its phraseology to the version recounted in William Camden's *Remains of a Greater Work concerning Britain*, which was published in 1605.

There is no record of any early performance of *Coriolanus*, but stylistic evidence and a few contemporary allusions point to a date of *c.* 1608–9. Menenius' 'coal of fire upon the ice' (*1*, 1, 165) may refer to the great freeze of 1607–8: a pamphlet written by Thomas Decker describes 'pans of coals' placed on the ice for people to warm their hands. Coriolanus' warning (*3*, 1, 98–9) that the tribune Sicinius could threaten to 'turn your current in a ditch And make your channel his' might be an allusion to a scheme for bringing water by channels into London; work was already started in February 1609 but was constantly interrupted by the owners of the land through which the passages were being cut. A phrase from Cominius' account of how Coriolanus, in combat with the Volsces, 'lurch'd all swords of the garland' (*2*, 2, 101) seems to have been repeated ('lurched all your friends of the better half of the garland') in Ben Jonson's play *Epicoene* (1609–10), suggesting that Shakespeare's play was already in production and catching the attention of his competitor.

Coriolanus was first published in 1623, in the collected edition of all Shakespeare's plays known as the First Folio. The text is divided into acts, but there is no division of scenes. From the unusual number and nature of the stage directions it seems likely that the manuscript from which the play was printed was Shakespeare's own (and not a transcript made by the prompter for use in the theatre). This edition makes use of the text established by R. B. Parker (Oxford Shakespeare, 1994).

People in the Play

THE ROMANS

Caius Martius	*later called* **Coriolanus**	
Menenius Agrippa	*his elderly friend*	
Cominius	*Consul and Commander-in Chief*	
Titus Lartius	*a general*	*patricians of Rome*
Volumnia	*mother of* Coriolanus	
Virgilia	Coriolanus' *wife*	
Young Martius	*his son*	
Valeria	*a noble lady*	

Sicinius Velutus	*tribunes of the people*	
Junius Brutus		
Citizens	*of Rome*	*plebeians of Rome*
Soldiers	*in the Roman army*	
Nicanor	*a traitor to Rome*	

A Gentlewoman, Usher, Herald, Aediles, Messengers, Senators, Lictors

THE VOLSCES

Tullus Aufidius *a general in the Volscian army*
Lieutenant
Servingmen
Conspirators *with* Aufidius
Adrian *a Volscian spy*

Lords, Senators, Citizens and Soldiers

The action of the play takes place in Rome, in the Volscian cities of Corioli and Antium, and in the territories between them.

Act I

The Roman citizens are threatening rebellion. Menenius calms them with his parable of the belly, but Martius stirs them to fresh anger with his insults. The situation is saved with the news that the Volsces are once again preparing to attack Rome, but the tribunes are still antagonistic.

1 *proceed any further*: i.e. in their advance on the Capitol, *and also*, in their case against Martius.
3 *die . . . famish*: These were the alternatives recognized by Stratford labourers in the riots of the early seventeenth century (see 'The Times', p.vi).

9 *Is't a verdict*: do you all agree.

10 *on't*: of it.

13 *authority*: those in authority.
14 *but*: merely.
16 *dear*: expensive.
17 *object*: spectacle.
18 *as an inventory . . . abundance*: like a calculator to itemize their own richness.
18–19 *our sufferance . . . them*: i.e. the more we suffer, the more they have.

Scene 1

Rome: enter a company of mutinous Citizens *with staves, clubs, and other weapons*

First Citizen
Before we proceed any further, hear me speak.
All
Speak, speak.
First Citizen
You are all resolved rather to die than to famish?
All
Resolved, resolved.
First Citizen
5 First, you know Caius Martius is chief enemy to the people.
All
We know't, we know't.
First Citizen
Let us kill him, and we'll have corn at our own price. Is't a verdict?
All
10 No more talking on't, let it be done. Away, away.
Second Citizen
One word, good citizens.
First Citizen
We are accounted poor citizens, the patricians good. What authority surfeits on would relieve us. If they would yield us but the superfluity while it were 15 wholesome, we might guess they relieved us humanely, but they think we are too dear. The leanness that afflicts us, the object of our misery, is as an inventory to particularize their abundance; our sufferance is a gain to them. Let us revenge this with

20 *pikes*: pitchforks.
rakes: i.e. lean as rakes.

25 *All*: Probably the line should be shared
between different speakers.
a very dog: a real enemy.
commonalty: common people.

29 *that*: i.e. for his service.

33 *to that end*: i.e. to win fame.
soft-conscienced: soft-headed, easy-going.

35 *partly proud*: proud of his ability.

36 *even . . . altitude of*: to the same high
degree as.
virtue: valiantness: 'Now in those days
valiantness was honoured in Rome
above all other virtues; which they call
virtus, by the name of virtue itself, as
including in that general name all other
special virtues besides. So that *virtus* in
the Latin was as much as valiantness'
(Plutarch).

40 *tire in repetition*: tire one out with
repeating them.

40s.d. *within*: offstage (within the 'tiring-
house' or dressing-room).

42 *prating*: jabbering on.
Capitol: Shakespeare assumes that the
meeting-house of the Senate was
located on the Capitoline Hill.

44 *Soft*: just a minute, gently now.

---

20 our pikes ere we become rakes; for the gods know,
speak this in hunger for bread, not in thirst for
revenge.

Second Citizen
Would you proceed especially against Caius
Martius?

All
25 Against him first. He's a very dog to the commonalty

Second Citizen
Consider you what services he has done for his
country?

First Citizen
Very well; and could be content to give him good
report for't, but that he pays himself with being
30 proud.

Second Citizen
Nay, but speak not maliciously.

First Citizen
I say unto you, what he hath done famously, he did
it to that end. Though soft-conscienced men can be
content to say it was for his country, he did it to
35 please his mother and to be partly proud—which he
is, even to the altitude of his virtue.

Second Citizen
What he cannot help in his nature you account a vice
in him. You must in no way say he is covetous.

First Citizen
If I must not, I need not be barren of accusations
40 He hath faults, with surplus, to tire in repetition.

Shouts within

What shouts are these? The other side o'th' city is
risen. Why stay we prating here? To th' Capitol!

All
Come, come.

Enter Menenius Agrippa

First Citizen
Soft, who comes here?

Second Citizen
45 Worthy Menenius Agrippa, one that hath always
loved the people.

would: I wish.

48–9 What . . . you: The regular blank verse lines mark the social distinction between Menenius and the Citizens.

48 What . . . hand: what's going on here.

49 bats: staves, cudgels.

50–1 Our business . . . fortnight: 'The Senate met many days in consultation about it; but in the end they concluded nothing' (Plutarch).

53 suitors: petitioners, beggars.
strong: foul.

60 dearth: famine.

62 will on: will keep on.

63 curbs: restraints (like the chain which is part of a horse's bridle bit).

65 your impediment: the obstruction you are making.

68 transported: being carried away.

69 Thither: i.e. to the point of mutiny.

70 helms o'th' state: helmsmen who steer the state.

74–8 make . . . poor: The oppression by usurers was, according to Plutarch, the first cause of the citizens' insurrection (see 'Plutarch', p. 143).

First Citizen
He's one honest enough. Would all the rest were so!

Menenius
What work's, my countrymen, in hand? Where go you
With bats and clubs? The matter? Speak, I pray you.

First Citizen
50 Our business is not unknown to th' Senate; they have had inkling this fortnight what we intend to do, which now we'll show 'em in deeds. They say poor suitors have strong breaths; they shall know we have strong arms too.

Menenius
55 Why, masters, my good friends, mine honest neighbours,
Will you undo yourselves?

First Citizen
We cannot, sir; we are undone already.

Menenius
I tell you, friends, most charitable care
Have the patricians of you. For your wants,
60 Your suffering in this dearth, you may as well
Strike at the heaven with your staves as lift them
Against the Roman state, whose course will on
The way it takes, cracking ten thousand curbs
Of more strong link asunder than can ever
65 Appear in your impediment. For the dearth,
The gods, not the patricians, make it, and
Your knees to them, not arms, must help. Alack,
You are transported by calamity
Thither where more attends you; and you slander
70 The helms o'th' state, who care for you like fathers,
When you curse them as enemies.

First Citizen
Care for us? True, indeed! They ne'er cared for us yet: suffer us to famish, and their storehouses crammed with grain; make edicts for usury, to
75 support usurers; repeal daily any wholesome act established against the rich, and provide more piercing statutes daily to chain up and restrain the poor. If the wars eat us not up, they will; and there's all the love they bear us.

Menenius
80 Either you must
Confess yourselves wondrous malicious
Or be accus'd of folly. I shall tell you
A pretty tale. It may be you have heard it,
But since it serves my purpose, I will venture
85 To stale't a little more.

First Citizen
Well, I'll hear it, sir; yet you must not think to fob
our disgrace with a tale. But an't please you, deliv

Menenius
There was a time when all the body's members,
Rebell'd against the belly, thus accus'd it:
90 That only like a gulf it did remain
I'th' midst o'th' body, idle and unactive,
Still cupboarding the viand, never bearing
Like labour with the rest; where th'other instrumen
Did see and hear, devise, instruct, walk, feel,
95 And, mutually participate, did minister
Unto the appetite and affection common
Of the whole body. The belly answer'd—

First Citizen
Well, sir, what answer made the belly?

Menenius
Sir, I shall tell you. With a kind of smile,
100 Which ne'er came from the lungs, but even thus—
For, look you, I may make the belly smile
As well as speak—it tauntingly replied
To th' discontented members, the mutinous parts
That envied his receipt; even so most fitly
105 As you malign our senators for that
They are not such as you.

First Citizen
                Your belly's answer—wha
The kingly, crowned head, the vigilant eye,
The counsellor heart, the arm our soldier,
Our steed the leg, the tongue our trumpeter,
110 With other muniments and petty helps
In this our fabric, if that they—

Menenius
                What then?
'Fore me, this fellow speaks! What then, what then

---

83 *pretty*: neat, apt.

85 *stale*: i.e. by repeating it once more.

86 *fob off*: push aside.
87 *disgrace*: injury, degrading misfortune.
    an't . . . deliver: if that's what you want, go ahead.

90 *gulf*: bottomless abyss, whirlpool.
92 *Still*: always, continually.
    cupboarding: stowing away; Shakespeare turns a noun into a verb.
93 *Like*: the same.
    instruments: organs of the body.
95 *mutually participate*: taking part together.
96 *affection*: desire.

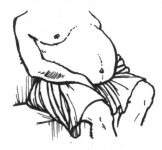

100 *thus*: Menenius somehow enacts the smile with a piece of comical stage business.
104 *his receipt*: what he received.
106 *Your belly's answer*: The First Citizen completes the blank verse line, adapting his speech to match the style of Menenius.
107 *crowned*: crownèd.
108 *counsellor heart*: The heart was considered to be the seat of understanding.
110 *muniments*: fortifications, equipment.
111 *fabric*: body.
112 *'Fore me . . . speaks*: 'My goodness, this man can really talk!'

3 *cormorant*: a proverbially greedy bird.

4 *sink*: sewer.

17 *small*: small amount.

20 *Your . . . belly*: i.e. this most serious belly we're talking about.

22 *incorporate*: joined into one body.

28 *Even . . . brain*: as far as the heart's court and the throne of the brain.

29 *cranks*: winding passages.
offices: those parts of a domestic property devoted to household works or services.

30 *nerves*: sinews.

31 *competency*: means of survival.

136 *audit*: balance-sheet.

137 *flour*: Menenius seems to be making a pun with 'flour' and 'flower' (= the best).

First Citizen
Should by the cormorant belly be restrain'd,
Who is the sink o'th' body—
      Menenius
                              Well, what then?
      First Citizen
115 The former agents, if they did complain,
What could the belly answer?
      Menenius
                              I will tell you,
If you'll bestow a small—of what you have little—
Patience a while, you'st hear the belly's answer.
      First Citizen
You're long about it.
      Menenius
                        Note me this, good friend:
120 Your most grave belly was deliberate,
Not rash like his accusers, and thus answer'd:
'True is it, my incorporate friends,' quoth he,
'That I receive the general food at first
Which you do live upon, and fit it is,
125 Because I am the storehouse and the shop
Of the whole body. But, if you do remember,
I send it through the rivers of your blood
Even to the court, the heart, to th'seat o'th' brain;
And through the cranks and offices of man
130 The strongest nerves and small inferior veins
From me receive that natural competency
Whereby they live. And though that all at once,
You, my good friends'—this says the belly, mark
      me—
      First Citizen
Ay, sir, well, well.
      Menenius
                        'Though all at once cannot
135 See what I do deliver out to each,
Yet I can make my audit up that all
From me do back receive the flour of all
And leave me but the bran.' What say you to't?
      First Citizen
It was an answer. How apply you this?

Menenius
140 The senators of Rome are this good belly,
    And you the mutinous members. For examine
    Their counsels and their cares, digest things rightly
    Touching the weal o'th' common, you shall find
    No public benefit which you receive
145 But it proceeds or comes from them to you,
    And no way from yourselves. What do you think,
    You, the great toe of this assembly?
        First Citizen
    I the great toe? Why the great toe?
        Menenius
    For that, being one o'th' lowest, basest, poorest
150 Of this most wise rebellion, thou goest foremost.
    Thou rascal, that art worst in blood to run,
    Lead'st first to win some vantage.
    But make you ready your stiff bats and clubs:
    Rome and her rats are at the point of battle;
155 The one side must have bale.

        Enter Caius Martius

                    Hail, noble Martius!
        Martius
    Thanks.—What's the matter, you dissentious rogues,
    That, rubbing the poor itch of your opinion,
    Make yourselves scabs?
        First Citizen
                    We have ever your good word
        Martius
    He that will give good words to thee will flatter
160 Beneath abhorring. What would you have, you curs
    That like nor peace nor war? The one affrights you,
    The other makes you proud. He that trusts to you,
    Where he should find you lions finds you hares,
    Where foxes, geese. You are no surer, no,
165 Than is the coal of fire upon the ice,
    Or hailstone in the sun. Your virtue is
    To make him worthy whose offence subdues him,
    And curse that justice did it. Who deserves greatness
    Deserves your hate, and your affections are
170 A sick man's appetite, who desires most that
    Which would increase his evil. He that depends

143 *Touching*: concerning.
    the weal o'th' common: general well-being.

151 *rascal*: The usual sense can incorporate the technical meaning of 'a young or inferior hound or deer that will run ahead of the pack or herd'.
153 *stiff bats*: stout cudgels.
154 *Rome . . . rats*: Presumably these lines are spoken 'aside' from the Citizens.

155 *bale*: injury, poison.
158 *Make . . . scabs*: give yourselves scabs, *and*, make yourselves into scabs.
159-60 *flatter . . . abhorring*: i.e. flatter those who are beneath abhorring.
162 *proud*: rebellious.
165 *coal . . . ice*: Shakespeare slips in a contemporary allusion to the Great Frost of 1607–8; see 'Source, Date, and Text', p. xxix).
166-8 *Your virtue . . . did it*: it's just like you to respect someone who has deserved punishment and to swear at the justice that punishes him.
168 *Who*: anyone who.
169 *affections*: inclinations.
171 *evil*: disease, sickness.

Upon your favours swims with fins of lead,
And hews down oaks with rushes. Hang ye! Trust ye?
With every minute you do change a mind,
175 And call him noble that was now your hate,
Him vile that was your garland. What's the matter,
That in these several places of the city
You cry against the noble Senate, who,
Under the gods, keep you in awe, which else
180 Would feed on one another? [*To* Menenius] What's
    their seeking?

Menenius
For corn at their own rates, whereof they say
The city is well stor'd.

Martius
                  Hang 'em! They say?
They'll sit by th' fire and presume to know
What's done i'th' Capitol, who's like to rise,
185 Who thrives and who declines; side factions and
    give out
Conjectural marriages, making parties strong
And feebling such as stand not in their liking
Below their cobbled shoes. They say there's grain
    enough!
Would the nobility lay aside their ruth
190 And let me use my sword, I'd make a quarry
With thousands of these quarter'd slaves as high
As I could pitch my lance.

Menenius
Nay, these are all most thoroughly persuaded,
For though abundantly they lack discretion,
195 Yet are they passing cowardly. But I beseech you,
What says the other troop?

Martius
              They are dissolved. Hang 'em!
They said they were an-hungry, sigh'd forth
    proverbs—
That hunger broke stone walls, that dogs must eat,
That meat was made for mouths, that the gods sent
    not
200 Corn for the rich men only. With these shreds
They vented their complainings, which being
    answer'd,

176 *garland*: hero (who in Rome was decorated with a garland).

177 *several*: different.
180 *feed on one another*: This was a commonplace image for total anarchy.

185 *side*: take sides with.

186 *marriages*: i.e. political unions.
187 *feebling*: disparaging.
188 *cobbled*: patched, roughly mended.

189 *ruth*: compassion.
190 *quarry*: heap of slaughtered bodies (particularly used of deer killed at a hunt).
191 *quarter'd*: butchered, cut to pieces.

193 *persuaded*: appeased.

195 *passing*: exceedingly.
196 *other troop*: i.e. the rebels said to be on the other side of the city (line 40s.d.).

201 *vented*: aired, expressed.

203 *To break . . . generosity*: to strike a death-blow against the nobility (from Latin *generosus*, of noble birth).

206 *Shouting . . . emulation*: striving to outdo one another in their shouts of delight.

209 *'Sdeath*: God's death (an Elizabethan oath, anachronistic here).

212 *Win upon power*: win even more power, get the better of those in authority. *themes*: topics.
213 *For . . . arguing*: to become grounds for rebellion.

215 *fragments*: scraps of uneaten food (hence, a general term of contempt).

218–19 *vent . . . superfluity*: get rid of the stale surplus of our energies.

220 *that*: that which.
lately: recently.

222 *put you to't*: put you to the test.

And a petition granted them—a strange one,
To break the heart of generosity
And make bold power look pale—they threw their
        caps
205 As they would hang them on the horns o'th' moon,
Shouting their emulation.
                                    Menenius
                                                What is granted them?
        Martius
Five tribunes to defend their vulgar wisdoms,
Of their own choice. One's Junius Brutus,
Sicinius Velutus, and I know not. 'Sdeath,
210 The rabble should have first unroof'd the city
Ere so prevail'd with me! It will in time
Win upon power and throw forth greater themes
For insurrection's arguing.
        Menenius
This is strange.
        Martius
215 [*To the* Citizens] Go get you home, you fragments.

                Enter a Messenger *hastily*

        Messenger
Where's Caius Martius?
        Martius
                                        Here. What's the matter?
        Messenger
The news is, sir, the Volsces are in arms.
        Martius
I am glad on't. Then we shall ha' means to vent
Our musty superfluity.—

                Enter Sicinius Velutus, Junius Brutus,
                Cominius, Titus Lartius, *with other*
                Senators

                                    See, our best elders!
        First Senator
220 Martius, 'tis true that you have lately told us.
The Volsces are in arms.
        Martius
                                        They have a leader,
Tullus Aufidius, that will put you to't.

I sin in envying his nobility,
And were I anything but what I am,
225 I would wish me only he.

Cominius
                                        You have fought together!

Martius

by th'ears: at odds, fighting together.
party: side.

Were half to half the world by th'ears and he
Upon my party, I'd revolt to make
Only my wars with him. He is a lion
That I am proud to hunt.

First Senator
                                        Then, worthy Martius,
230 Attend upon Cominius to these wars.

Cominius
[*To* Martius] It is your former promise.

Martius
                                                    Sir, it is,
And I am constant. Titus Lartius, thou
Shalt see me once more strike at Tullus' face.
What, art thou stiff? Stand'st out?

Lartius

art thou . . . out: Lartius is probably stiff
from earlier wounds (rather than old
age); Martius puns on 'stiff' = obstinate.

                                        No, Caius Martius.
235 I'll lean upon one crutch and fight with t'other
Ere stay behind this business.

Menenius
                                        O true bred!

First Senator
Your company to th' Capitol, where I know
Our greatest friends attend us.

Lartius
[*To* Cominius]   Lead you on.
[*To* Martius] Follow Cominius. We must follow you,
240 Right worthy your priority.

Right . . . priority: you are most worthy
to have first place.

Cominius
                                        Noble Martius.

First Senator
[*To the* Citizens] Hence to your homes, be gone.

Martius
                                        Nay, let them follow.
The Volsces have much corn. Take these rats thither
To gnaw their garners.   [Citizens *steal away*
                        Worshipful mutineers,

garners: granaries; in the forays against
Actium, Coriolanus and his army 'met
with great plenty of corn' (Plutarch).

244 *puts well forth*: is very promising.

> Your valour puts well forth. [*To the* Senators] Pray
> follow.
>>> [*Exeunt all but* Sicinius *and* Bru[

Sicinius
245 Was ever man so proud as is this Martius?
Brutus
He has no equal.
Sicinius
When we were chosen tribunes for the people—
Brutus
Mark'd you his lip and eyes?
Sicinius
>>>>> Nay, but his taunts.

Brutus

249 *gird*: scoff at, deride.

Being mov'd, he will not spare to gird the gods—
Sicinius

250 *Bemock*: mock at.
    modest moon: The moon was associated
    with the virgin goddess Diana.
251 *The . . . him*: May the present wars
    consume him.
252 *Too proud . . . valiant*: over-conceited in
    his own valour.

250 Bemock the modest moon.
Brutus
The present wars devour him. He is grown
Too proud to be so valiant.
Sicinius
>>>> Such a nature,
Tickled with good success, disdains the shadow
Which he treads on at noon. But I do wonder

255 *brook*: tolerate.

255 His insolence can brook to be commanded
Under Cominius!
Brutus
>>>> Fame, at the which he aims,

257 *In whom*: in which—i.e. fame.

In whom already he's well grac'd, cannot
Better be held nor more attain'd than by
A place below the first; for what miscarries

259 *miscarries*: goes wrong.

260 Shall be the general's fault, though he perform

261 *giddy censure*: the fickleness of popular
    opinion.

To th'utmost of a man, and giddy censure
Will then cry out of Martius 'O, if he

263 *borne*: been responsible for.

Had borne the business!'
Sicinius
>>>> Besides, if things go well,

264 *Opinion*: reputation, popular opinion.
265 *demerits*: deserts, merits.
    Come: Brutus encourages Sicinius to go
    even further with this idea.

Opinion, that so sticks on Martius, shall
265 Of his demerits rob Cominius.
Brutus
>>>> Come:
Half all Cominius' honours are to Martius,
Though Martius earn'd them not; and all his faults

59 *aught*: anything.

70 *dispatch*: order for war.

71 *More . . . singularity*: besides his own
self-importance.

To Martius shall be honours, though indeed
In aught he merit not.
>   **Sicinius**
>   Let's hence and hear
270 How the dispatch is made, and in what fashion,
More than his singularity, he goes
Upon this present action.
>   **Brutus**
>   Let's along.

>   [*Exeunt*

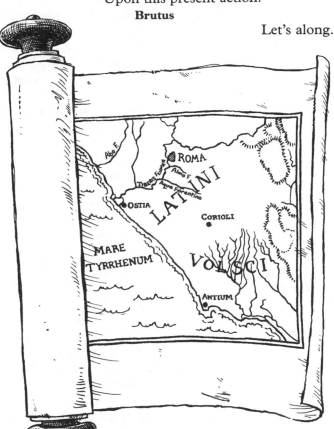

Act 1   Scene 2

Aufidius warns the Senators of Corioles that
there is a new threat from Rome.

Scene 2

Corioles: enter Tullus Aufidius, *with*
Senators *of Corioles*

2 *enter'd in*: informed about, privy to.

First Senator
So, your opinion is, Aufidius,
That they of Rome are enter'd in our counsels
And know how we proceed.

Aufidius

                Is it not yours?
What ever have been thought on in this state
5 That could be brought to bodily act, ere Rome
Had circumvention? 'Tis not four days gone
Since I heard thence. These are the words. I think
I have the letter here—yes, here it is.
[*He reads*] 'They have press'd a power, but it is not known
10 Whether for east or west. The dearth is great,
The people mutinous, and it is rumour'd
Cominius, Martius your old enemy,
Who is of Rome worse hated than of you,
And Titus Lartius, a most valiant Roman,
15 These three lead on this preparation
Whither 'tis bent. Most likely 'tis for you.
Consider of it.'
    First Senator
              Our army's in the field.
We never yet made doubt but Rome was ready
To answer us.
    Aufidius
               Nor did you think it folly
20 To keep your great pretences veil'd till when
They needs must show themselves, which in the hatching,
It seem'd, appear'd to Rome. By the discovery
We shall be shorten'd in our aim, which was
To take in many towns ere, almost, Rome
25 Should know we were afoot.
    Second Senator
                Noble Aufidius,
Take your commission, hie you to your bands.
Let us alone to guard Corioles.
If they set down before's, for the remove
Bring up your army, but I think you'll find
30 They've not prepar'd for us.
    Aufidius
                   O, doubt not that.
I speak from certainties. Nay, more,
Some parcels of their power are forth already,
And only hitherward. I leave your honours.
If we and Caius Martius chance to meet,

4–6 *What ever . . . circumvention*: what is there that has been decided in this state that has not been foiled by Rome.

6 *gone*: past, ago.

9 *press'd*: conscripted.
power: army.

10 *east or west*: The Volscian territories lay south-east and south-west of Rome (see map, p. 11).
dearth: famine, shortages.

13 *of Rome*: by Rome.

15 *preparation*: military force prepared for war.

16 *bent*: intended.

19 *answer us*: respond to our attack.

20 *pretences*: designs, intentions.

21 *in the hatching*: while they were still being contrived.

23 *be shorten'd . . . aim*: be forced to lower our sights.

24 *take in*: capture.
ere, almost: almost before.

26 *hie*: hasten.
bands: troops.

27 *Let us . . . Corioles*: leave us to guard Corioles ourselves.

28 *set down*: lay siege.
remove: raising of the siege.

32 *parcels*: portions, divisions.
are forth: have started out.

35 'Tis sworn between us we shall ever strike
Till one can do no more.

All the Senators
                           The gods assist you!

Aufidius
And keep your honours safe.

First Senator
                           Farewell.

Second Senator
                                  Farewell.

All
                                        Farewell.

[*Exeunt* Aufidius *at one door,* Senators *at another door*

Act 1   Scene 3

The boyhood of Martius: Volumnia talks
about her son.

2 *comfortable sort*: cheerful manner.
3 *should*: would.

Scene 3

Rome: *the house of* Caius Martius. *Enter*
Volumnia *and* Virgilia, *mother and wife to*
Martius. *They set them down on two low
stools and sew*

Volumnia
I pray you, daughter, sing, or express yourself in a
more comfortable sort. If my son were my husband,
I should freelier rejoice in that absence wherein he
won honour than in the embracements of his bed
5 where he would show most love. When yet he was
but tender-bodied and the only son of my womb,

7–8 *plucked . . . way*: drew all eyes in his
    direction.

9 *should*: would.

10 *become*: suit, enhance.

10–11 *such a person*: such an attractive
    appearance.

12 *renown*: i.e. the desire for 'renown'.
    made . . . stir: did not bring it to life.

13 *like*: likely.

14 *cruel war*: Volumnia refers to the wars
    (*c.* 510 BC) which drove the tyrant
    Tarquin from Rome.

15 *brows . . . oak*: 'crowned with a garland
    of oaken boughs' (Plutarch); this was
    an award given to a Roman citizen who
    had saved another citizen's life in battle.

16 *sprang*: i.e. my heart sprang.

20 *report*: reputation.

25s.d. *Gentlewoman*: lady-in-waiting; she
    addresses Volumnia as mistress of the
    house (Martius took a wife 'at her
    desire . . . and yet never left his
    mother's house therefore').

28 *retire*: withdraw.

30 *hither*: coming this way.

32 *As children . . . him*: the Volsces running
    away from him as children flee from a
    bear.

30–8 *Methinks I hear . . . hire*: Volumnia's
    words anticipate the actions of Martius
    in the scenes (4 and 5) that follow.

34 *got*: begotten.

36 *mail'd*: armoured.

37–8 *task'd . . . hire*: commanded to mow
    the whole harvest or get no pay.

when youth with comeliness plucked all gaze his
way, when for a day of kings' entreaties a mother
should not sell him an hour from her beholding, I
10 considering how honour would become such a
person—that it was no better than, picture-like, to
hang by th' wall if renown made it not stir—was
pleased to let him seek danger where he was like to
find fame. To a cruel war I sent him, from whence he
15 returned his brows bound with oak. I tell thee,
daughter, I sprang not more in joy at first hearing he
was a man-child than now in first seeing he had
proved himself a man.

Virgilia
But had he died in the business, madam, how then?

Volumnia
20 Then his good report should have been my son. I
therein would have found issue. Hear me profess
sincerely: had I a dozen sons, each in my love alike,
and none less dear than thine and my good Martius,
I had rather had eleven die nobly for their country
25 than one voluptuously surfeit out of action.

Enter a Gentlewoman

Gentlewoman
[*To* Volumnia] Madam, the Lady Valeria is come to
visit you.

Virgilia
Beseech you give me leave to retire myself.

Volumnia
Indeed you shall not.
30 Methinks I hear hither your husband's drum,
See him pluck Aufidius down by th' hair;
As children from a bear, the Volsces shunning him.
Methinks I see him stamp thus, and call thus:
'Come on, you cowards, you were got in fear
35 Though you were born in Rome!' His bloody brow
With his mail'd hand then wiping, forth he goes,
Like to a harvest-man that's task'd to mow
Or all or lose his hire.

Virgilia
His bloody brow? O Jupiter, no blood!

Volumnia

40 Away, you fool! It more becomes a man
Than gilt his trophy. The breasts of Hecuba
When she did suckle Hector look'd not lovelier
Than Hector's forehead when it spit forth blood
At Grecian sword, contemning.—
[*To the* Gentlewoman]   Tell Valeria
45 We are fit to bid her welcome.   [*Exit* Gentlewoman

Virgilia

Heavens bless my lord from fell Aufidius!

Volumnia

He'll beat Aufidius' head below his knee
And tread upon his neck.

Enter Valeria *with an* Usher *and the*
Gentlewoman

Valeria

My ladies both, good day to you.

Volumnia

50 Sweet madam.

Virgilia

I am glad to see your ladyship.

Valeria

How do you both? You are manifest housekeepers.
[*To* Volumnia] What are you sewing here? A fine
spot, in good faith.
55 [*To* Virgilia] How does your little son?

Virgilia

I thank your ladyship; well, good madam.

Volumnia

He had rather see the swords and hear a drum than
look upon his schoolmaster.

Valeria

O' my word, the father's son! I'll swear 'tis a very
60 pretty boy. O' my troth, I looked upon him o'
Wednesday half an hour together: 'has such a
confirmed countenance! I saw him run after a gilded
butterfly, and when he caught it he let it go again,
and after it again, and over and over he comes, and
65 up again, catched it again. Or whether his fall
enraged him, or how 'twas, he did so set his teeth
and tear it! O, I warrant, how he mammocked it!

---

41 *gilt*: gilding.
   trophy: monument, memorial to his
   triumphs.
41-2 *Hecuba . . . Hector*: The queen of Troy
   and her son, its champion, from whose
   family the Romans claimed descent.
44 *contemning*: spurning, showing
   contempt.
45 *fit*: prepared, ready.
46 *fell*: cruel.

48s.d *Usher*: male escort in attendance on
   noble lady.

52 *manifest housekeepers*: really domesticated,
   determined to stay at home.
53-4 *A fine spot*: a nicely worked piece of
   embroidery.
61 *'has*: he has.
62 *confirmed countenance*: determined
   expression.
   gilded: painted, coloured.
64 *over and over*: head over heels.
66 *how*: however.
67 *mammocked*: savaged, tore apart.

68 *on's*: of his.
    moods: furies, rages.

70 *crack*: little rascal.

71–2 *play . . . with me*: be lazy sluts like me.

73 *not out of doors*: It was the duty of a
    Roman wife to remain at home when
    her husband was away in the army or
    on business.

76 *by your patience*: by your leave.

79 *lies in*: is expecting a baby.

80 *speedy strength*: a quick recovery.

83 *want*: lack.

84–6 *Penelope . . . moths*: Penelope, wife of
    Ulysses, king of Ithaca, was a model for
    faithful wives; she persisted in weaving
    her tapestry and repelling all suitors
    during the absence of her husband at
    the siege of Troy and in his mysterious
    voyagings (the subject of Homer's
    Odyssey).
86 *cambric*: fine linen.
87 *sensible*: sensitive.
    leave: leave off, give over.

Volumnia
One on's father's moods.
    Valeria
Indeed, la, 'tis a noble child.
    Virgilia
70 A crack, madam.
    Valeria
Come, lay aside your stitchery. I must have you pl[ay]
the idle housewife with me this afternoon.
    Virgilia
No, good madam, I will not out of doors.
    Valeria
Not out of doors?
    Volumnia
75 She shall, she shall.
    Virgilia
Indeed, no, by your patience. I'll not over th[e]
threshold till my lord return from the wars.
    Valeria
Fie, you confine yourself most unreasonably. Com[e,]
you must go visit the good lady that lies in.
    Virgilia
80 I will wish her speedy strength, and visit her with m[y]
prayers, but I cannot go thither.
    Volumnia
Why, I pray you?
    Virgilia
'Tis not to save labour, nor that I want love.
    Valeria
You would be another Penelope. Yet they say all th[e]
85 yarn she spun in Ulysses' absence did but fill Ithac[a]
full of moths. Come, I would your cambric wer[e]
sensible as your finger, that you might leave pricking
it for pity. Come, you shall go with us.
    Virgilia
No, good madam, pardon me, indeed I will no[t]
90 forth.
    Valeria
In truth, la, go with me, and I'll tell you excellen[t]
news of your husband.
    Virgilia
O, good madam, there can be none yet.

Valeria

Verily, I do not jest with you: there came news from
95 him last night.

Virgilia

Indeed, madam?

Valeria

In earnest, it's true. I heard a senator speak it. Thus
it is: the Volsces have an army forth, against whom
Cominius the general is gone with one part of our
100 Roman power. Your lord and Titus Lartius are set
down before their city Corioles. They nothing doubt
prevailing, and to make it brief wars. This is true, on
mine honour; and so, I pray, go with us.

Virgilia

Give me excuse, good madam, I will obey you in
105 everything hereafter.

Volumnia

[*To* Valeria] Let her alone, lady. As she is now, she
will but disease our better mirth.

Valeria

In truth, I think she would. Fare you well, then.
Come, good sweet lady. Prithee, Virgilia, turn thy
110 solemness out o' door and go along with us.

Virgilia

No, at a word, madam. Indeed, I must not. I wish
you much mirth.

Valeria

Well then, farewell.

[*Exeunt* Valeria, Volumnia, *and* Usher *at one door,*
Virgilia *and* Gentlewoman *at another door*

98 *forth*: in the battlefield.

00 *power*: fighting force.

01–2 *set down*: in siege.

02 *to make . . . wars*: that the fighting will
be quickly over.

07 *disease*: trouble, make uneasy.

11 *at a word*: in short.

Act 1   Scene 4

Martius leads an assault on Corioles

os.d *colours*: banners.

before: outside; the balcony at the back
of the stage would serve as the city wall
(line 12s.d.), and the Volscian army
could enter through the central doors
beneath.

to them: The side of the stage from
which the Messenger enters will
represent (for this scene) the direction
of Cominius' force.

1   *met*: encountered in battle.

4   *spoke*: fought.
7   *Summon*: i.e. summon to parley.
9   *'larum*: alarum, call to arms with drums
     or trumpets.

10   *Mars*: the Roman god of war.
12   *fielded*: still on the battlefield.
     Come . . . blast: Although Lartius is
     superior officer, the trumpeters do not
     respond until Martius repeats the
     command.

Scene 4

Corioles: enter Martius, Titus Lartius, *with
a drummer, a trumpeter, and colours, with*
Captains *and* Soldiers *carrying scaling
ladders, as before the city Corioles; to them a*
Messenger

Martius
Yonder comes news. A wager they have met.
Lartius
My horse to yours, no.
Martius
                                'Tis done.
Lartius
                                         Agreed.
Martius
[*To the* Messenger] Say, has our general met the
   enemy?
Messenger
They lie in view, but have not spoke as yet.
Lartius
5 So, the good horse is mine.
Martius
                                      I'll buy him of you.
Lartius
No, I'll nor sell nor give him. Lend you him I will,
For half a hundred years. [*To the* trumpeter]
   Summon the town.
Martius
[*To the* Messenger] How far off lie these armies?
Messenger
                                Within this mile and half.
Martius
Then shall we hear their 'larum, and they ours.
10 Now Mars, I prithee, make us quick in work,
   That we with smoking swords may march from
      hence
To help our fielded friends. [*To the* trumpeter]
   Come, blow thy blast.

They sound a parley. Enter two Senators,
with others, *on the walls of Corioles.*

[*To the* Senators] Tullus Aufidius, is he within your
    walls?

First Senator

No, nor a man that fears you less than he:
15 That's lesser than a little.

Drum afar off

[*To the* Volscians]   Hark, our drums
Are bringing forth our youth. We'll break our walls
Rather than they shall pound us up. Our gates,
Which yet seem shut, we have but pinn'd with
    rushes;

7 *pound us up*: shut us in like animals in a
    compound.
8 *pinn'd . . . rushes*: i.e. lightly fastened.

They'll open of themselves.

Alarum far off

[*To the* Romans]   Hark you, far off
20 There is Aufidius. List what work he makes
Amongst your cloven army.
                              [*Exeunt* Volscians *from the wall*
Martius
                              O, they are at it!
Lartius
Their noise be our instruction. Ladders, ho!

Enter the army of the Volsces *from the gates*

Martius
They fear us not, but issue forth their city.
Now put your shields before your hearts, and fight
25 With hearts more proof than shields. Advance,
       brave Titus.
They do disdain us much beyond our thoughts,
Which makes me sweat with wrath. Come on, my
       fellows.
He that retires, I'll take him for a Volsce,
And he shall feel mine edge.

Alarum. The Romans *are beat back and
exeunt to their trenches, the* Volsces *following*

21 *cloven*: divided (under two commanders); cut to pieces.

22 *our instruction*: a lesson to us.
22s.d. *Enter . . . gates*: This is a surprise sortie by the defenders of Corioles, not the troops led by Aufidius.

25 *proof*: of tested strength.

29 *edge*: sword edge.
29s.d. *beat . . . trenches*: The direction echoes the words of Shakespeare's source; presumably the soldiers will leave through one of the side doors and enter again, pursued by Martius, at the other side of the stage.

Act 1   Scene 5

The Romans are in retreat. Martius leads a fresh assault.

1 *contagion*: infection; it was thought that the plague afflicting London when *Coriolanus* was being written was carried by the warm damp winds from the south.
2 *Boils*: a symptom of bubonic plague.
3–4 *abhorr'd . . . seen*: shunned (because of the smell) before you are even seen.
7 *Pluto*: god of the underworld.

Scene 5

Enter Roman Soldiers *in retreat, followed by*
Martius, *cursing*

Martius
All the contagion of the south light on you,
You shames of Rome! You herd of—Boils and plagues
Plaster you o'er, that you may be abhorr'd
Farther than seen, and one infect another
5 Against the wind a mile! You souls of geese
That bear the shapes of men, how have you run
From slaves that apes would beat! Pluto and hell:

All hurt behind! Backs red, and faces pale
With flight and agued fear! Mend and charge home,
10 Or by the fires of heaven I'll leave the foe
And make my wars on you. Look to't. Come on.
If you'll stand fast, we'll beat them to their wives,
As they us to our trenches. Follow's!

Another alarum, and as the Volsces *re-enter
to attack,* Martius *beats them back and
follows them to the gates*

So, now the gates are ópe. Now prove good seconds.
15 'Tis for the followers fortune widens them,
Not for the fliers. Mark me, and do the like.

He enters the gates

First Soldier
Foolhardiness! Not I.
Second Soldier
Nor I.

Alarum continues. The gates close, and
Martius *is shut in*

First Soldier
See, they have shut him in.
Third Soldier
20 To th' pot, I warrant him.

Enter Titus Lartius *with* Soldiers *carrying
ladders*

Lartius
What is become of Martius?
Third Soldier
Slain, sir, doubtless.
First Soldier
Following the fliers at the very heels,
With them he enters, who upon the sudden
Clapp'd-to their gates. He is himself alone
25 To answer all the city.
Lartius
O noble fellow,
Who sensibly outdares his senseless sword
And, when it bows, stand'st up! Thou art lost,
Martius.

9 *agued*: shivering (as though feverish
with the plague).
home: all the way.

14 *seconds*: followers.

20 *pot*: stew-pot.

24 *Clapp'd-to*: slammed shut.
himself alone: all by himself.
25 *answer*: deal with.

26 *sensibly*: sensitive to pain.
senseless: unfeeling.
27 *bows*: bends.
stand'st up: stands firm.

28 *carbuncle*: ruby (or other red gem).

29–30 *a soldier . . . wish*: Cato (234–149 BC) was a great advocate of traditional military values—but this praise of Martius, copied from Plutarch, is anachronistic here.

34 *tremble*: i.e. as in an earthquake.

35 *fetch him off*: rescue him.
make remain alike: stay there with him.

A carbuncle entire, as big as thou art,
Were not so rich a jewel. Thou wast a soldier
30 Even to Cato's wish, not fierce and terrible
Only in strokes, but with thy grim looks and
The thunder-like percussion of thy sounds
Thou mad'st thine enemies shake as if the world
Were feverous and did tremble.

Enter Martius *bleeding, assaulted by the enemy*

First Soldier
                              Look, sir.
Lartius
                                        O, 'tis Martius
35 Let's fetch him off, or make remain alike.

They fight, and all enter the city

Act I   Scene 6

The Romans are victorious.

3 *murrain*: cattle plague.

4 *movers*: Martius scorns the looters.
5 *drachma*: Greek coin of little value.
6 *Irons*: weapons, fire-irons.
doit: Dutch coin of little value.
6–7 *doublets . . . them*: The hangmen took possession of the clothes of those they had executed.
doublets: short jackets, with or without sleeves.

Scene 6

Enter certain Romans *with spoils*

First Roman
This will I carry to Rome.
Second Roman
And I this.
Third Roman
A murrain on't, I took this for silver.

Alarum continues still afar off. Enter
Martius, *bleeding, and* Titus Lartius *with a*
trumpeter

Martius
See here these movers that do prize their hours
5 At a crack'd drachma! Cushions, leaden spoons,
Irons of a doit, doublets that hangmen would
Bury with those that wore them, these base slaves,
Ere yet the fight be done, pack up. Down with them!
[*Exeunt* Romans *with spoils*

And hark what noise the general makes. To him!
10 There is the man of my soul's hate, Aufidius,
Piercing our Romans. Then, valiant Titus, take
Convenient numbers to make good the city,
Whilst I, with those that have the spirit, will haste
To help Cominius.

Lartius
                    Worthy sir, thou bleed'st.
15 Thy exercise hath been too violent
For a second course of fight.

Martius
                        Sir, praise me not.
My work hath yet not warm'd me. Fare you well.
The blood I drop is rather physical
Than dangerous to me. To Aufidius thus
20 I will appear and fight.

Lartius
                    Now the fair goddess Fortune
Fall deep in love with thee, and her great charms
Misguide thy opposers' swords! Bold gentleman,
Prosperity be thy page.

12 *make good*: secure.

16 *course*: onslaught.
18 *physical*: good for my health; medicinal
blood-letting was a common Elizabethan
practice for choleric temperaments.

21 *charms*: magic spells.

23 *be thy page*: attend upon you.

Martius
                                        Thy friend no less
Than those she placeth highest. So farewell.

Lartius
25 Thou worthiest Martius!   [*Exit* Martius
Go sound thy trumpet in the market-place.
Call thither all the officers o'th' town,
Where they shall know our mind. Away.
                              [*Exeunt severally*

23–4 *no less . . . highest*: i.e. no less than her best friend.

28s.d. *severally*: i.e. in different directions.

Act 1   Scene 7

In another part of the battlefield, Cominius rallies his troops.

Scene 7

The battlefield: enter Cominius, *as it were in retire, with* Soldiers

Cominius
Breathe you, my friends. Well fought. We are come off
Like Romans, neither foolish in our stands
Nor cowardly in retire. Believe me, sirs,
We shall be charg'd again. Whiles we have struck,
5 By interims and conveying gusts we have heard
The charges of our friends. Ye Roman gods,
Lead their successes as we wish our own,
That both our powers, with smiling fronts encount'ring,
May give you thankful sacrifice!

Enter a Messenger

                                        Thy news?

Messenger
10 The citizens of Corioles have issued,
And given to Lartius and to Martius battle.
I saw our party to their trenches driven,
And then I came away.

Cominius
                          Though thou speak'st truth,
Methinks thou speak'st not well. How long is't since?

Messenger
15 Above an hour my lord.

Cominius
'Tis not a mile; briefly we heard their drums.

1 *are come off*: have got out of this.

3 *retire*: retreat.
4 *charg'd*: attacked.
  struck: been fighting.
5 *By interims . . . gusts*: by rumours from time to time.
7 *Lead . . . own*: guide our friends' fortunes, as we wish our own.
8 *fronts*: faces.

10 *issued*: come outside the gates.

16 *not a mile*: at *1, 4, 8* it was a 'mile and half'; presumably Cominius' troops have retired in the direction of the other Roman force.
  briefly: a short time ago.

confound: waste.

How couldst thou in a mile confound an hour,
And bring thy news so late?

Messenger
                                              Spies of the Volsces

that: so that.

Held me in chase, that I was forc'd to wheel
20 Three or four miles about; else had I, sir,
Half an hour since brought my report.   [*Exit*

Enter Martius, *bloody*

Cominius
                                              Who's yonder,

2 *as . . . flay'd*: like a newly skinned
   carcass.
3 *stamp*: form, bearing.
4 *Beforetime*: before now.

That does appear as he were flay'd? O gods!
He has the stamp of Martius, and I have
Beforetime seen him thus.

Martius
                              Come I too late?

Cominius

5 *tabor*: small drum used by dancers and
   revellers.

25 The shepherd knows not thunder from a tabor
More than I know the sound of Martius' tongue
From every meaner man.

Martius
                              Come I too late?

Cominius
Ay, if you come not in the blood of others,
But mantled in your own.

Martius
                              O, let me clip ye

27 *meaner*: ordinary.
29 *mantled*: covered, cloaked.
   clip: embrace.

30 In arms as sound as when I woo'd, in heart
As merry as when our nuptial day was done,
And tapers burnt to bedward!

They embrace

Cominius
Flower of warriors! How is't with Titus Lartius?

Martius
As with a man busied about decrees,

36 *Ransoming . . . pitying*: releasing a man
   for ransom or for pity.

35 Condemning some to death and some to exile,
Ransoming him or pitying, threat'ning th'other;
Holding Corioles in the name of Rome
Even like a fawning greyhound in the leash,
To let him slip at will.

Cominius

Where is that slave
40 Which told me they had beat you to your trenches
Where is he? Call him hither.

Martius

Let him alone.
He did inform the truth—but for our gentlemen,
The common file—a plague! tribunes for them!—
The mouse ne'er shunn'd the cat as they did budge
45 From rascals worse than they.

Cominius

But how prevail'd you

Martius

Will the time serve to tell? I do not think.
Where is the enemy? Are you lords o'th' field?
If not, why cease you till you are so?

Cominius

Martius, we have at disadvantage fought,
50 And did retire to win our purpose.

Martius

How lies their battle? Know you on which side
They have plac'd their men of trust?

Cominius

As I guess, Martius
Their bands i'th' vanguard are the Antiates,
Of their best trust; o'er them Aufidius,
55 Their very heart of hope.

Martius

I do beseech you
By all the battles wherein we have fought,
By th' blood we have shed together,
By th' vows we have made
To endure friends, that you directly set me
60 Against Aufidius and his Antiates,
And that you not delay the present, but,
Filling the air with swords advanced and darts,
We prove this very hour.

Cominius

Though I could wish
You were conducted to a gentle bath
65 And balms applied to you, yet dare I never
Deny your asking. Take your choice of those
That best can aid your action.

42 *inform*: report.
43 *common file*: rank and file.
44 *budge*: flinch from.
45 *rascals*: rogues (see *1, 1, 151*n).

51 *battle*: battle formation.

53 *Antiates*: men of Antium (the chief city of the Volsces, and Aufidius' home town).
55 *heart of hope*: highest hope.

61 *delay the present*: make any delay now.
62 *advanced*: raised before us.
63 *prove*: try what we can do.
   this very hour: right now.

Martius

                                        Those are they
That most are willing. If any such be here—
As it were sin to doubt—that love this painting
70 Wherein you see me smear'd; if any fear
Lesser his person than an ill report;
If any think brave death outweighs bad life,
And that his country's dearer than himself,
Let him alone, or so many so minded,
75 Wave thus to express his disposition,
And follow Martius.

> *He waves his sword. They all shout and*
> *wave their swords, take him up in their arms*
> *and cast up their caps*

O, me alone! Make you a sword of me?
If these shows be not outward, which of you
But is four Volsces? None of you but is
80 Able to bear against the great Aufidius
A shield as hard as his. A certain number—
Though thanks to all—must I select from all.
The rest shall bear the business in some other fight
As cause will be obey'd. Please you to march,
85 And I shall quickly draw out my command,
Which men are best inclin'd.
            Cominius
                                        March on, my fellows.
Make good this ostentation, and you shall
Divide in all with us.
                                        [*Exeunt*

69 *painting*: i.e. the blood.

71 *Lesser*: less for.

84 *As . . . obey'd*: as occasion may demand.
85 *draw . . . command*: pick out my
command-force.
86 *inclin'd*: suited.

Act I   Scene 8

Corioles is well guarded.

1 *ports*: gates.

3 *centuries*: companies consisting of one hundred men under the command of a centurion.

8 *guider*: guide, escort.

Scene 8

Corioles. Titus Lartius, *having set a guard upon* Corioles, *going with drummer and trumpeter toward* Cominius *and* Caius Martius, *enters with a* Lieutenant, *other* Soldiers *and a* Scout

Lartius
[*To the* Lieutenant] So, let the ports be guarded.
    Keep your duties
As I have set them down. If I do send, dispatch
Those centuries to our aid. The rest will serve
For a short holding. If we lose the field
5 We cannot keep the town.
    Lieutenant
Fear not our care, sir.
    Lartius
Hence, and shut your gates upon's.
                              [*Exit* Lieutenant
[*To the* Scout] Our guider, come; to th' Roman
    camp conduct us.
                              [*Exeunt*

Act I   Scene 9

Martius encounters Aufidius.

os.d. *several doors*: i.e. from different directions.

Scene 9

The battlefield. Alarum, as in battle. Enter Martius *and* Aufidius, *at several doors*

Martius
I'll fight with none but thee, for I do hate thee
Worse than a promise-breaker.
    Aufidius
                              We hate alike.
Not Afric owns a serpent I abhor
More than thy fame and envy. Fix thy foot.
    Martius
5 Let the first budger die the other's slave,
And the gods doom him after.
    Aufidius
                              If I fly, Martius,
Holloa me like a hare.

Martius

              Within these three hours, Tullus,
Alone I fought in your Corioles' walls,
And made what work I pleas'd. 'Tis not my blood
10 Wherein thou seest me mask'd. For thy revenge,
Wrench up thy power to th' highest.

Aufidius

              Wert thou the Hector
That was the whip of your bragg'd progeny,
Thou shouldst not 'scape me here.

11–12 *the Hector . . . progeny*: i.e. that original Hector which your people ('progeny' = race) brag of as being their scourge; see *1, 3, 41–2n.*

> *Here they fight, and certain* Volsces *come in the aid of* Aufidius. Martius *fights till they be driven in breathless,* Martius *following*

Officious and not valiant, you have sham'd me
15 In your condemned seconds.

                        [*Exit*

15 *In . . . seconds*: with your damned support.
condemned: condemnèd.

Act 1   Scene 10

Victory! The Romans return to their encampment with Martius as hero of the day.

os.d. *retreat*: trumpet-call to fetch back the troops chasing the enemy.
Flourish: trumpet-call sounded to herald the entrance of the victors.
at one door . . . another door: The Romans, entering from both sides of the stage, have complete command of the battle.
2 *Thou't*: thou wouldst.
4 *shrug*: i.e. in an expression of incredulity.
5 *admire*: wonder, marvel.
6 *quak'd*: thrilled, agitated.
dull: sullen, spiritless.
7 *fusty*: mouldy, stale.
plébeians: stressed on the first syllable.

10 *morsel*: leftover scrap: the fight with Aufidius was nothing compared to Martius' other achievements—*or*, perhaps, Cominius is claiming some success for himself.

Scene 10

> *The Roman camp. Alarum. A retreat is sounded. Flourish. Enter at one door* Cominius *with the* Romans, *at another door* Martius *with his left arm in a scarf*

Cominius

[*To* Martius] If I should tell thee o'er this thy day's work
Thou't not believe thy deeds. But I'll report it
Where senators shall mingle tears with smiles,
Where great patricians shall attend, and shrug,
5 I'th' end admire; where ladies shall be frighted
And, gladly quak'd, hear more; where the dull tribunes,
That with the fusty plebeians hate thine honours,
Shall say against their hearts 'We thank the gods
Our Rome hath such a soldier.'
10 Yet cam'st thou to a morsel of this feast,
Having fully din'd before.

> *Enter* Lartius, *with his power, from the pursuit*

Lartius

                                    O general,
Here is the steed, we the caparison.
Hadst thou beheld—
    Martius

                              Pray now, no more. My mother,
Who has a charter to extol her blood,
15 When she does praise me, grieves me.
I have done as you have done, that's what I can;
Induc'd as you have been, that's for my country.
He that has but effected his good will
Hath overta'en mine act.
    Cominius

                                    You shall not be
20 The grave of your deserving. Rome must know
The value of her own. 'Twere a concealment
Worse than a theft, no less than a traducement,
To hide your doings and to silence that
Which, to the spire and top of praises vouch'd,
25 Would seem but modest. Therefore, I beseech you—
In sign of what you are, not to reward
What you have done—before our army hear me.
    Martius
I have some wounds upon me, and they smart
To hear themselves remember'd.
    Cominius

                                        Should they not,
30 Well might they fester 'gainst ingratitude,
And tent themselves with death. Of all the horses—
Whereof we have ta'en good, and good store—of all
The treasure in this field achiev'd and city,
We render you the tenth, to be ta'en forth
35 Before the common distribution
At your only choice.
    Martius

                              I thank you, general,
But cannot make my heart consent to take
A bribe to pay my sword. I do refuse it,
And stand upon my common part with those
40 That have upheld the doing.

A long flourish. They all cry 'Martius,
Martius!', *casting up their caps and lances.*
Cominius *and* Lartius *stand bare*

---

12 *Here . . . caparison*: i.e. Martius here is the main force and we are merely the trappings.

14 *charter*: prerogative, legal right.

18–19 *He . . . act*: He who has simply carried out his resolution has accomplished more than I.

20 *deserving*: deserts.
must know: needs to know, has a right to know.
22 *traducement*: slander.

24 *to the spire . . . vouch'd*: given the very highest praises, 'commended beyond the moon' (Plutarch).
26 *sign*: recognition.
what you are: i.e. your unique individuality.

30 *'gainst*: in the face of.
31 *tent*: clean up; a 'tent' was a roll of linen used to probe and clean wounds.

32 *good store*: plenty of them.
36 *only*: own.

40 *upheld*: sustained.
40s.d. *stand bare*: take off their headgear (in mark of respect for Martius).

1 *instruments*: i.e. the trumpets sounding the 'long flourish'.

2–4 *When drums . . . soothing*: i.e. if drums and trumpets are going to be flatterers in the battlefield, there will be nothing but lies and hypocrisy in civilian life; embarrassment, here (and below, 45–6) makes Martius incoherent.

4 *soothing*: deception, corruption.

5–6 *When steel . . . wars*: i.e. when the warrior's armour (and conduct) become soft as silk, the court parasite will praise warfare.

5 *parasite*: flatterer (one who earns his meals by flattery).

7 *For that*: because.

8 *foil'd*: overcome, overthrown.
  debile: feeble.

9 *without note*: unnoticed.

50 *shout me forth*: acclaim me.

52 *little*: small achievement.

52–3 *dieted In*: fattened up on.

53 *sauc'd*: spiced, seasoned.

55 *give*: report.

57 *means . . . harm*: intends to injure himself.

62 *trim belonging*: i.e. the 'caparison' and equipment.

65 *Martius Caius Coriolanus*: Shakespeare departs from the usual Roman sequence of personal name + family name + addition ('Caius Martius Coriolanus').

66 *addition*: title: 'The third [name] was in addition given either for some act or notable service . . . or else for some virtue' (Plutarch).

68 *Coriolanus*: The hero's speech prefix is changed at this point by most editors, although Folio retains 'Martius' until the return to Rome (*Act 2, Scene 1*).

72–3 *To undercrest . . . power*: i.e. 'bear like an heraldic crest the noble title you have given me, and do my best to live up to it'.

May these same instruments which you profane
Never sound more. When drums and trumpets shall
I'th' field prove flatterers, let courts and cities be
Made all of false-fac'd soothing!
45 When steel grows soft as the parasite's silk,
Let him be made an ovator for th' wars!
No more, I say! For that I have not wash'd
My nose that bled, or foil'd some debile wretch,
Which without note here's many else have done,
50 You shout me forth
In acclamations hyperbolical;
As if I lov'd my little should be dieted
In praises sauc'd with lies.

    Cominius
                          Too modest are you,
More cruel to your good report than grateful
55 To us that give you truly. By your patience,
If 'gainst yourself you be incens'd we'll put you,
Like one that means his proper harm, in manacles,
Then reason safely with you. Therefore be it known,
As to us, to all the world, that Caius Martius
60 Wears this war's garland, in token of the which
My noble steed, known to the camp, I give him,
With all his trim belonging; and from this time,
For what he did before Corioles, call him,
With all th'applause and clamour of the host,
65 Martius Caius Coriolanus!
Bear th'addition nobly ever!

    Flourish. Trumpets sound, and drums

    All
Martius Caius Coriolanus!
    Coriolanus
I will go wash,
And when my face is fair you shall perceive
70 Whether I blush or no. Howbeit, I thank you.
    [*To* Cominius] I mean to stride your steed, and at all times
To undercrest your good addition
To th' fairness of my power.
    Cominius
                    So, to our tent,
Where, ere we do repose us, we will write

77 *best*: leading citizens of Corioles.
    articulate: negotiate.

75 To Rome of our success. You, Titus Lartius,
    Must to Corioles back. Send us to Rome
    The best, with whom we may articulate
    For their own good and ours.
            Lartius
                                        I shall, my lord.
            Coriolanus
    The gods begin to mock me. I, that now
80 Refus'd most princely gifts, am bound to beg
    Of my lord general.
            Cominius
                            Take't, 'tis yours. What is't?
            Coriolanus

82–90 *I . . . forgot*: The episode is taken
    from Plutarch (who describes the host
    as having been rich).
83 *us'd*: treated.

    I sometime lay here in Corioles,
    At a poor man's house. He us'd me kindly.
    He cried to me; I saw him prisoner;
85 But then Aufidius was within my view,
    And wrath o'erwhelm'd my pity. I request you
    To give my poor host freedom.
            Cominius
                                        O, well begg'd!
    Were he the butcher of my son, he should
    Be free as is the wind. Deliver him, Titus.
            Lartius
90 Martius, his name?
            Coriolanus
                            By Jupiter, forgot!
    I am weary, yea, my memory is tir'd.
    Have we no wine here?
            Cominius
                            Go we to our tent.
    The blood upon your visage dries; 'tis time
    It should be look'd to. Come.

            A flourish of cornetts.   [*Exeun*.

ct 1   Scene 11

he defeated Aufidius is determined to get
venge.

2 *good condition*: The soldier means
'favourable terms'—but Aufidius will
take up the sense 'satisfactory state' to
make a bitter pun.

7 *part . . . mercy*: defeated side absolutely
in the power of the victor.

14 *in . . . force*: on equal ground.
15 *potch*: jab, poke.
16 *Or . . . or*: either . . . or.

19 *fly . . . itself*: i.e. betray its own nature.
20 *naked*: defenceless.
    fane: temple.
22 *Embargements . . . fury*: all situations in
which anger is prohibited.
23 *rotten*: corrupt with age.
25 *upon . . . guard*: under my brother's
protection.
26 *hospitable canon*: the law of hospitality.
27 *heart*: heart's blood.

Scene 11

Outside Corioles: *enter* Tullus Aufidius,
bloody, with two or three Soldiers

Aufidius
The town is ta'en.
        A Soldier
'Twill be deliver'd back on good condition.
        Aufidius
Condition?
I would I were a Roman, for I cannot,
5 Being a Volsce, be that I am. Condition!
What good condition can a treaty find
I'th' part that is at mercy? Five times, Martius,
I have fought with thee; so often hast thou beat me,
And wouldst do so, I think, should we encounter
10 As often as we eat. By th'elements,
If e'er again I meet him beard to beard,
He's mine, or I am his! Mine emulation
Hath not that honour in't it had, for where
I thought to crush him in an equal force,
15 True sword to sword, I'll potch at him some way,
Or wrath or craft may get him.
        A Soldier
                        He's the devil.
        Aufidius
Bolder, though not so subtle. My valour, poison'd
With only suff'ring stain by him, for him
Shall fly out of itself. Nor sleep nor sanctuary,
20 Being naked, sick, nor fane or Capitol,
The prayers of priests nor times of sacrifice—
Embargements all of fury—shall lift up
Their rotten privilege and custom 'gainst
My hate to Martius. Where I find him, were it
25 At home upon my brother's guard, even there,
Against the hospitable canon, would I
Wash my fierce hand in's heart. Go you to th' city.
Learn how 'tis held, and what they are that must
Be hostages for Rome.
        A Soldier
                        Will not you go?

Aufidius

30   I am attended at the cypress grove. I pray you—
     'Tis south the city mills—bring me word thither
     How the world goes, that to the pace of it
     I may spur on my journey.

A Soldier

                                   I shall, sir.

[*Exeunt* Aufidius *at one door,* Soldiers *at the other doo*

Act 2

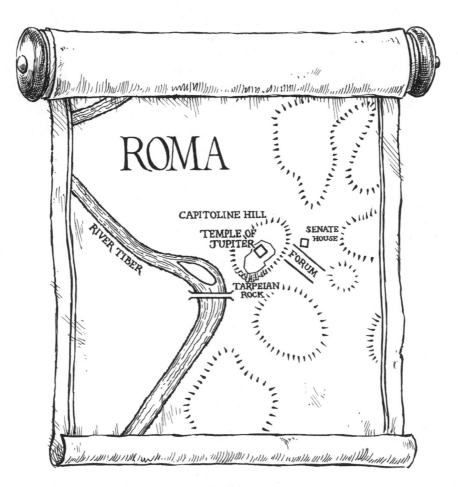

ROMA

CAPITOLINE HILL

TEMPLE OF
JUPITER

SENATE
HOUSE

RIVER TIBER

FORUM

TARPEIAN
ROCK

Scene 1

> *Rome*: enter Menenius *with the two tribunes*
> *of the people* Sicinius *and* Brutus

Menenius
The augurer tells me we shall have news tonight.
    Brutus
Good or bad?
    Menenius
Not according to the prayer of the people, for they
love not Martius.

Sicinius

5 Nature teaches beasts to know their friends.

Menenius

Pray you, who does the wolf love?

Sicinius

The lamb.

Menenius

Ay, to devour him, as the hungry plebeians wou[ld]
the noble Martius.

Brutus

10 He's a lamb indeed that baas like a bear.

Menenius

He's a bear indeed that lives like a lamb. You two a[re]
old men. Tell me one thing that I shall ask you.

Sicinius and **Brutus**

Well, sir?

Menenius

In what enormity is Martius poor in that you tw[o]
15 have not in abundance?

Brutus

He's poor in no one fault, but stored with all.

Sicinius

Especially in pride.

Brutus

And topping all others in boasting.

Menenius

This is strange now. Do you two know how you a[re]
20 censured here in the city—I mean of us o'th' rig[ht]
hand file? Do you?

Sicinius and **Brutus**

Why, how are we censured?

Menenius

Because you talk of pride now—will you not [be]
angry?

Sicinius and **Brutus**

25 Well, well, sir, well?

Menenius

Why, 'tis no great matter, for a very little thief [of]
occasion will rob you of a great deal of patience. Gi[ve]
your dispositions the reins, and be angry at yo[ur]
pleasures—at the least, if you take it as a pleasure [to]
30 you in being so. You blame Martius for being prou[d]

---

12 *old men*: Menenius implies that they should therefore be wise.

13 *Sicinius and Brutus*: The Folio text reads '*Both*', suggesting that the two tribunes speak together; modern editors sometimes divide the speeches.

14 *enormity*: irregularity of conduct, wickedness.

20–1 *right-hand file*: right wing, i.e. the patricians.

26–7 *very little . . . occasion*: i.e. the slightest occasion.

Brutus
We do it not alone, sir.

Menenius
I know you can do very little alone, for your helps are many, or else your actions would grow wondrous single. Your abilities are too infant-like for doing
35 much alone. You talk of pride. O that you could turn your eyes toward the napes of your necks, and make but an interior survey of your good selves! O that you could!

Sicinius and **Brutus**
What then, sir?

Menenius
40 Why, then you should discover a brace of unmeriting, proud, violent, testy magistrates, alias fools, as any in Rome.

Sicinius
Menenius, you are known well enough too.

Menenius
I am known to be a humorous patrician, and one
45 that loves a cup of hot wine with not a drop of allaying Tiber in't; said to be something imperfect in favouring the first complaint, hasty and tinder-like upon too trivial motion; one that converses more with the buttock of the night than with the forehead
50 of the morning. What I think, I utter, and spend my malice in my breath. Meeting two such wealsmen as you are, I cannot call you Lycurguses. If the drink you give me touch my palate adversely, I make a crooked face at it. I cannot say your worships have
55 delivered the matter well, when I find the ass in compound with the major part of your syllables. And though I must be content to bear with those that say you are reverend grave men, yet they lie deadly that tell you have good faces. If you see this in the map of
60 my microcosm, follows it that I am known well enough too? What harm can your bisson conspectuities glean out of this character, if I be known well enough too?

Brutus
Come, sir, come, we know you well enough.

4 *humorous*: whimsical, temperamental.

46 *Tiber*: the river of Rome.
46–7 *something . . . complaint*: rather too ready to decide in favour of the plaintiff (who is first to speak).
47 *tinder-like*: quick to flare up.
48 *motion*: provocation.
48–50 *converses . . . morning*: is more accustomed to staying up late than rising early.
51 *wealsmen*: men devoted to the common weal (= public good). Menenius seems to be making some kind of pun with *wealsmen* and 'wellsmen' (= men who draw water from a well, *and* those who repeatedly say 'well').
52 *Lycurguses*: Lycurgus was a legendary Spartan law-giver who was the subject of one of Plutarch's *Lives*.
55–6 *ass . . . syllables*: something asinine in almost everything you say; Menenius mocks the tribunes with an affectation of learning.
59 *good*: honest, handsome.
59–60 *map . . . microcosm*: i.e. my face (which is an indication of what the 'little world' of the man is like).
61–2 *bisson conspectuities*: bleary-eyed insights.

66 *caps and legs*: i.e. respect (shown in the raising of caps and bowing down).
68 *orange-wife*: woman who sells oranges. *faucet-seller*: pedlar of taps for wine-barrels.
69 *rejourn*: adjourn.
71 *party*: i.e. party to a dispute, litigant.
72–3 *make . . . mummers*: pull faces like actors in mimes or dumb-shows.
73 *bloody flag*: i.e. the red flag of battle.

75 *bleeding*: unhealed, unsettled.
80 *giber . . . table*: dinner table wit. *bencher*: magistrate.
83 *subjects*: creatures, topics.
86 *botcher*: one who patches clothes.

88–9 *in a . . . estimation*: even at the lowest valuation.
90 *since Deucalion*: i.e. since the flood; Deucalion was the Greek equivalent of Noah.
91 *e'en*: evening (the expression could be used any time after noon).
92 *conversation*: company, society.

95 *moon*: i.e. Diana, goddess of the moon; see *1, 1, 250*.

99 *Juno*: queen of the Roman gods.

Menenius

65 You know neither me, yourselves, nor anything. You are ambitious for poor knaves' caps and legs. You wear out a good wholesome forenoon in hearing cause between an orange-wife and a faucet-seller, and then rejourn the controversy of threepence to a

70 second day of audience. When you are hearing a matter between party and party, if you chance to be pinched with the colic, you make faces like mummers, set up the bloody flag against all patience, and in roaring for a chamber-pot, dismiss

75 the controversy bleeding, the more entangled by your hearing. All the peace you make in their cause is calling both the parties knaves. You are a pair of strange ones.

Brutus

Come, come, you are well understood to be a

80 perfecter giber for the table than a necessary bencher in the Capitol.

Menenius

Our very priests must become mockers if they shall encounter such ridiculous subjects as you are. When you speak best unto the purpose, it is not worth the

85 wagging of your beards, and your beards deserve not so honourable a grave as to stuff a botcher's cushion or to be entombed in an ass's pack-saddle. Yet you must be saying Martius is proud, who, in a cheap estimation, is worth all your predecessors since

90 Deucalion, though peradventure some of the best of 'em were hereditary hangmen. Good e'en to your worships. More of your conversation would infect my brain, being the herdsmen of the beastly plebeians. I will be bold to take my leave of you.

He leaves Brutus *and* Sicinius, *who stand aside. Enter* Volumnia, Virgilia, *and* Valeria

95 How now, my as fair as noble ladies—and the moon, were she earthly, no nobler—whither do you follow your eyes so fast?

Volumnia

Honourable Menenius, my boy Martius approaches. For the love of Juno, let's go.

Menenius

100 Ha, Martius coming home?

Volumnia

Ay, worthy Menenius, and with most prosperous approbation.

Menenius

[*Throwing up his cap*] Take my cap, Jupiter, and I thank thee! Hoo, Martius coming home?

Virgilia and **Valeria**

105 Nay, 'tis true.

Volumnia

Look, here's a letter from him. The state hath another, his wife another, and I think there's one at home for you.

Menenius

I will make my very house reel tonight. A letter for
110 me?

Virgilia

Yes, certain, there's a letter for you; I saw't.

Menenius

A letter for me? It gives me an estate of seven years' health, in which time I will make a lip at the physician. The most sovereign prescription in Galen
115 is but empiricutic and, to this preservative, of no better report than a horse-drench. Is he not wounded? He was wont to come home wounded.

Virgilia

O, no, no, no!

Volumnia

O, he is wounded, I thank the gods for't!

Menenius

120 So do I, too, if it be not too much. Brings a victory in his pocket, the wounds become him.

Volumnia

On's brows, Menenius. He comes the third time home with the oaken garland.

Menenius

Has he disciplined Aufidius soundly?

Volumnia

125 Titus Lartius writes they fought together, but Aufidius got off.

101–2 *prosperous approbation*: confirmed success.

112 *gives . . . estate*: endows me with.

113 *make a lip at*: scoff at.

114 *Galen*: a famous physician of the second century AD whose authority was still respected in Shakespeare's time (but the reference is anachronistic here).

115 *empiricutic*: the prescription of an empiric (= quack-doctor); Menenius coins the word on the analogy of 'pharmaceutic'.

116 *horse-drench*: dose of horse medicine.

120 *Brings a*: if he brings.

122 *On's brows*: i.e. crowned with glory.

124 *disciplined*: thrashed.

127 *An*: if.

129 *'fidiussed*: Menenius coins a word from
Aufidius' name to make a pun with the
legal term 'fidejussor', meaning 'one
who goes bail for another'.
130 *possessed*: informed.

133 *name*: credit, glory.

137 *purchasing*: earning, deserving.

146 *cicatrices*: scars.
146–7 *stand . . . place*: offer himself for
election.
147 *repulse of Tarquin*: Tarquinius Superbus,
the last king of Rome, was finally
defeated in the battle of Lake Regillus
(496 BC), when Martius first attracted
military attention (*1, 3, 14*note).

Menenius
And 'twas time for him too, I'll warrant him that. A
he had stayed by him, I would not have been o
'fidiussed for all the chests in Corioles and the gol
130   that's in them. Is the Senate possessed of this?
Volumnia
Good ladies, let's go. Yes, yes, yes. The Senate ha
letters from the general, wherein he gives my son th
whole name of the war. He hath in this actio
outdone his former deeds doubly.
Valeria
135   In truth, there's wondrous things spoke of him.
Menenius
Wondrous, ay, I warrant you; and not without hi
true purchasing.
Virgilia
The gods grant them true.
Volumnia
True? Pooh-whoo!
Menenius
140   True? I'll be sworn they are true. Where is he
wounded? [*To the* Tribunes] God save your good
worships. Martius is coming home. He has more
cause to be proud. [*To* Volumnia] Where is he
wounded?
Volumnia
145   I'th' shoulder and i'th' left arm. There will be large
cicatrices to show the people when he shall stand for
his place. He received in the repulse of Tarquin seven
hurts i'th' body.
Menenius
One i'th' neck and two i'th' thigh—there's nine that
150   I know.
Volumnia
He had before this last expedition twenty-five
wounds upon him.
Menenius
Now it's twenty-seven. Every gash was an enemy's
grave.

A shout and flourish

155 Hark, the trumpets.

Volumnia
These are the ushers of Martius. Before him
He carries noise, and behind him he leaves tears.
Death, that dark spirit, in's nervy arm doth lie,
Which being advanc'd, declines; and then men die.

> *A sennet. Enter* Cominius *the general and*
> Titus Lartius: *between them* Coriolanus
> *crowned with an oaken garland, with*
> Captains *and* Soldiers, *and a* Herald.
> *Trumpets sound*

Herald
160 Know, Rome, that all alone Martius did fight
Within Corioles' gates, where he hath won
With fame a name to 'Martius Caius'; these
In honour follows 'Coriolanus'.
Welcome to Rome, renowned Coriolanus!

> *A flourish sounds*

All
165 Welcome to Rome, renowned Coriolanus!

Coriolanus
No more of this, it does offend my heart.
Pray now, no more.

Cominius   Look, sir, your mother.

Coriolanus
[*To* Volumnia]   O!
You have, I know, petition'd all the gods
For my prosperity!

> *He kneels*

Volumnia
                        Nay, my good soldier, up,
170 My gentle Martius, worthy Caius,
And, by deed-achieving honour newly nam'd—
What is it?—'Coriolanus' must I call thee?

> *He rises*

But O, thy wife!

158 *nervy*: sinewy.
159 *advanc'd*: raised.
     declines: falls.
159s.d. *sennet*: ceremonial flourish on the
     trumpets.
     Lartius: In the theatre it would probably
     not be noticed that Lartius had been
     left behind in Corioles (*1*, 10, 75–6) and
     will be found there in the next scene
     (*2, 2, 38*).
164 *renowned*: renownèd.

165 *renowned*: renownèd.

171 *deed-achieving honour*: honour which is
     achieved by deeds.

Coriolanus

[*To* Virgilia] My gracious silence, hail.

175 Wouldst thou have laugh'd had I come coffin'd home
That weep'st to see me triumph? Ah, my dear,
Such eyes the widows in Corioles wear,
And mothers that lack sons.

Menenius

                              Now the gods crown the

Coriolanus

And live you yet? [*To* Valeria] O my sweet lady,
pardon.

Volumnia

180 I know not where to turn. O, welcome home!
And welcome, general, and you're welcome all.

Menenius

A hundred thousand welcomes! I could weep
And I could laugh, I am light and heavy. Welcome
A curse begin at very root on's heart

185 That is not glad to see thee. You are three
That Rome should dote on. Yet, by the faith of men
We have some old crab-trees here at home that wi
not
Be grafted to your relish. Yet welcome, warriors!
We call a nettle but a nettle, and

190 The faults of fools but folly.

Cominius

Ever right.

Coriolanus

Menenius, ever, ever.

Herald

Give way there, and go on.

Coriolanus

[*To* Volumnia *and* Virgilia]   Your hand, and your
Ere in our own house I do shade my head

195 The good patricians must be visited,
From whom I have receiv'd not only greetings,
But with them change of honours.

Volumnia

                              I have liv'd

To see inherited my very wishes,
And the buildings of my fancy. Only

200 There's one thing wanting, which I doubt not but
Our Rome will cast upon thee.

188 *grafted*: altered.
   relish: taste.
189–90 *We call . . . folly*: i.e. that's the way
   things are and we must accept them.

Coriolanus

                      Know, good mother,
I had rather be their servant in my way
Than sway with them in theirs.

Cominius

                     On, to the Capitol.

*A flourish of cornetts. Exeunt in state, as
before, all but* Brutus *and* Sicinius, *who
come forward*

206 *rapture*: paroxysm, fit.
207 *malkin*: wench (diminutive of 'Maud').
208 *lockram*: linen cloth.
    reechy: greasy, sweaty.
209 *bulks*: projecting framework in front of
    shop.
210 *leads*: lead-covered roofs.
    ridges hors'd: i.e. people are sitting
    astride the roof ridges.
211 *variable complexions*: all sorts of people
    (*literally*, the complexions of the four
    humours: sanguine, phlegmatic,
    melancholic, and choleric).
212 *Seld-shown flamens*: priests who rarely
    show themselves.
214 *vulgar station*: place to stand among the
    common people.
215–17 *Commit . . . kisses*: i.e. expose their
    beautifully made-up cheeks to the risk
    of sunburn.
217 *pother*: uproar, commotion.

Brutus

All tongues speak of him, and the blear'd sights
205 Are spectacled to see him. Your prattling nurse
Into a rapture lets her baby cry
While she chats him; the kitchen malkin pins
Her richest lockram 'bout her reechy neck,
Clamb'ring the walls to eye him. Stalls, bulks,
    windows
210 Are smother'd up, leads fill'd and ridges hors'd
With variable complexions, all agreeing
In earnestness to see him. Seld-shown flamens
Do press among the popular throngs, and puff
To win a vulgar station. Our veil'd dames
215 Commit the war of white and damask in
Their nicely guarded cheeks to th' wanton spoil
Of Phoebus' burning kisses. Such a pother

As if that whatsoever god who leads him
Were slily crept into his human powers
220 And gave him graceful posture.
Sicinius
                                    On the sudden
I warrant him consul.
Brutus
                        Then our office may
During his power go sleep.
Sicinius

223 *temp'rately*: moderately, reasonably.

He cannot temp'rately transport his honours
From where he should begin and end, but will
225 Lose those he hath won.
Brutus
                            In that there's comfort.
Sicinius
                                        Doubt not
The commoners, for whom we stand, but they

227 *Upon*: on the ground of.
   ancient: former, earlier.

Upon their ancient malice will forget
With the least cause these his new honours, which
That he will give them make I as little question
230 As he is proud to do't.
Brutus
                        I heard him swear,
Were he to stand for consul, never would he
Appear i'th' market-place nor on him put

233 *napless vesture*: threadbare garment;
according to Plutarch, the candidate for
office wore only a toga, without a tunic
underneath.

The napless vesture of humility,
Nor, showing, as the manner is, his wounds
235 To th' people, beg their stinking breaths.
Sicinius
                                    'Tis right.
Brutus
It was his word. O, he would miss it rather
Than carry it, but by the suit of the gentry to him,
And the desire of the nobles.
Sicinius
                            I wish no better
Than have him hold that purpose, and to put it
240 In execution.
Brutus
                'Tis most like he will.

Sicinius

It shall be to him then, as our good wills,
A sure destruction.

Brutus
                                    So it must fall out
To him, or our authority's for an end.
We must suggest the people in what hatred
245 He still hath held them; that to's power he would
Have made them mules, silenc'd their pleaders,
And dispropertied their freedoms, holding them
In human action and capacity
Of no more soul nor fitness for the world
250 Than camels in the war, who have their provand
Only for bearing burdens, and sore blows
For sinking under them.

Sicinius
                                    This, as you say, suggested
At some time when his soaring insolence
Shall touch the people—which time shall not want
255 If he be put upon't, and that's as easy
As to set dogs on sheep—will be his fire
To kindle their dry stubble, and their blaze
Shall darken him for ever.

Enter a Messenger

Brutus
                                    What's the matter?

Messenger

You are sent for to the Capitol.
260 'Tis thought that Martius shall be consul.
I have seen the dumb men throng to see him,
And the blind to hear him speak. Matrons flung
    gloves,
Ladies and maids their scarves and handkerchiefs,
Upon him as he pass'd. The nobles bended
265 As to Jove's statue, and the commons made
A shower and thunder with their caps and shouts.
I never saw the like.

Brutus
                                    Let's to the Capitol,
And carry with us ears and eyes for th' time,
But hearts for the event.

Sicinius
                                    Have with you.

                                    [*Exeunt*

---

41 *our good wills*: our interest demands.

244 *suggest*: persuade.
245 *still*: always.

247 *dispropertied*: dispossessed them of.
248 *capacity*: understanding.

250 *provand*: provender, food rations.

252 *suggested*: insinuated.

254 *touch*: spark off.
255 *put upon't*: provoked to it.

268 *for th' time*: appropriate for what's going on.
269 *for the event*: committed to the outcome.

Act 2   Scene 2

Cominius presents Coriolanus to the Senators and tribunes as a candidate for election.

os.d. *cushions*: i.e. the seats of office: Aufidius observes (*4, 7, 43*) that Coriolanus may not be able to adapt from 'th' casque to th' cushion'.
Capitol: Shakespeare assumes that this was the meeting-place of the Senate.

5 *vengeance*: exceedingly.

8 *loved them*: i.e. loved the people.
9 *they*: the people.

14 *out of*: owing to.
noble carelessness: aristocratic nonchalance.

Scene 2

The Senate House: enter two Officers, *to lay cushions, as it were in the Capitol*

First Officer
Come, come, they are almost here. How many stand for consulships?
Second Officer
Three, they say, but 'tis thought of everyone Coriolanus will carry it.
First Officer
5 That's a brave fellow, but he's vengeance proud and loves not the common people.
Second Officer
Faith, there hath been many great men that have flattered the people who ne'er loved them; and there be many that they have loved they know not
10 wherefore, so that if they love they know not why, they hate upon no better a ground. Therefore for Coriolanus neither to care whether they love or hate him manifests the true knowledge he has in their disposition, and out of his noble carelessness lets
15 them plainly see't.

First Officer

If he did not care whether he had their love or no he
waved indifferently 'twixt doing them neither good
nor harm; but he seeks their hate with greater
devotion than they can render it him, and leaves
20 nothing undone that may fully discover him their
opposite. Now to seem to affect the malice and
displeasure of the people is as bad as that which he
dislikes, to flatter them for their love.

Second Officer

He hath deserved worthily of his country, and his
25 ascent is not by such easy degrees as those who,
having been supple and courteous to the people,
bonneted, without any further deed to have them at
all into their estimation and report. But he hath so
planted his honours in their eyes and his actions in
30 their hearts that for their tongues to be silent and not
confess so much were a kind of ingrateful injury. To
report otherwise were a malice that, giving itself the
lie, would pluck reproof and rebuke from every ear
that heard it.

First Officer

35 No more of him. He's a worthy man. Make way, they
are coming.

> *A sennet. Enter the* Patricians, *and* Sicinius
> *and* Brutus, *the tribunes of the people,*
> Lictors *before them;* Coriolanus,
> Menenius, Cominius *the consul. The*
> Patricians *take their places and sit.* Sicinius
> *and* Brutus *take their places by themselves.*
> Coriolanus *stands*

Menenius

Having determin'd of the Volsces, and
To send for Titus Lartius, it remains
As the main point of this our after-meeting
40 To gratify his noble service that
Hath thus stood for his country. Therefore please
      you,
Most reverend and grave elders, to desire
The present consul and last general
In our well-found successes to report
45 A little of that worthy work perform'd

7 *he waved*: he would have wavered.
   indifferently: impartially.

0 *discover*: disclose.
1 *opposite*: adversary.
   seem to affect: give the impression of
   preferring.

25 *degrees*: steps, stages.
26 *supple*: charming, flattering.
27 *bonneted*: went cap-in-hand to them.
36s.d. *sennet*: trumpet flourish.
   Lictors: attendants who preceded the
   Roman magistrates bearing the *fasces*—
   rods bound together around an axe, the
   Roman symbol of strength in unity.

37 *determin'd of*: settled the matter of.
38 *Titus Lartius*: Lartius had been
   necessary for the triumph of
   Coriolanus' homecoming (2, 1, 159s.d.)
   but he seems to have returned to his
   charge in Corioles (1, 7, 37).
40 *gratify*: show gratitude to, reward.
41 *stood for*: defended, stood up for.

44 *well-found*: fortunate, of good report.

By Martius Caius Coriolanus, whom
We met here both to thank and to remember
With honours like himself.

Coriolanus sits

First Senator
                                    Speak, good Cominius.
Leave nothing out for length, and make us think
50 Rather our state's defective for requital
Than we to stretch it out. [*To the* Tribunes] Master
    o'th' people,
We do request your kindest ears and, after,
Your loving motion toward the common body
To yield what passes here.
        Sicinius
                                    We are convented
55 Upon a pleasing treaty, and have hearts
Inclinable to honour and advance
The theme of our assembly.
        Brutus
                                    Which the rather
We shall be bless'd to do if he remember
A kinder value of the people than
60 He hath hereto priz'd them at.
        Menenius
                                    That's off, that's off.
I would you rather had been silent. Please you
To hear Cominius speak?
        Brutus
                                    Most willingly,
But yet my caution was more pertinent
Than the rebuke you give it.
        Menenius
                                    He loves your people,
65 But tie him not to be their bedfellow.
Worthy Cominius, speak.

Coriolanus rises and offers to go away

[*To* Coriolanus]   Nay, keep your place.
        First Senator
Sit, Coriolanus. Never shame to hear
What you have nobly done.

---

47 *met*: assembled, are met with.
   remember: acknowledge our debt to.
48 *like himself*: appropriate for him.

49 *for length*: for fear of going on too long.
50 *defective for requital*: lacking in resources
   for repayment.
51 *we . . . out*: that we are unwilling to
   stretch our resources.
52 *after*: afterwards.
53 *motion . . . body*: influence with the
   general public.
54 *yield*: report.
   convented: convened, summoned.

55 *treaty*: matter to be treated of.

58 *bless'd*: happy.
59 *kinder*: more generous.

60 *off*: beside the point.

66s.d. *offers*: attempts to.

Coriolanus
                                        Your honours' pardon,
I had rather have my wounds to heal again
70 Than hear say how I got them.
                    Brutus
                                        Sir, I hope
My words disbench'd you not?
                    Coriolanus
                                        No, sir, yet oft
When blows have made me stay I fled from words.
You sooth'd not, therefore hurt not; but your people,
I love them as they weigh—
                    Menenius
                                        Pray now, sit down.
                    Coriolanus
75 I had rather have one scratch my head i'th' sun
When the alarum were struck than idly sit
To hear my nothings monster'd.   [*Exit*
                    Menenius
                                        Masters of the people,
Your multiplying spawn how can he flatter—
That's thousand to one good one—when you now see
80 He had rather venture all his limbs for honour
Than one on's ears to hear it? Proceed, Cominius.
                    Cominius
I shall lack voice; the deeds of Coriolanus
Should not be utter'd feebly. It is held
That valour is the chiefest virtue, and
85 Most dignifies the haver. If it be,
The man I speak of cannot in the world
Be singly counterpois'd. At sixteen years,
When Tarquin made a head for Rome, he fought
Beyond the mark of others. Our then dictator,
90 Whom with all praise I point at, saw him fight
When with his Amazonian chin he drove
The bristl'd lips before him. He bestrid
An o'erpress'd Roman, and, i'th' consul's view,
Slew three opposers. Tarquin's self he met,
95 And struck him on his knee. In that day's feats,
When he might act the woman in the scene,
He prov'd best man i'th' field, and for his meed
Was brow-bound with the oak. His pupil age
Man-enter'd thus, he waxed like a sea,

71 *disbench'd you*: made you leave your place, disturbed you.

73 *sooth'd*: flattered.
74 *as they weigh*: for what they are worth.

76 *alarum*: summons to battle.
77 *monster'd*: shown forth with exaggeration.
78 *multiplying spawn*: A literal translation of the Latin '*proletarii*' (= good breeders of children).
82–122 *I shall . . . panting*: Cominius' eulogy is a fine speech of epic praise—but it is frequently in danger of undercutting itself with its exaggerated images.
84 *valour . . . virtue*: i.e. the Roman *virtus*; see *1, 1, 36*.
87 *singly counterpois'd*: matched by any one person.
88 *made a head*: raised an army against.
89 *mark*: reach.
   our then dictator: The military governor (not named by Plutarch).
90 *point at*: refer to.
91 *Amazonian*: i.e. beardless; the Amazons (in classical mythology) were a tribe of female warriors.
92–4 *he bestrid . . . opposers*: Plutarch tells how 'a Roman soldier being thrown to the ground even hard by him, Martius straight bestrid him, and after slew the enemy with his own hands'.
96 *act . . . scene*: have been able to act a woman's part on the stage (because his voice had not broken).
97 *meed*: reward.
98–9 *His . . . thus*: being initiated into manhood while still in his minority.
   pupil age: pupillage, apprenticeship.
99 *waxed*: waxèd.

100 *brunt*: shock, violence.
101 *lurch'd . . . garland*: stole the garland from all other contenders.
103 *speak him home*: say too much in his praise; in fact Cominius himself was not present at Corioles.
108 *it took*: it made its impression.
110 *tim'd*: regularly accompanied.
111 *mortal*: fatal (because Martius risked his own death when he entered the gate to bring death to the inhabitants of Corioles).
111–12 *painted . . . destiny*: marked out with blood for a destiny it could not avoid.
114 *like a planet*: like the malignant influence shed by a planet (perhaps bringing plague).
116 *ready*: keen, eager.
       doubled: of redoubled vigour.
117 *Requicken'd*: reinvigorated.
       fatigate: fatigued.
119 *reeking*: smoking with blood.
120 *spoil*: slaughter.
123 *with measure*: appropriately, moderately.

124 *spoils*: booty, plunder.

128–9 *content . . . end it*: satisfied that time [well] spent should be an end in itself.

100 And in the brunt of seventeen battles since
He lurch'd all swords of the garland. For this last
Before and in Corioles, let me say
I cannot speak him home. He stopp'd the fliers,
And by his rare example made the coward
105 Turn terror into sport. As weeds before
A vessel under sail, so men obey'd
And fell below his stem. His sword, death's stamp,
Where it did mark, it took. From face to foot
He was a thing of blood, whose every motion
110 Was tim'd with dying cries. Alone he enter'd
The mortal gate of th' city, which he painted
With shunless destiny, aidless came off,
And with a sudden reinforcement struck
Corioles like a planet. Now all's his.
115 When by and by the din of war gan pierce
His ready sense, then straight his doubled spirit
Requicken'd what in flesh was fatigate,
And to the battle came he, where he did
Run reeking o'er the lives of men as if
120 'Twere a perpetual spoil; and till we call'd
Both field and city ours he never stood
To ease his breast with panting.

Menenius
                                         Worthy man.

First Senator
He cannot but with measure fit the honours
Which we devise him.

Cominius
                              Our spoils he kick'd at,
125 And look'd upon things precious as they were
The common muck of the world. He covets less
Than misery itself would give, rewards
His deeds with doing them, and is content
To spend the time to end it.

Menenius
                                      He's right noble.
130 Let him be call'd for.

First Senator
Call Coriolanus.

Officer
He doth appear.

Enter Coriolanus

Menenius
The Senate, Coriolanus, are well pleas'd
To make thee consul.
                Coriolanus
                                I do owe them still
135 My life and services.
                Menenius
                        It then remains
That you do speak to the people.
                        Coriolanus
                                        I do beseech you,
Let me o'erleap that custom, for I cannot
Put on the gown, stand naked, and entreat them
For my wounds' sake to give their suffrage.
140 Please you that I may pass this doing.
                Sicinius
                                        Sir, the people
Must have their voices, neither will they bate
One jot of ceremony.
                Menenius
[*To* Coriolanus]   Put them not to't.
Pray you, go fit you to the custom and
Take to you, as your predecessors have,
145 Your honour with your form.
                        Coriolanus
                                        It is a part
That I shall blush in acting, and might well
Be taken from the people.
                Brutus
[*To* Sicinius]   Mark you that?
                Coriolanus
To brag unto them 'Thus I did, and thus',
Show them th'unaching scars, which I should hide,
150 As if I had receiv'd them for the hire
Of their breath only!
                Menenius
                        Do not stand upon't.—
We recommend to you, tribunes of the people,
Our purpose to them; and to our noble consul
Wish we all joy and honour.

---

134 *still*: as ever.

138 *naked*: i.e. naked beneath the outer gown.
139 *suffrage*: vote.
140 *pass*: be excused.

141 *voices*: votes.
bate: omit.

142 *Put . . . to't*: don't push it with them, don't tempt them.

145 *your form*: i.e. the form prescribed by custom.

151 *stand upon't*: insist upon it.
152 *recommend*: commit.
153 *purpose to them*: intentions towards the people.

Senators

155 To Coriolanus come all joy and honour!

A flourish of cornetts. Then exeunt all but
Sicinius *and* Brutus

Brutus

You see how he intends to use the people.

Sicinius

May they perceive's intent! He will require them
As if he did contemn what he requested
Should be in them to give.

Brutus

Come, we'll inform the

160 Of our proceedings here. On th' market-place
I know they do attend us.

[*Exeu*

157 *require them*: ask for their votes.
158–9 *As if . . . give*: as though he were
  contemptuous [of the fact] that it
  should be in their power to give what he
  requested.

Act 2   Scene 3

The citizens prepare to encounter Coriolanus
in the election. When they have given their
votes in his favour, their minds are swayed by
the tribunes to deny their choice.

1 *First*: The numbering of the Citizens in
  this scene is quite independent of any
  other numbering.
  Once: once and for all; there has clearly
  been a discussion of this matter before.

4–5 *a power . . . to do*: i.e. 'a legal
  prerogative that we don't have the moral
  right to exercise'.

14–15 *to make . . . serve*: it won't take much
  to make the patricians think us no better
  than monsters.
15 *once*: once when.

Scene 3

Rome: *the market place. Enter seven or eigh*
Citizens

First Citizen

Once, if he do require our voices we ought not
deny him.

Second Citizen

We may, sir, if we will.

Third Citizen

We have power in ourselves to do it, but it is a pow
5 that we have no power to do. For if he show us h
wounds and tell us his deeds, we are to put ou
tongues into those wounds and speak for them; so
he tell us his noble deeds we must also tell him ou
noble acceptance of them. Ingratitude is monstrou
10 and for the multitude to be ingrateful were to mak
a monster of the multitude, of the which we, bein
members, should bring ourselves to be monstrou
members.

First Citizen

And to make us no better thought of, a little help wi
15 serve; for once we stood up about the corn, h

5–17 *many-headed multitude*: A proverbial
description, of classical origin, of the
politically unstable masses.

8 *of*: by.

9 *abram*: auburn (i.e. fair).

3–4 *consent . . . compass*: decision about a
single route would be to fly off at once
in every direction.

9 *southward*: i.e. towards the source of the
'contagion' referred to in *1, 5, 1*.

2–3 *for conscience' . . . wife*: The sense of
the joke is not apparent—even to the
Second Citizen.

42 *by particulars*: to each one of us
separately.

43 *single honour*: individual right.

himself stuck not to call us the many-headed
multitude.

Third Citizen

We have been called so of many, not that our heads
are some brown, some black, some abram, some
20 bald, but that our wits are so diversely coloured; and
truly I think if all our wits were to issue out of one
skull, they would fly east, west, north, south, and
their consent of one direct way should be at once to
all the points o'th' compass.

Second Citizen

25 Think you so? Which way do you judge my wit
would fly?

Third Citizen

Nay, your wit will not so soon out as another man's
will, 'tis strongly wedged up in a blockhead. But if it
were at liberty, 'twould sure southward.

Second Citizen

30 Why that way?

Third Citizen

To lose itself in a fog where, being three parts melted
away with rotten dews, the fourth would return for
conscience' sake, to help to get thee a wife.

Second Citizen

You are never without your tricks. You may, you
35 may.

Third Citizen

Are you all resolved to give your voices? But that's no
matter, the greater part carries it. I say, if he would
incline to the people there was never a worthier man.

Enter Coriolanus *in a gown of humility and
a hat, with* Menenius

Here he comes, and in the gown of humility. Mark
40 his behaviour. We are not to stay all together, but to
come by him where he stands by ones, by twos, and
by threes. He's to make his requests by particulars,
wherein every one of us has a single honour in giving
him our own voices with our own tongues. Therefore
45 follow me, and I'll direct you how you shall go by
him.

All the Citizens
Content, content.   [*Exeunt Citizer*

    Menenius
O sir, you are not right. Have you not known
The worthiest men have done't?

    Coriolanus
                  What must I say?
50 'I pray, sir'? Plague upon't, I cannot bring
My tongue to such a pace. 'Look, sir, my wounds.
I got them in my country's service, when
Some certain of your brethren roar'd and ran
From th' noise of our own drums'?

    Menenius
                    O me, the gods
55 You must not speak of that, you must desire them
To think upon you.

    Coriolanus
              Think upon me? Hang 'em!
I would they would forget me like the virtues
Which our divines lose by 'em.

    Menenius
                  You'll mar all.
I'll leave you. Pray you, speak to 'em, I pray you,
60 In wholesome manner.

    Coriolanus
              Bid them wash their faces
And keep their teeth clean.   [*Exit Meneniu*

Enter three of the Citizens

              So, here comes a brace.
You know the cause, sir, of my standing here.

    Third Citizen
We do, sir. Tell us what hath brought you to't.

    Coriolanus
Mine own desert.

    Second Citizen
65 Your own desert?

    Coriolanus
Ay, but not mine own desire.

    Third Citizen
How not your own desire?

---

51 *to such a pace*: to speak in this way; the image is of the measured gait of a trained horse.

56 *think upon*: remember, think kindly about.

57 *virtues*: moral precepts.
58 *divines*: clergymen.
lose: waste.

60 *wholesome*: decent, proper; Martius proceeds to make a pun with the meaning 'clean'.

61s.d. *three*: This is the number given in the Folio text—although Coriolanus sees only a 'brace' (= a pair of game birds).

64–107 *Mine own desert . . . no farther*: Coriolanus now speaks to the citizens in their own language—i.e. prose.

Coriolanus
No, sir, 'twas never my desire yet to trouble the poor
with begging.

Third Citizen
70 You must think if we give you anything we hope to
gain by you.

Coriolanus
Well then, I pray, your price o'th' consulship?

First Citizen
The price is to ask it kindly.

Coriolanus
Kindly, sir, I pray let me ha't. I have wounds to show
75 you which shall be yours in private. [*To* Second
Citizen] Your good voice, sir. What say you?

Second Citizen
You shall ha't, worthy sir.

Coriolanus
A match, sir. There's in all two worthy voices
begged. I have your alms. Adieu.

Third Citizen
80 [*To the other* Citizens] But this is something odd.

Second Citizen
An 'twere to give again—but 'tis no matter.
                        [*Exeunt* Citizens

Enter two other Citizens

Coriolanus
Pray you now, if it may stand with the tune of your
voices that I may be consul, I have here the
customary gown.

Fourth Citizen
85 You have deserved nobly of your country, and you
have not deserved nobly.

Coriolanus
Your enigma?

Fourth Citizen
You have been a scourge to her enemies, you have
been a rod to her friends. You have not, indeed,
90 loved the common people.

Coriolanus
You should account me the more virtuous that I
have not been common in my love. I will, sir, flatter
my sworn brother the people to earn a dearer

73 *kindly*: nicely, pleasantly—*and also*
recognizing common 'kind', kinship,
with the citizens as Romans and human
beings.

81 *An 'twere*: if it were.

82 *stand*: accord.

88–9 *a scourge . . . rod*: The phrase is that of
Psalm 89:32, 'I will visit their offences
with the rod, and their sin with
scourges'.

92 *common*: vulgar, indiscriminate.

93–4 *dearer estimation*: higher valuation.

94 *condition*: form of behaviour
95 *gentle*: aristocratic.

97 *be off*: take off my hat.
98 *counterfeitly*: hypocritically.

estimation of them. 'Tis a condition they accoun
95 gentle. And since the wisdom of their choice is rathe
to have my hat than my heart, I will practise th
insinuating nod and be off to them mos
counterfeitly; that is, sir, I will counterfeit th
bewitchment of some popular man, and give i
100 bountiful to the desirers. Therefore, beseech you
may be consul.

Fifth Citizen
We hope to find you our friend, and therefore giv
you our voices heartily.

Fourth Citizen
You have received many wounds for your country.

Coriolanus
105 I will not seal your knowledge with showing them. I
will make much of your voices, and so trouble you
no farther.

Both Citizens
The gods give you joy, sir, heartily.

Coriolanus
Most sweet voices.   [*Exeunt* Citizens

105 *seal*: authenticate, confirm.
110–21 *Better . . . I do*: Coriolanus' contempt
expresses itself in the rhymed couplets.
111 *hire . . . deserve*: reward which is already
merited.
112 *wolvish toge*: i.e. the 'napless vesture of
humility' (2, 1, 233); Coriolanus sees
himself as the proverbial wolf in sheep's
clothing ('toge' = toga).

110 Better it is to die, better to starve,
Than crave the hire which first we do deserve.
Why in this wolvish toge should I stand here
To beg of Hob and Dick that does appear
Their needless vouches? Custom calls me to't.
115 What custom wills, in all things should we do't,
The dust on antique time would lie unswept,
And mountainous error be too highly heap'd
For truth to o'erpeer. Rather than fool it so,
Let the high office and the honour go
120 To one that would do thus. I am half through.
The one part suffer'd, the other will I do.

Enter three Citizens *more*

113 *Hob . . . appear*: i.e. any Tom, Dick, or
Harry that turns up; 'Hob' = familiar
form of 'Robin'.
114 *needless vouches*: superfluous votes;
Coriolanus believes the people's
allowance to be unnecessary now that
he has been made consul by the senate
(2, 2, 133).
116 *antique time*: ancient traditions.
118 *o'erpeer*: see over.
124 *Watch'd*: done guard duty.

Here come more voices.—
Your voices! For your voices I have fought,
Watch'd for your voices, for your voices bear
125 Of wounds two dozen odd; battles thrice six
I have seen and heard of; for your voices
Have done many things, some less, some more.
Your voices! Indeed I would be consul.

Sixth Citizen
He has done nobly, and cannot go without any
130 honest man's voice.

Seventh Citizen
Therefore let him be consul. The gods give him joy
and make him good friend to the people!

All the Citizens
Amen, amen, God save thee, noble consul!

Coriolanus
Worthy voices.   [*Exeunt* Citizens

Enter Menenius *with* Brutus *and* Sicinius

35 *limitation*: allotted time.

Menenius
135 You have stood your limitation, and the tribunes
Endue you with the people's voice. Remains
That in th'official marks invested, you
Anon do meet the Senate.

37 *official marks*: insignia of office.

Coriolanus
                                   Is this done?

Sicinius
The custom of request you have discharg'd.
140 The people do admit you, and are summon'd
To meet anon upon your approbation.

39 *custom of request*: required custom.

41 *anon*: immediately.
upon your approbation: i.e. to ratify your
election (see line 206, 'He's not
confirm'd, we may deny him yet').

Coriolanus
Where, at the Senate-house?

Sicinius
                                   There, Coriolanus.

Coriolanus
May I change these garments?

Sicinius
                                        You may, sir.

Coriolanus
That I'll straight do, and, knowing myself again,
145 Repair to th' Senate-house.

Menenius
I'll keep you company. [*To the* Tribunes] Will you
along?

Brutus
We stay here for the people.

Sicinius
                                   Fare you well.
                              [*Exeunt* Coriolanus *and* Menenius
He has it now, and by his looks methinks
'Tis warm at's heart.

149 *warm at's heart*: very gratifying to him.

Brutus

                             With a proud heart he wore
150 His humble weeds. Will you dismiss the people?

Enter the Plebeians

150s.d. *Plebeians*: Shakespeare several times uses this word when he thinks of the citizens as a political faction.

Sicinius
How now, my masters, have you chose this man?
First Citizen
He has our voices, sir.
Brutus
We pray the gods he may deserve your loves.
Second Citizen
Amen, sir. To my poor unworthy notice
155 He mock'd us when he begg'd our voices.
Third Citizen
Certainly. He flouted us downright.
First Citizen
No, 'tis his kind of speech. He did not mock us.
Second Citizen
Not one amongst us save yourself but says
He us'd us scornfully. He should have show'd us
160 His marks of merit, wounds receiv'd for's country.
Sicinius
Why, so he did, I am sure.
All the Citizens
No, no; no man saw 'em.
Third Citizen
He said he had wounds which he could show in
    private,
And with his hat, thus waving it in scorn,

165 *Aged*: Agèd.

165 'I would be consul,' says he. 'Aged custom
But by your voices will not so permit me;
Your voices therefore.' When we granted that,
Here was 'I thank you for your voices, thank you.
Your most sweet voices. Now you have left your
    voices
170 I have no further with you.' Was not this mockery?
Sicinius
Why, either were you ignorant to see't,
Or, seeing it, of such childish friendliness
To yield your voices?

Brutus

                         Could you not have told him

174 *lesson'd*: instructed.

As you were lesson'd: when he had no power

175 But was a petty servant to the state,

He was your enemy, ever spake against

Your liberties and the charters that you bear

178 *weal*: commonwealth, state.
arriving: reaching.

I'th' body of the weal; and now arriving

179 *sway o'th'state*: state authority.

A place of potency and sway o'th' state,

180 If he should still malignantly remain

181 *plebeii*: plebeians, common people.

Fast foe to th' plebeii, your voices might

Be curses to yourselves? You should have said

That as his worthy deeds did claim no less

Than what he stood for, so his gracious nature

185 *Would*: i.e. should, ought to.
think upon: have consideration of.

185 Would think upon you for your voices and

Translate his malice towards you into love,

187 *Standing . . . lord*: speaking out for you
as your patron.

Standing your friendly lord.

Sicinius

                              Thus to have said

188 *touch'd*: tested.

As you were fore-advis'd had touch'd his spirit

189 *tried his inclination*: found out which way
he was inclined.

And tried his inclination, from him pluck'd

190 Either his gracious promise which you might,

191 *cause*: occasion.

As cause had call'd you up, have held him to,

192 *gall'd*: rubbed, scraped against.

Or else it would have gall'd his surly nature,

193 *article*: condition.

Which easily endures not article

Tying him to aught. So putting him to rage,

195 You should have ta'en th'advantage of his choler

And pass'd him unelected.

Brutus

                              Did you perceive

197 *free*: open, undisguised.

He did solicit you in free contempt

When he did need your loves, and do you think

That his contempt shall not be bruising to you

200 When he hath power to crush? Why, had your
bodies

201 *heart*: i.e. spirit (both wit and courage).
201–2 *to cry . . . judgement*: to rebel against
the rule of reason.

No heart among you? Or had you tongues to cry

Against the rectorship of judgement?

Sicinius

                                   Have you

Ere now denied the asker, and now again,

204 *Of*: on.

Of him that did not ask but mock, bestow

205 Your sued-for tongues?

Third Citizen

He's not confirm'd, we may deny him yet.

Second Citizen

And will deny him.

I'll have five hundred voices of that sound.

First Citizen

209 *piece 'em*: join to them.

I twice five hundred, and their friends to piece 'em.

Brutus

210 Get you hence instantly, and tell those friends
They have chose a consul that will from them take
Their liberties, make them of no more voice
Than dogs that are as often beat for barking,

214 *therefor*: for that purpose.

As therefor kept to do so.

Sicinius

Let them assemble

215 *safer*: sounder.

215 And on a safer judgement all revoke

216 *Enforce*: emphasize.

Your ignorant election. Enforce his pride
And his old hate unto you. Besides, forget not

218 *weed*: garment.

With what contempt he wore the humble weed,
How in his suit he scorn'd you; but your loves,

220 Thinking upon his services, took from you

221 *apprehension*: appreciation,
understanding.
portance: bearing, conduct.

Th'apprehension of his present portance,
Which most gibingly, ungravely he did fashion

222 *gibingly*: mockingly.
ungravely: casually.

After the inveterate hate he bears you.

Brutus

Lay

A fault on us your tribunes, that we labour'd

224-5 *labour'd . . . between*: urged that
nothing should stand in your way.

225 No impediment between, but that you must
Cast your election on him.

Sicinius

Say you chose him
More after our commandment than as guided

228 *affections*: inclinations.

By your own true affections, and that your minds,
Preoccupied with what you rather must do

230 *against the grain*: contrary to your
natures.

230 Than what you should, made you against the grain
To voice him consul. Lay the fault on us.

232 *read*: delivered.

Brutus

235-42 *The noble . . . ancestor*: This account
of Coriolanus' ancestry (taken from
Plutarch) is calculated to enrage the
plebeians.

Ay, spare us not. Say we read lectures to you,
How youngly he began to serve his country,
How long continued, and what stock he springs of,

236-7 *Ancus Martius . . . Numa . . . Hostilius
. . . king*: (Numa Pompilius, 715–673 BC,
Tullus Hostilius, 673–642 BC, Ancus
Martius, 642–617 BC).

235 The noble house o'th' Martians, from whence came
That Ancus Martius, Numa's daughter's son,
Who after great Hostilius here was king;

38   *Publius*: This character has not been
     *identified.
     Quintus: This allusion is anachronistic:
     the water conduit built by Quintus
     Martius Rex was not started until
     144 BC.

240–1   *And Censorinus . . . censor*: Another
        anachronism: Caius Martius Rutilus
        received his title in 265 BC; line 240 is
        an editorial addition, supplying an
        obvious omission in the Folio text.
246   *Scaling*: weighing, balancing.
248   *sudden*: hasty.
249   *Harp . . . still*: always keep coming back
      to that.
      but . . . on: if we hadn't put you up to it.
250   *drawn your number*: got your supporters
      together.
253   *put in hazard*: ventured, risked.
254   *Than . . . greater*: rather than wait for the
      bigger uprising that will undoubtedly
      follow.
256–7   *answer . . . anger*: take advantage of
        his anger.

Of the same house Publius and Quintus were,
That our best water brought by conduits hither;
240 And Censorinus that was so surnam'd,
And nobly nam'd so, twice being censor,
Was his great ancestor.

Sicinius
                                    One thus descended,
That hath beside well in his person wrought
To be set high in place, we did commend
245 To your remembrances, but you have found,
Scaling his present bearing with his past,
That he's your fix'd enemy, and revoke
Your sudden approbation.

Brutus
                              Say you ne'er had done't—
Harp on that still—but by our putting on;
250 And presently when you have drawn your number,
Repair to th' Capitol.

A Citizen
                          We will so.

Another Citizen
                                        Almost all
Repent in their election.   [*Exeunt* Plebeians

Brutus
                          Let them go on.
This mutiny were better put in hazard
Than stay, past doubt, for greater.
255 If, as his nature is, he fall in rage
With their refusal, both observe and answer
The vantage of his anger.

Sicinius
                              To th' Capitol, come.
We will be there before the stream o'th' people,
And this shall seem, as partly 'tis, their own,
260 Which we have goaded onward.

                                              [*Exeunt*

Act 3

Confrontation! Coriolanus quarrels with the
ribunes when they bar his way to the
market-place. A riot is narrowly avoided, but
he matter must come to trial.

os.d. *Cornetts . . . Senators*: The procession
   is heading towards the market-place
   (and will meet the tribunes (line 22) as
   these are going to the Capitol).
   all the gentry: i.e. the patricians;
   according to Plutarch, Coriolanus was
   accompanied by the 'young nobility'.
1 *made new head*: raised another army.
3 *swifter composition*: coming to terms
   more quickly than we expected;
   probably Lartius refers to the terms for
   restoring Corioles (1, 10, 75–8,
   2, 2, 37–8).
4 *stand . . . first*: are just as they used to
   be (i.e. nothing has been gained by the
   fighting).
5 *road*: raids, inroads.
6 *worn*: exhausted.
   lord consul: Coriolanus has perhaps
   changed his attire—but Cominius' form
   of address is (ironically) premature.
9 *safeguard*: safe-conduct.

Scene 1

Rome. Cornetts. Enter Coriolanus,
Menenius, *all the gentry*; Cominius,
Titus Lartius, *and other* Senators

Coriolanus
Tullus Aufidius then had made new head?

Lartius
He had, my lord, and that it was which caus'd
Our swifter composition.

Coriolanus
So then the Volsces stand but as at first,
5 Ready when time shall prompt them to make road
Upon's again.

Cominius
                    They are worn, lord consul, so
That we shall hardly in our ages see
Their banners wave again.

Coriolanus
[*To* Lartius]   Saw you Aufidius?

Lartius
On safeguard he came to me, and did curse
10 Against the Volsces for they had so vilely
Yielded the town. He is retired to Antium.

Coriolanus
Spoke he of me?

Lartius
                    He did, my lord.

Coriolanus
                                         How? What?

Lartius
How often he had met you sword to sword;
That of all things upon the earth he hated

16 *To . . . restitution*: beyond all hope of
recovery.
so: provided that.

24 *prank them*: dress themselves up.
25 *noble sufferance*: endurance of the
nobility.

31 *pass'd*: been approved by.

15 Your person most; that he would pawn his fortune
To hopeless restitution, so he might
Be called your vanquisher.

Coriolanus
At Antium lives he?

Lartius
At Antium.

Coriolanus
20 I wish I had a cause to seek him there,
To oppose his hatred fully. Welcome home.

[*Exit* Lartius]

Enter Sicinius *and* Brutus

Behold, these are the tribunes of the people,
The tongues o'th' common mouth. I do despise
them,
For they do prank them in authority
25 Against all noble sufferance.

Sicinius
Pass no further.

Coriolanus
Ha, what is that?

Brutus
It will be dangerous to go on. No further.

Coriolanus
What makes this change?

Menenius
30 The matter?

Cominius
Hath he not pass'd the noble and the common?

Brutus
Cominius, no.

Coriolanus
                  Have I had children's voices?

First Senator
Tribunes, give way. He shall to th' market-place.

Brutus
The people are incens'd against him.

Sicinius
                                        Stop,
35 Or all will fall in broil!

Coriolanus

Are these your herd?
Must these have voices, that can yield them now
And straight disclaim their tongues? What are your
    offices?
You being their mouths, why rule you not their
    teeth?
Have you not set them on?

Menenius

Be calm, be calm.

Coriolanus

40 It is a purpos'd thing, and grows by plot
To curb the will of the nobility.
Suffer't, and live with such as cannot rule
Nor ever will be rul'd.

Brutus

Call't not a plot.
The people cry you mock'd them, and of late

45 When corn was given them gratis, you repin'd,
Scandall'd the suppliants for the people, call'd them
Time-pleasers, flatterers, foes to nobleness.

Coriolanus

Why, this was known before.

Brutus

Not to them all.

Coriolanus

Have you inform'd them sithence?

Brutus

How! I inform them?

[Coriolanus]

50 You are like to do such business.

Brutus

Not unlike,
Each way to better yours.

Coriolanus

Why then should I be consul? By yon clouds,
Let me deserve so ill as you, and make me
Your fellow tribune.

Sicinius

You show too much of that

55 For which the people stir. If you will pass
To where you are bound, you must enquire your
    way,

---

37 *straight*: immediately.

40 *purpos'd thing*: put-up job.

44–5 *of late . . . repin'd*: Coriolanus had objected to a recommendation that a large amount of corn, purchased cheaply, should be distributed as a dole among the plebeians.

46 *Scandall'd*: slandered.

49 *sithence*: since then.

50 *[Coriolanus]*: The Folio text ascribes this comment to Cominius.

50–1 *Not . . . yours*: Brutus seems to mean that Coriolanus can alienate the people quite well by himself, without any assistance—but Coriolanus understands from the double negative that Brutus is claiming superiority in any 'business'.

54 *that*: that characteristic.

56 *where . . . bound*: i.e. to the market-place—and to the consulship.

37 *are out of*: have strayed from.

59 *yoke with him*: be paired with Brutus.

60 *abus'd*: misled, deceived.
    set on: incited.
    palt'ring: deceit, trickery.
62 *dishonour'd rub*: dishonourable
    impediment; the tribunes are seen as
    cheating at a game of bowls.

69 *mutable*: changeable.
    meinie: multitude, crew.
70-1 *Let them . . . themselves*: i.e. 'let them
    regard me (as a mirror) and I'll give
    them a true picture of themselves'.
72-4 *nourish . . . scatter'd*: 'Moreover he
    said they nourished against themselves
    the naughty seed and cockle of
    insolence and sedition, which had been
    sowed and scattered abroad amongst
    the people' (Plutarch).
73 *cockle*: weeds, tares.
75 *honour'd*: honourable.
76 *virtue*: i.e. the Roman *virtus*, valiantness;
    see *1, 1, 36* note.

81 *Coin . . . against*: speak out against,
    recite charms to protect from.
    measles: scabs.
82 *tetter*: infect with skin eruptions.

Which you are out of, with a gentler spirit,
Or never be so noble as a consul,
Nor yoke with him for tribune.
                Menenius
                                    Let's be calm.
        Cominius
60 The people are abus'd, set on. This palt'ring
    Becomes not Rome, nor has Coriolanus
    Deserv'd this so dishonour'd rub, laid falsely
    I'th' plain way of his merit.
        Coriolanus
                                    Tell me of corn!
    This was my speech, and I will speak't again—
                Menenius
65 Not now, not now.
        First Senator
    Not in this heat, sir, now.
        Coriolanus
    Now as I live,
    I will. My nobler friends, I crave their pardons.
    For the mutable, rank-scented meinie,
70 Let them regard me, as I do not flatter,
    And therein behold themselves. I say again,
    In soothing them we nourish 'gainst our Senate
    The cockle of rebellion, insolence, sedition,
    Which we ourselves have plough'd for, sow'd, and
        scatter'd
75 By mingling them with us, the honour'd number
    Who lack not virtue, no, nor power, but that
    Which they have given to beggars.
        Menenius
                                    Well, no more.
        First Senator
    No more words, we beseech you.
        Coriolanus
                                    How, no more?
    As for my country I have shed my blood,
80 Not fearing outward force, so shall my lungs
    Coin words till their decay against those measles
    Which we disdain should tetter us, yet sought
    The very way to catch them.

Brutus
You speak o'th' people as if you were a god
85 To punish, not a man of their infirmity.
    Sicinius
'Twere well we let the people know't.
        Menenius
                                        What, what? His choler?
        Coriolanus
Choler! Were I as patient as the midnight sleep,
By Jove, 'twould be my mind.
        Sicinius
                                    It is a mind
That shall remain a poison where it is,
90 Not poison any further.
        Coriolanus
                                    'Shall remain'?
Hear you this Triton of the minnows? Mark you
His absolute 'shall'?
        Cominius
                                    'Twas from the canon.
        Coriolanus
                                                        'Shall'?
O good but most unwise patricians, why,
You grave but reckless senators, have you thus
95 Given Hydra here to choose an officer
That, with his peremptory 'shall', being but
The horn and noise o'th' monster's, wants not spirit
To say he'll turn your current in a ditch
And make your channel his? If he have power,
100 Then vail your impotence; if none, awake
Your dangerous lenity. If you are learned,
Be not as common fools; if you are not,
Let them have cushions by you. You are plebeians
If they be senators, and they are no less
105 When, both your voices blended, the great'st taste
Most palates theirs. They choose their magistrate,
And such a one as he, who puts his 'shall',
His popular 'shall', against a graver bench
Than ever frown'd in Greece. By Jove himself,
110 It makes the consuls base, and my soul aches
To know, when two authorities are up,
Neither supreme, how soon confusion

---

87 *patient*: long-suffering.

91 *Triton . . . minnows*: lord god of the tiddlers; in classical mythology Triton was a minor sea-god.

92 *from the canon*: i.e. out of order.
95 *Given*: allowed.
Hydra: a many-headed monster (in Greek mythology) which was killed by Hercules as one of his twelve labours— see 4, 1, 18note).

97 *horn and noise*: noisy horn (Triton (line 91) was the trumpeter for Neptune).

98–9 *turn . . . his*: divert your power and resources to his own ends; see 'Source, Date, and Text', p. xxix for the possible contemporary allusion.

100 *vail your impotence*: bow down in your own weakness.

100–1 *awake . . . lenity*: snap out of this dangerous acquiescence.
101 *learned*: wise.

103 *have . . . by you*: seats beside you (or instead of you) in the government (see 2, 2, os.d.).

105–6 *great'st taste . . . theirs*: i.e. the majority will prefer (*or* will constitute) the people's—as opposed to the patricians'— choice.

108 *popular*: belonging to the people.
bench: governing body.

111 *up*: roused up.

112 *confusion*: chaos.

113 14 *take   other*, use one to destroy the
    other.

115–18 *Whoever . . . power*: Plutarch's account
    tells how Coriolanus denounced those
    who thought that 'corn should be given
    out to the common people *gratis*, as they
    used to do in cities of Greece, where the
    people had more absolute power'.

119 *they*: i.e. 'Whoever gave that counsel'
    (line 115).

123 *recompense*: i.e. payment for services
    rendered.

124 *press'd*: impressed, conscripted.

125 *the navel*: i.e. the vital centre.
    touch'd: threatened.

126 *thread . . . gates*: go through the gates;
    Coriolanus refers to the gates of
    Rome—but his phrasing inevitably
    recalls the soldiers' refusal to follow him
    into Corioles.

129 *accusation*: i.e. that corn is being
    hoarded.

131 *All cause unborn*: without any cause.
    native: origin, motive.

132 *frank donation*: free gift.

133 *bosom multiplied*: monster of many
    stomachs.
    digest: assimilate, understand.

136 *poll*: number of heads.
    true: great.

137 *They*: i.e. the patricians.

139 *cares*: concern, solicitude.

141 *crows*: carrion birds *and* crowbars (for
    breaking open the locks).
    eagles: The eagle, chief among birds,
    was the emblem of Roman power.

May enter 'twixt the gap of both and take
The one by th'other.

Cominius
                                        Well, on to th' market-place.

Coriolanus
115 Whoever gave that counsel to give forth
The corn o'th' storehouse gratis, as 'twas us'd
Sometime in Greece—

Menenius
                                        Well, well, no more of that.

Coriolanus
Though there the people had more absolute power
I say they nourish'd disobedience, fed
120 The ruin of the state.

Brutus
                                        Why shall the people give
One that speaks thus their voice?

Coriolanus
                                        I'll give my reason
More worthier than their voices. They know the corn
Was not our recompense, resting well assur'd
They ne'er did service for't. Being press'd to th' war
125 Even when the navel of the state was touch'd,
They would not thread the gates. This kind of service
Did not deserve corn gratis. Being i'th' war,
Their mutinies and revolts, wherein they show'd
Most valour, spoke not for them. Th'accusation
130 Which they have often made against the Senate,
All cause unborn, could never be the native
Of our so frank donation. Well, what then?
How shall this bosom multiplied digest
The Senate's courtesy? Let deeds express
135 What's like to be their words: 'We did request it,
We are the greater poll, and in true fear
They gave us our demands.' Thus we debase
The nature of our seats, and make the rabble
Call our cares fears, which will in time
140 Break ope the locks o'th' Senate and bring in
The crows to peck the eagles.

Menenius
                                        Come, enough.

Brutus

Enough with over-measure.

Coriolanus

                              No, take more.

What may be sworn by, both divine and human,

Seal what I end withal! This double worship,

145 Where one part does disdain with cause, the other

Insult without all reason, where gentry, title, wisdom

Cannot conclude but by the yea and no

Of general ignorance, it must omit

Real necessities, and give way the while

150 To unstable slightness. Purpose so barr'd, it follows

Nothing is done to purpose. Therefore beseech

       you—

You that will be less fearful than discreet,

That love the fundamental part of state

More than you doubt the change on't, that prefer

155 A noble life before a long, and wish

To jump a body with a dangerous physic

That's sure of death without it—at once pluck out

The multitudinous tongue; let them not lick

The sweet which is their poison. Your dishonour

160 Mangles true judgement, and bereaves the state

Of that integrity which should become't,

Not having the power to do the good it would

For th'ill which doth control't.

Brutus

                              He's said enough.

Sicinius

He's spoken like a traitor, and shall answer

165 As traitors do.

Coriolanus

                    Thou wretch, despite o'erwhelm thee!

What should the people do with these bald tribunes,

On whom depending, their obedience fails

To th' greater bench? In a rebellion,

When what's not meet but what must be was law,

170 Then were they chosen. In a better hour

Let what is meet be said it must be meet,

And throw their power i'th' dust.

Brutus

Manifest treason.

---

44 *double worship*: divided authority (see line 111).

146 *without all*: beyond all.

147 *conclude*: reach a decision.

148 *general*: common, popular.
   it: i.e. the 'double worship' (line 144).
   omit: neglect.

150 *slightness*: triviality.
   Purpose so barr'd: when planning is obstructed like this.

151 *to purpose*: according to plan.

152 *will be . . . discreet*: wish to be less cowardly than discerning.

153 *fundamental . . . state*: i.e. constitution of the government.

156 *jump*: risk.

158 *multitudinous tongue*: i.e. those—the tribunes—who speak for the many.

158–9 *lick . . . poison*: i.e. taste the power that will ruin them.

159 *Your dishonour*: i.e. in granting power to the citizens.

163 *control*: overpower, overmaster.

164 *answer*: take the consequences.

165 *despite*: contempt.

166 *bald*: poorly endowed (both literally and metaphorically—with hair and with intelligence).

168 *greater bench*: i.e. the Senate.

169 *When . . . must be*: when what is not right but could not be avoided.

171 *Let . . . be meet*: let it be said that the right thing to do shall be done.

Sicinius
                    This a consul? No.

Brutus
The aediles, ho!

Enter an Aedile

                    Let him be apprehended.

Sicinius
175 Go call the people,   [*Exit Aedile*
[*To* Coriolanus]   in whose name myself
Attach thee as a traitorous innovator,
A foe to th' public weal. Obey, I charge thee,
And follow to thine answer.

He tries to seize Coriolanus

Coriolanus
                              Hence, old goat!

All the Patricians
We'll surety him.

Cominius
[*To* Sicinius]   Aged sir, hands off.

Coriolanus
180 [*To* Sicinius] Hence, rotten thing, or I shall shake
     thy bones
Out of thy garments.

Sicinius
                         Help, ye citizens!

Enter a rabble of Plebeians, *with the*
Aediles

Menenius
On both sides more respect.

Sicinius
Here's he that would take from you all your power.

Brutus
Seize him, aediles!

All the Citizens
185 Down with him!—down with him!—down with
     him!—

Second Senator
Weapons!—weapons!—weapons!—

They all bustle about Coriolanus

---

174 *aediles*: police officers (plebeians appointed to assist the tribunes and carry out their decisions).

176 *Attach*: arrest.
     innovator: revolutionary.

179 *Aged*: Agèd.

All
Tribunes!—Patricians!—Citizens!—What ho!
Sicinius!—Brutus!—Coriolanus!—Citizens!
Peace!—Peace!—Peace!—Stay!—Hold!—Peace!
Menenius
190 What is about to be?—I am out of breath.—
Confusion's near.—I cannot speak.—You tribunes,
To th'people!—Coriolanus, patience!—
Speak, good Sicinius
Sicinius
                              Hear me, people, peace!
All the Citizens
Let's hear our tribune! Peace! Speak, speak, speak!
Sicinius
195 You are at point to lose your liberties.
Martius would have all from you, Martius
Whom late you have named for consul.
Menenius
                                        Fie, fie, fie!
This is the way to kindle, not to quench.
First Senator
To unbuild the city, and to lay all flat.
Sicinius
200 What is the city but the people?
All the Citizens
                                        True,
The people are the city.
Brutus
                                By the consent of all
We were establish'd the people's magistrates.
All the Citizens
You so remain.
Menenius
                        And so are like to do.
Coriolanus
That is the way to lay the city flat,
205 To bring the roof to the foundation,
And bury all which yet distinctly ranges
In heaps and piles of ruin.
Sicinius
                                This deserves death.

91   *Confusion*: anarchy, chaos.
91–2 *You, tribunes . . . people*: Menenius
      seems to be asking the tribunes to speak
      to the people.

195 *at point to*: on the point of.
196 *Martius*: Sicinius refuses to use the
      addition 'Coriolanus'.

198 *This*: i.e. Coriolanus' move to abolish
      the tribunate.

208 *Or:* either.

213 *rock Tarpeian:* A promontory at the end
of the Capitoline Hill (from which
traitors were thrown in execution).

Brutus
Or let us stand to our authority,
Or let us lose it. We do here pronounce,
210 Upon the part o'th' people in whose power
We were elected theirs, Martius is worthy
Of present death.
      Sicinius
               Therefore lay hold of him,
Bear him to th' rock Tarpeian; and from thence
Into destruction cast him.
      Brutus
                 Aediles, seize him.
All the Citizens
215 Yield, Martius, yield.
      Menenius
               Hear me one word.
Beseech you, tribunes, hear me but a word.
      Aediles
Peace, peace!
      Menenius
[*To* Brutus] Be that you seem, truly your country's
    friend,
And temp'rately proceed to what you would
220 Thus violently redress.
      Brutus
               Sir, those cold ways
That seem like prudent helps are very poisons
Where the disease is violent. Lay hands upon him,
And bear him to the rock.

     Coriolanus *draws his sword*

      Coriolanus
               No, I'll die here.
There's some among you have beheld me fighting.
225 Come, try upon yourselves what you have seen me.
      Menenius
Down with that sword! Tribunes, withdraw a while.
      Brutus
Lay hands upon him.
      Menenius
               Help Martius, help!
You that be noble, help him, young and old.

All the Citizens
Down with him, down with him!

In this mutiny the Tribunes, *the* Aediles,
and the people are beat in, and exeunt

Menenius
230 [*To* Coriolanus] Go get you to your house. Be gone,
away!
All will be naught else.
Second Senator
[*To* Coriolanus]   Get you gone.
[Coriolanus]
                                    Stand fast.
We have as many friends as enemies.
Menenius
Shall it be put to that?
First Senator
                        The gods forbid!
[*To* Coriolanus] I prithee, noble friend, home to thy
house.
235 Leave us to cure this cause.
Menenius
                              For 'tis a sore
Upon us you cannot tent yourself.
Be gone, beseech you.
[Cominius]
                        Come, sir, along with us.
[Coriolanus]
I would they were barbarians, as they are,
Though in Rome litter'd; not Romans, as they are
not,
240 Though calv'd i'th' porch o'th' Capitol.
[Menenius]
                                          Be gone.
Put not your worthy rage into your tongue.
One time will owe another.
Coriolanus
                          On fair ground
I could beat forty of them.
Menenius
                          I could myself
Take up a brace o'th' best of them—
245 Yea, the two tribunes!

Side notes:

9s.d. *beat in*: i.e. driven off the stage and into the tiring house.

31 *naught*: lost, ruined.
[Coriolanus]: This speech (like those at 237, 238, 240) has been re-allocated: Coriolanus is eager to continue the struggle, but Cominius and Menenius urge withdrawal.

35 *cause*: disease.
35–6 *sore . . . us*: an affliction upon us all (i.e. not personal to Coriolanus alone).
36 *tent*: treat (see *1*, 10, 31note).

38 *I would . . . barbarians*: Presumably Coriolanus would have no hesitation in attacking barbarians.

42 *One . . . another*: there will be another opportunity to compensate for this one.

43 *forty*: any [large] number.

44 *Take up*: take on.

Cominius

But now 'tis odds beyond arithmetic,
And manhood is called foolery when it stands
Against a falling fabric. [*To* Coriolanus] Will you hence
Before the tag return, whose rage doth rend
250 Like interrupted waters, and o'erbear
What they are used to bear?

Menenius

[*To* Coriolanus]   Pray you, be gone.
I'll try whether my old wit be in request
With those that have but little. This must be patch'
With cloth of any colour.

Cominius

255 Nay, come away.

[*Exeunt* Coriolanus *and* Cominiu

A Patrician

This man has marr'd his fortune.

Menenius

His nature is too noble for the world.
He would not flatter Neptune for his trident
Or Jove for's power to thunder. His heart's his mouth.
260 What his breast forges, that his tongue must vent,
And, being angry, does forget that ever
He heard the name of death.

A noise within

Here's goodly work!

A Patrician

                              I would they were abec

Menenius

I would they were in Tiber! What the vengeance,
265 Could he not speak 'em fair?

Enter Brutus *and* Sicinius, *with the rabble again*

Sicinius

                              Where is this viper
That would depopulate the city and
Be every man himself?

Menenius

                              You worthy tribunes—

---

246 *odds beyond arithmetic*: i.e. they infinitely outnumber us.
247 *stands*: holds out.
248 *falling fabric*: collapsing building.

249 *tag*: rabble, rag-tag.
250–1 *o'erbear . . . bear*: i.e. burst the banks that usually restrain them.

252 *whether*: The word is colloquially contracted to 'wh'er'.
in request: have any effect.

259 *His heart . . . mouth*: i.e. he speaks out everything he feels.

260 *vent*: utter.

264 *What the vengeance*: i.e. why the hell.
265 *viper*: A symbol of treachery: the young viper was traditionally said to eat its way out of the parent snake.

Sicinius

He shall be thrown down the Tarpeian rock

With rigorous hands. He hath resisted law,

270 And therefore law shall scorn him further trial

Than the severity of the public power,

Which he so sets at naught.

First Citizen

         He shall well know

The noble tribunes are the people's mouths,

And we their hands.

All the Citizens

       He shall, sure on't.

Menenius

            Sir, sir.

Sicinius

              Peace!

Menenius

275 Do not cry havoc where you should but hunt

With modest warrant.

Sicinius

       Sir, how comes't that you

Have holp to make this rescue?

Menenius

          Hear me speak.

As I do know the consul's worthiness,

So can I name his faults.

Sicinius

280 Consul? What consul?

Menenius

The consul Coriolanus.

Brutus

He consul?

All the Citizens

No, no, no, no, no!

Menenius

If, by the tribunes' leave and yours, good people,

285 I may be heard, I would crave a word or two,

The which shall turn you to no further harm

Than so much loss of time.

Sicinius

        Speak briefly then,

For we are peremptory to dispatch

This viperous traitor. To eject him hence

---

275 *cry havoc*: give order for the slaughter to begin.

276 *modest warrant*: restricted licence (setting limits on the kill).

276–7 *how comes . . . rescue*: Sicinius turns the weight of his authority against Menenius, using 'rescue' in a legal sense (= take by force out of legal custody).

277 *holp*: helped.

286 *turn you to*: bring about for you.

288 *peremptory*: resolutely determined.

290 Were but our danger, and to keep him here
Our certain death. Therefore it is decreed
He dies tonight.

Menenius
                 Now the good gods forbid
That our renowned Rome, whose gratitude
Towards her deserved children is enroll'd
295 In Jove's own book, like an unnatural dam
Should now eat up her own!

Sicinius
He's a disease that must be cut away.

Menenius
O, he's a limb that has but a disease;
Mortal to cut it off, to cure it easy.
300 What has he done to Rome that's worthy death?
Killing our enemies, the blood he hath lost—
Which I dare vouch is more than that he hath
By many an ounce—he dropp'd it for his country;
And what is left, to lose it by his country
305 Were to us all that do't and suffer it
A brand to th'end o'th' world.

Sicinius
                    This is clean cam.

Brutus
Merely awry. When he did love his country
It honour'd him.

Sicinius
            The service of the foot,
Being once gangren'd, is not then respected
310 For what before it was.

Brutus
                We'll hear no more.
[*To the* Citizens] Pursue him to his house and pluck
   him thence,
Lest his infection, being of catching nature,
Spread further.

Menenius
              One word more, one word!
This tiger-footed rage, when it shall find
315 The harm of unscann'd swiftness, will too late
Tie leaden pounds to's heels. Proceed by process,
Lest parties—as he is belov'd—break out
And sack great Rome with Romans.

293 *renowned*: renownèd.
294 *deserved*: deservèd, deserving.
295 *Jove's own book*: This probably refers to the registers of the Capitol, which was Jove's temple.

299 *Mortal*: fatal.

306 *brand*: stigma, mark of infamy.
clean cam: utterly perverse.

307 *Merely awry*: completely out of line.

312 *infection . . . nature*: Gangrene is not 'of catching nature' but it does 'spread further' within the affected body.

315 *unscann'd*: unthinking.
316 *to's*: to its.
by process: i.e. by process of law.
317 *parties*: factions.

Brutus

If it were so?

Sicinius

320 [*To* Menenius] What do ye talk?
Have we not had a taste of his obedience:
Our aediles smote, ourselves resisted? Come.

Menenius

Consider this: he has been bred i'th' wars
Since a could draw a sword, and is ill-school'd
325 In bolted language. Meal and bran together
He throws without distinction. Give me leave,
I'll go to him and undertake to bring him
Where he shall answer by a lawful form—
In peace—to his utmost peril.

First Senator

Noble tribunes,
330 It is the humane way. The other course
Will prove too bloody, and the end of it
Unknown to the beginning.

Sicinius

Noble Menenius,
Be you then as the people's officer.
[*To the* Citizens] Masters, lay down your weapons.

Brutus

Go not home.

Sicinius

335 Meet on the market-place. [*To* Menenius] We'll
     attend you there,
Where if you bring not Martius, we'll proceed
In our first way.

Menenius

I'll bring him to you.
[*To the* Senators] Let me desire your company. He
     must come,
Or what is worst will follow.

First Senator

Pray you, let's to him.
     [*Exeunt* Tribunes *and* Citizens *at one door,*
          Patricians *at another door*

---

325 *bolted*: refined, sifted; the image is of milling flour, and anticipates 'Meal and bran'.

328–9 *answer . . . peril*: i.e. be amenable to stand trial for his life.

329 *Noble tribunes*: The Senator appeals to the better part of the tribunes' nature.

330 *humane*: properly human.

335 *attend*: wait for.

Act 3   Scene 2

The Senators and Menenius persuade
Coriolanus to face his trial; Volumnia
rehearses him in his part.

0s.d. *Nobles*: patricians.

4 *precipitation*: drop, precipice.

5 *Below . . . sight*: farther than eye can
see.

6s.d. *Enter Volumnia*: Volumnia apparently
enters in the course of Coriolanus'
speech.

7 *muse*: wonder.

9 *woollen*: wool-clad.

10 *buy . . . groats*: i.e. petty tradesmen; a
'groat' was worth about 2p.

12 *ordinance*: rank, status.

18 *Let 't go*: that's enough.

21 *tryings*: testings.
dispositions: purposes, inclinations.
23 *Ere . . . you*: i.e. until they were
powerless to deny you.

Scene 2

The House of Coriolanus: *enter* Coriolanus
with Nobles

Coriolanus
Let them pull all about mine ears, present me
Death on the wheel or at wild horses' heels,
Or pile ten hills on the Tarpeian rock,
That the precipitation might down stretch
5 Below the beam of sight, yet will I still
Be thus to them.

Enter Volumnia

A Patrician
You do the nobler.

Coriolanus
                        I muse my mother
Does not approve me further, who was wont
To call them woollen vassels, things created
10 To buy and sell with groats, to show bare heads
In congregations, to yawn, be still, and wonder,
When one but of my ordinance stood up
To speak of peace or war. [*To* Volumnia] I talk of
      you.
Why did you wish me milder? Would you have me
15 False to my nature? Rather say I play
The man I am.

Volumnia
                        O, sir, sir, sir,
I would have had you put your power well on
Before you had worn it out.

Coriolanus
                              Let 't go.

Volumnia
You might have been enough the man you are
20 With striving less to be so. Lesser had been
The tryings of your dispositions if
You had not show'd them how ye were dispos'd
Ere they lack'd power to cross you.

Coriolanus
                              Let them hang.

Volumnia
Ay, and burn too.

Enter Menenius, *with the* Senators

Menenius

25 [*To* Coriolanus] Come, come, you have been too
        rough, something too rough.
  You must return and mend it.

First Senator

                            There's no remedy
  Unless, by not so doing, our good city
  Cleave in the midst and perish.

Volumnia

[*To* Coriolanus]   Pray be counsell'd.
  I have a heart as little apt as yours,
30 But yet a brain that leads my use of anger
  To better vantage.

Menenius

                    Well said, noble woman.
  Before he should thus stoop to th' herd, but that
  The violent fit o'th' time craves it as physic
  For the whole state, I would put mine armour on,
35 Which I can scarcely bear.

Coriolanus

  What must I do?

Menenius

  Return to th' tribunes.

Coriolanus

  Well, what then, what then?

Menenius

  Repent what you have spoke.

Coriolanus

40 For them? I cannot do it to the gods,
  Must I then do't to them?

Volumnia

                          You are too absolute,
  Though therein you can never be too noble,
  But when extremities speak. I have heard you say,
  Honour and policy, like unsever'd friends,
45 I'th' war do grow together. Grant that, and tell me
  In peace what each of them by th'other lose
  That they combine not here.

Coriolanus

                            Tush, tush!

29 *apt*: yielding, compliant.

30–1 *leads . . . vantage*: teaches me to make
        better use of my anger.

33 *fit*: frenzy, madness.

41 *absolute*: uncompromising, inflexible.

43 *extremities speak*: necessity demands.

44 *policy*: stratagems.
        unsever'd: inseparable.

Menenius

A good demand

Volumenia

If it be honour in your wars to seem
The same you are not, which for your best ends
50 You adopt your policy, how is it less or worse
That it shall hold companionship in peace
With honour, as in war, since that to both
It stands in like request?

Coriolanus

Why force you this?

Volumnia

Because that now it lies you on to speak
55 To th' people; not by your own instruction,
Nor by th' matter which your heart prompts you,
But with such words that are but roted in
Your tongue, though but bastards and syllables
Of no allowance to your bosom's truth.
60 Now this no more dishonours you at all
Than to take in a town with gentle words,
Which else would put you to your fortune and
The hazard of much blood.
I would dissemble with my nature where
65 My fortunes and my friends at stake requir'd
I should do so in honour. I am in this
Your wife, your son, these senators, the nobles;
And you will rather show our general louts
How you can frown than spend a fawn upon 'em
70 For the inheritance of their loves and safeguard
Of what that want might ruin.

Menenius

Noble lady!
[*To* Coriolanus] Come, go with us, speak fair. You
     may salve so,
Not what is dangerous present, but the loss
Of what is past.

Volumnia

I prithee now, my son [*She takes his bonnet*]
75 Go to them with this bonnet in thy hand,
And thus far having stretch'd it—here be with
     them—
Thy knee bussing the stones—for in such business
Action is eloquence, and the eyes of th'ignorant

48–53 *If it be . . . request*: 'If you think it is honourable in wartime to use deceit for your own purposes, why should it be any less honourable in peacetime, since it's necessary for both war and peace'.

53 *force*: enforce, urge.

54 *lies you on*: is incumbent on you.
55 *instruction*: inclination, feelings.

57 *but roted*: only learned by rote.
58–9 *bastards . . . truth*: words and sounds not coming in honesty from your heart.

61 *take in*: capture.
62 *put . . . fortune*: make you try your luck.
63 *The . . . blood*: risk shedding much blood. The short line allows Volumnia an emphatic pause before proceeding in her argument from the general to the personal.
64–6 *I would . . . honour*: 'I would be deceitful if honour required this for the sake of my fortunes and my friends': Volumnia does not share the personal integrity of her son.
66 *I am in this*: in this I represent.
68 *our general louts*: the vulgar louts of our community.
70 *inheritance*: acquisition.
71 *that want*: i.e. failure to 'spend a fawn upon 'em'.

73 *Not . . . but*: not only . . . but also.
     dangerous: in danger.
     present: in the present—i.e. Coriolanus' life.
74 *what is past*: i.e. the consulship.
76 *stretch'd it*: held it out.
     here . . . them: play along with them like this.
77 *bussing*: kissing, kneeling on.
78 *Action is eloquence*: i.e. gestures speak louder than words.

79 *waving*: bowing in all directions.

80 *Which offer . . . heart*: Volumnia
(perhaps) bows in different directions,
beating her breast.
stout: proud.

81-2 *Now humble . . . handling*: 'with your
heart, now humble, all soft and yielding
in their hands'; the ripe mulberry was
occasionally used as emblem of a
yielding disposition.

82 *hold*: bear.
or: or, again.

85 *fit*: appropriate.

87 *theirs*: according to their wishes.

90 *free*: generous, easily given.

93 *in fiery gulf*: through hell-fire.

94 *bower*: lady's chamber.

More learned than the ears—waving thy head,
80 Which offer thus, correcting thy stout heart,
Now humble as the ripest mulberry
That will not hold the handling; or say to them
Thou art their soldier and, being bred in broils,
Hast not the soft way which, thou dost confess,
85 Were fit for thee to use as they to claim,
In asking their good loves; but thou wilt frame
Thyself, forsooth, hereafter theirs so far
As thou hast power and person.
     Menenius
[*To* Coriolanus]   This but done
Even as she speaks, why, their hearts were yours;
90 For they have pardons, being ask'd, as free
As words to little purpose.
     Volumnia
                              Prithee now,
Go, and be rul'd, although I know thou hadst rather
Follow thine enemy in a fiery gulf
Than flatter him in a bower.

     .*Enter* Cominius

                         Here is Cominius.
     Cominius
95 I have been i'th' market-place; and, sir, 'tis fit
You make strong party, or defend yourself
By calmness or by absence. All's in anger.
     Menenius
Only fair speech.
     Cominius
               I think 'twill serve, if he
Can thereto frame his spirit.
     Volumnia
                         He must, and will.
100 Prithee now, say you will, and go about it.
     Coriolanus
Must I go show them my unbarbed sconce?
Must I with my base tongue give to my noble heart
A lie that it must bear? Well, I will do't.
Yet were there but this single plot to lose,
105 This mould of Martius, they to dust should grind it
And throw't against the wind. To th' market-place.

101 *unbarbed*: unbarbèd; defenceless,
uncovered.

102 *noble*: i.e. patrician.

104 *single plot*: piece of earth—i.e. his body.

105 *mould of Martius*: clay which is Martius.

107 *part*: i.e. actor's part.
108 *discharge*: perform.

114 *harlot*: prostitute, beggar.
115 *choir'd*: harmonized.
116 *Small*: i.e. small in volume and high in pitch.
eunuch: small, flute-shaped, musical instrument.

117 *lull*: The plural object 'babies' has attracted the plural verb form.
118 *Tent*: camp, take up residence.
119 *glasses . . . sight*: eyeballs.
123 *surcease*: cease.
125 *inherent*: permanently indwelling.
129 *stoutness*: obstinacy.
132 *owe*: own.
134 *mountebank*: i.e. 'sell myself like a quack doctor' (who mounted a platform—'bank'—to attract customers with his patter).

135 *Cog*: swindle.
136 *trades*: workers.

You have put me now to such a part which never
I shall discharge to th' life.

Cominius

Come, come, we'll prompt you

Volumnia

I prithee now, sweet son, as thou hast said
110 My praises made thee first a soldier, so,
To have my praise for this, perform a part
Thou hast not done before.

Coriolanus

Well, I must do't.
Away, my disposition; and possess me
Some harlot's spirit! My throat of war be turn'd,
115 Which choir'd with my drum, into a pipe
Small as an eunuch or the virgin voice
That babies lull asleep! The smiles of knaves
Tent in my cheeks, and schoolboys' tears take up
The glasses of my sight! A beggar's tongue
120 Make motion through my lips, and my arm'd knees
Who bow'd but in my stirrup, bend like his
That hath receiv'd an alms!—I will not do't,
Lest I surcease to honour mine own truth,
And by my body's action teach my mind
125 A most inherent baseness.

Volumnia

At thy choice, then!
To beg of thee it is my more dishonour
Than thou of them. Come all to ruin. Let
Thy mother rather feel thy pride than fear
Thy dangerous stoutness, for I mock at death
130 With as big heart as thou. Do as thou list.
Thy valiantness was mine, thou suck'st it from me,
But owe thy pride thyself.

Coriolanus

Pray be content.
Mother, I am going to the market-place.
Chide me no more. I'll mountebank their loves,
135 Cog their hearts from them, and come home belov'd
Of all the trades in Rome. Look, I am going.
Commend me to my wife. I'll return consul,
Or never trust to what my tongue can do
I'th' way of flattery further.

Volumnia

Do your will.   [*Exit*

Cominius

140 Away! The tribunes do attend you. Arm yourself
To answer mildly, for they are prepar'd
With accusations, as I hear, more strong
Than are upon you yet.

Coriolanus

The word is 'mildly'. Pray you let us go.
145 Let them accuse me by invention, I
Will answer in mine honour.

Menenius

Ay, but mildly.

Coriolanus

Well, mildly be it, then—mildly!

[*Exeunt*

---

ct 3   Scene 3

ae tribunes gather their forces for the
nfrontation. Coriolanus loses his temper
d is exiled from Rome.

1 *charge him home*: press home your
charges.
affects: is aiming for.
3 *envy to*: malice against.
4–5 *spoil . . . distributed*: 'they charged him
. . . that he had not made the common
distribution of the spoil he had gotten
in invading the territory of the Antiates'
(Plutarch).

9 *voices*: votes.
10 *poll*: head.

Scene 3

The Market-place: *enter* Sicinius *and*
Brutus

Brutus

In this point charge him home: that he affects
Tyrannical power. If he evade us there,
Enforce him with his envy to the people,
And that the spoil got on the Antiates
5 Was ne'er distributed.

Enter an Aedile

What, will he come?

Aedile

He's coming.

Brutus

How accompanied?

Aedile

With old Menenius, and those senators
That always favour'd him.

Sicinius

Have you a catalogue
Of all the voices that we have procur'd,
10 Set down by th' poll?

Aedile

I have, 'tis ready.

Sicinius

Have you collected them by tribes?

Aedile

I have.

Sicinius

Assemble presently the people hither,
And when they hear me say 'It shall be so
I'th' right and strength o'th' commons', be it eithe
15 For death, for fine, or banishment, then let them,
If I say 'Fine', cry 'Fine!', if 'Death', cry 'Death!',
Insisting on the old prerogative
And power i'th' truth o'th' cause.

Aedile

I shall inform then

Brutus

And when such time they have begun to cry,
20 Let them not cease, but with a din confus'd
Enforce the present execution
Of what we chance to sentence.

Aedile

Very well.

Sicinius

Make them be strong, and ready for this hint
When we shall hap to give't them.

Brutus

Go about it.

[*Exit* Aedil

25 [*To* Sicinius] Put him to choler straight. He hath
been us'd
Ever to conquer and to have his worth
Of contradiction. Being once chaf'd, he cannot
Be rein'd again to temperance. Then he speaks
What's in his heart, and that is there which looks
30 With us to break his neck.

Sicinius

Well, here he comes.

Enter Coriolanus, Menenius, *and*
Cominius, *with other* Senators *and*
Patricians

11 *by tribes*: Plutarch describes how the tribunes organized the voting to be by tribes (in which each tribe had one vote determined by simple majority) instead of by centuries (where voting power was weighted according to wealth).
12 *presently*: immediately.

17 *old prerogative*: traditional precedent.
18 *power . . . cause*: i.e. the power that the justice of their cause gives to them.

21–2 *Enforce . . . sentence*: insist on the immediate execution of whatever we happen to decree.

26–7 *Ever . . . contradiction*: always to have his own way and to be as contradictory as he pleases.

29 *looks*: looks likely, promises well.
30 *With us*: i.e. with our help.

Menenius

[*To* Coriolanus] Calmly, I do beseech you.

Coriolanus

[*To* Menenius] Ay, as an hostler that for th' poorest piece

Will bear the knave by th' volume.—[*Aloud*] Th'honour'd gods

Keep Rome in safety and the chairs of justice

35 Supplied with worthy men, plant love among's,

Throng our large temples with the shows of peace,

And not our streets with war!

First Senator

                Amen, amen.

Menenius

                    A noble wish.

Enter the Aedile *with the* Citizens

Sicinius

Draw near, ye people.

Aedile

          List to your tribunes. Audience!

Peace, I say.

Coriolanus

        First, hear me speak.

Sicinius and **Brutus**

              Well, say.—Peace ho!

Coriolanus

40 Shall I be charg'd no further than this present?

Must all determine here?

Sicinius

              I do demand

If you submit you to the people's voices,

Allow their officers, and are content

To suffer lawful censure for such faults

45 As shall be prov'd upon you.

Coriolanus

              I am content.

Menenius

Lo, citizens, he says he is content.

The warlike service he has done, consider. Think

Upon the wounds his body bears, which show

Like graves i'th' holy churchyard.

---

2 *piece*: coin.

3 *bear . . . volume*: will tolerate being called 'knave' any number of times.

36 *shows*: ceremonies.

38 *Audience*: attention.

41 *determine*: be concluded.
demand: require to know.

43 *Allow*: acknowledge.

Coriolanus
                                    Scratches with brier
50 Scars to move laughter only.
      Menenius
                              Consider further
      That when he speaks not like a citizen,
      You find him like a soldier. Do not take
      His rougher accents for malicious sounds,
      But, as I say, such as become a soldier
55 Rather than envy you.
      Cominius
      Well, well, no more.
      Coriolanus
      What is the matter
      That, being pass'd for consul with full voice,
      I am so dishonour'd that the very hour
60 You take it off again?
      Sicinius
      Answer to us.
      Coriolanus
      Say then!—'Tis true, I ought so.
      Sicinius
      We charge you that you have contriv'd to take
      From Rome all season'd office, and to wind
65 Yourself into a power tyrannical,
      For which you are a traitor to the people.
      Coriolanus
      How, traitor!
      Menenius
                        Nay, temperately—your promise.
      Coriolanus
      The fires i'th' lowest hell fold in the people!
      Call me their traitor, thou injurious tribune!
70 Within thine eyes sat twenty thousand deaths,
      In thy hands clutch'd as many millions, in
      Thy lying tongue both numbers, I would say
      'Thou liest' unto thee with a voice as free
      As I do pray the gods.
      Sicinius
75 Mark you this, people?
      All the Citizens
      To th' rock, to th' rock with him!

---

55 *envy you*: show malice towards you.

58 *with full voice*: unanimously.

63 *contriv'd*: plotted.
64 *season'd*: old-established.
65 *power tyrannical*: According to Plutarch, the tribunes tried to prove that all Martius' actions 'tended to usurp tyrannical power over Rome'.

69 *injurious*: insulting.
70 *Within*: i.e. if within.

73 *free*: clear.

Sicinius
Peace!
We need not put new matter to his charge.
What you have seen him do and heard him speak,
80 Beating your officers, cursing yourselves,
Opposing laws with strokes, and here defying
Those whose great power must try him—even this,
So criminal and in such capital kind,
Deserves th'extremest death.

Brutus
                              But since he hath
85 Serv'd well for Rome—

Coriolanus
                    What do you prate of service?

Brutus
I talk of that that know it.

Coriolanus
                    You?

Menenius
Is this the promise that you made your mother?

Cominius
Know, I pray you—

Coriolanus
                    I'll know no further.
Let them pronounce the steep Tarpeian death,
90 Vagabond exile, flaying, pent to linger
But with a grain a day, I would not buy
Their mercy at the price of one fair word,
Nor check my courage for what they can give
To have't with saying 'Good morrow'.

Sicinius
                              For that he has,
95 As much as in him lies, from time to time
Envied against the people, seeking means
To pluck away their power, as now at last
Given hostile strokes, and that not in the presence
Of dreaded justice, but on the ministers
100 That doth distribute it, in the name o'th' people,
And in the power of us the tribunes, we
E'en from this instant banish him our city
In peril of precipitation
From off the rock Tarpeian, never more

81 *Opposing . . . strokes*: taking arms
against legal authority.

83 *capital*: deserving of capital punishment.

85 *prate*: prattle, talk rubbish.

86 *I talk . . . You?*: Brutus talks of civic
service—which Coriolanus will not
recognize.

90 *pent*: being imprisoned.

93 *courage*: spirit, mettle.

94 *For that*: inasmuch as; the legalistic
phraseology suggests that Sicinius is
reading from a prepared charge-sheet.

96 *Envied*: shown malice.

105 To enter our Rome gates. I'th' people's name
I say it shall be so.

All the Citizens
It shall be so, it shall be so! Let him away!
He's banish'd, and it shall be so!

Cominius
Hear me, my masters and my common friends.

Sicinius
110 He's sentenc'd. No more hearing.

Cominius
                                    Let me speak.
I have been consul, and can show for Rome
Her enemies' marks upon me. I do love
My country's good with a respect more tender
More holy and profound, than mine own life,

115 estimate: reputation, honour.
115–16 womb's . . . loins: i.e. children;
    Cominius shows the patrician
    sentiments of Volumnia (1, 3, 3–20).

115 My dear wife's estimate, her womb's increase,
And treasure of my loins. Then if I would
Speak that—

Sicinius
                    We know your drift. Speak what?

Brutus
There's no more to be said, but he is banish'd
As enemy to the people and his country.
120 It shall be so!

All the Citizens
                    It shall be so, it shall be so!

Coriolanus
121 cry: pack.

You common cry of curs, whose breath I hate
As reek o'th' rotten fens, whose loves I prize
As the dead carcasses of unburied men
That do corrupt my air: I banish you!
125 And here remain with your uncertainty:
Let every feeble rumour shake your hearts;
Your enemies, with nodding of their plumes,
Fan you into despair! Have the power still
To banish your defenders, till at length

130 finds . . . feels: i.e. 'sees nothing until it
    happens'.
131–2 Making . . . foes: i.e. 'leaving no one
    in the city but yourselves—who are, as
    always, your own worst enemies'.
133 abated: abject, miserable.

130 Your ignorance—which finds not till it feels—
Making but reservation of yourselves—
Still your own foes—deliver you
As most abated captives to some nation
That won you without blows! Despising

135 For you the city, thus I turn my back.
There is a world elsewhere.

[*Exeunt* Coriolanus, Cominius, *and* Menenius
with the rest of the Patricians

The Citizens *all shout, and throw up their caps*

Aedile
The people's enemy is gone, is gone.
All the Citizens
Our enemy is banish'd, he is gone. Hoo-hoo!
Sicinius
Go see him out at gates, and follow him
140 As he hath follow'd you, with all despite.
Give him deserv'd vexation. Let a guard
Attend us through the city.
All the Citizens
Come, come, let's see him out at gates. Come.
The gods preserve our noble tribunes! Come.

[*Exeunt*

Act 4

Coriolanus takes his leave of Rome.

1–2 *The beast . . . heads*: i.e. the multitude.

3 *ancient*: old, former.
  used: accustomed.
4 *extremities*: great crises.

7–9 *fortune's . . . cunning*: i.e. 'when fate does its worst, it takes a high class training to endure with dignity'.

9 *cunning*: knowledge, ability.

11 *conn'd*: studied, learnt.

14 *red pestilence*: spotted fever (typhus).
15 *occupations*: handicrafts, trades.

18 *Hercules*: the demigod of Greek mythology who demonstrated his divinity by completing twelve 'labours', all demanding superhuman strength and skill (see *3, 1, 95*note).

Scene 1

The Gates of Rome: enter Coriolanus, Volumnia, Virgilia, Menenius, Cominius, *with the young nobility of Rome*

Coriolanus
Come, leave your tears. A brief farewell. The beast
With many heads butts me away. Nay, mother,
Where is your ancient courage? You were used
To say extremities was the trier of spirits,
5 That common chances common men could bear,
That when the sea was calm all boats alike
Showed mastership in floating; fortune's blows
When most struck home, being gentle wounded craves
A noble cunning. You were used to load me
10 With precepts that would make invincible
The heart that conn'd them.
    Virgilia
O heavens, O heavens!
    Coriolanus
Nay, I prithee, woman—
    Volumnia
Now the red pestilence strike all trades in Rome,
15 And occupations perish!
    Coriolanus
                    What, what, what!
I shall be lov'd when I am lack'd. Nay, mother,
Resume that spirit when you were wont to say,
If you had been the wife of Hercules
Six of his labours you'd have done, and sav'd
20 Your husband so much sweat. Cominius,
Droop not; adieu. Farewell, my wife, my mother;
I'll do well yet. Thou old and true Menenius,

27 *fond*: foolish.

28 *wot*: know.

29 *My hazards . . . solace*: you have always
enjoyed the risks I have taken.

30 *Believe't not lightly*: i.e. take this
assurance seriously.

33 *or . . . or*: either . . . or.
exceed the common: surpass the common
expectation.

34 *cautelous . . . practice*: deceitful tricks
and sharp practices.
first: best, most noble; Volumnia seems
to have had only the one child (see
1, 3, 6) but thinks of herself (*1, 3, 20–3*)
as the Roman mother of many sons.

38 *starts*: starts up, arises.

42 *cause*: occasion.
repeal: recall.

50 *noble touch*: proven nobility (the
metaphor is from the touchstone used
to test gold); these are perhaps the
friends who protected Coriolanus
(*3, 3, 141*) from the 'vexation'
threatened by the tribunes.

Thy tears are salter than a younger man's
And venomous to thine eyes. My sometime general
25 I have seen thee stern, and thou hast oft beheld
Heart-hard'ning spectacles. Tell these sad women
'Tis fond to wail inevitable strokes
As 'tis to laugh at 'em. My mother, you wot well
My hazards still have been your solace, and—
30 Believe't not lightly—though I go alone,
Like to a lonely dragon that his fen
Makes fear'd and talk'd of more than seen, your son
Will or exceed the common or be caught
With cautelous baits and practice.

Volumnia
                                        My first son,
35 Whither wilt thou go? Take good Cominius
With thee a while. Determine on some course
More than a wild exposure to each chance
That starts i'th' way before thee.

Virgilia
                                        O the gods!

Cominius
I'll follow thee a month, devise with thee
40 Where thou shalt rest, that thou mayst hear of us
And we of thee. So, if the time thrust forth
A cause for thy repeal, we shall not send
O'er the vast world to seek a single man,
And lose advantage, which doth ever cool
45 I'th' absence of the needer.

Coriolanus
                                        Fare ye well.
Thou hast years upon thee, and thou art too full
Of the wars' surfeits to go rove with one
That's yet unbruis'd. Bring me but out at gate.
Come, my sweet wife, my dearest mother, and
50 My friends of noble touch. When I am forth,
Bid me farewell, and smile. I pray you, come.
While I remain above the ground you shall
Hear from me still, and never of me aught
But what is like me formerly.

Menenius
                                        That's worthily
55 As any ear can hear. Come, let's not weep.
If I could shake off but one seven years

From these old arms and legs, by the good gods,
I'd with thee every foot.

Coriolanus

                Give me thy hand. Come.

                        [*Exeunt*

Act 4   Scene 2

Volumnia meets the tribunes.

Scene 2

        Inside the City: *enter the two tribunes,*
        Sicinius *and* Brutus, *with the* Aedile

Sicinius
[*To the* Aedile] Bid them all home. He's gone, and
  we'll no further.
The nobility are vex'd, whom we see have sided
In his behalf.

Brutus

              Now we have shown our power,
Let us seem humbler after it is done

5 Than when it was a-doing.

Sicinius
[*To the* Aedile]   Bid them home.
Say their great enemy is gone, and they
Stand in their ancient strength.

Brutus

                  Dismiss them home.

                  [*Exit* Aedile

Here comes his mother.

        Enter Volumnia, Virgilia, *weeping, and*
        Menenius

Sicinius
Let's not meet her.

Brutus

10 Why?

Sicinius
They say she's mad.

Brutus
They have ta'en note of us. Keep on your way.

Volumnia
O, you're well met! Th'hoarded plague o'th' gods
Requite your love!

11 *mad*: furious.

Menenius
                              Peace, peace, be not so loud.
Volumnia
15 If that I could for weeping, you should hear—
   Nay, and you shall hear some. [*To* Sicinius] Will
   you be gone?
Virgilia
[*To* Brutus] You shall stay too! I would I had the
   power
To say so to my husband.
Sicinius
[*To* Volumnia]   Are you mankind?
Volumnia
Ay, fool. Is that a shame? Note but this, fool:
20 Was not a man my father? Hadst thou foxship
To banish him that struck more blows for Rome
Than thou hast spoken words?
Sicinius
                              O blessed heavens!
Volumnia
More noble blows than ever thou wise words,
And for Rome's good. I'll tell thee what—yet go!
25 Nay, but thou shalt stay too. I would my son
Were in Arabia, and thy tribe before him,
His good sword in his hand.
Sicinius
                                 What then?
Virgilia
                                      What then?
He'd make an end of thy posterity.
Volumnia
Bastards and all.
30 Good man, the wounds that he does bear for Rome!
Menenius
Come, come, peace.
Sicinius
I would he had continu'd to his country
As he began, and not unknit himself
The noble knot he made.
Brutus
                              I would he had.

18 *mankind*: Sicinius means 'behaving like
a man'—but Volumnia interprets the
word as 'belonging to the human race'.
20 *foxship*: i.e. the qualities—cunning and
ingratitude—attributed to the fox.

22 *blessed*: blessèd.
26 *Arabia*: i.e. the desert (where he would
be free to slaughter them without
interference).

33 *unknit*: untied.
34 *noble knot*: the bond by which he bound
Rome to himself.

36   *Cats*: Volumnia's term of revulsion and
abuse.

Volumnia
35   'I would he had'! 'Twas you incens'd the rabble:
Cats, that can judge as fitly of his worth
As I can of those mysteries which heaven
Will not have earth to know.
Brutus
[*To* Sicinius] Pray, let's go.
Volumnia
40   Now pray, sir, get you gone.
You have done a brave deed. Ere you go, hear this:
As far as doth the Capitol exceed
The meanest house in Rome, so far my son—
This lady's husband here, this, do you see?—
45   Whom you have banish'd does exceed you all.
Brutus
Well, well, we'll leave you.
Sicinius
                                    Why stay we to be baited

46   *baited*: harassed.

With one that wants her wits?   [*Exeunt* Tribunes
Volumnia
                                    Take my prayers with you!
I would the gods had nothing else to do
But to confirm my curses. Could I meet 'em

50   *unclog*: release.

50   But once a day, it would unclog my heart
Of what lies heavy to't.
Menenius
                                    You have told them home,
And, by my troth, you have cause. You'll sup with
me?
Volumnia
Anger's my meat: I sup upon myself

54   *starve with feeding*: i.e. kill myself by
indulging my anger.

And so shall starve with feeding. [*To* Virgilia]
Come, let's go.

55   *Leave*: cease.
puling: whimpering.
56   *Juno*: queen of the Roman gods.

55   Leave this faint puling and lament as I do,
In anger, Juno-like. Come, come, come.
                                    [*Exeunt* Volumnia *and* Virgilia
Menenius
                                    Fie, fie, fie.
                                    [*Exit

Act 4   Scene 3

A Roman deserter encounters a Volscian spy.

5 *against 'em*: i.e. the Romans; Nicanor is in the pay of the Volscians.

9 *favour . . . tongue*: your appearance is confirmed by the way you speak.

13–14 *There . . . nobles*: This is the state of affairs described by Plutarch—but here it is contradicted by the opening of Scene 6, a scene of Shakespeare's own invention.

16–17 *They . . . them*: i.e. the Volscians . . . the Romans.

23 *glowing*: i.e. like the embers of the fire.

Scene 3

Between Rome and Antium: enter Nicanor *a Roman, and* Adrian, *a Volsce*

Nicanor
I know you well, sir, and you know me. Your nam
I think, is Adrian.

Adrian
It is so, sir. Truly, I have forgot you.

Nicanor
I am a Roman, and my services are, as you ar
5 against 'em. Know you me yet?

Adrian
Nicanor, no?

Nicanor
The same, sir.

Adrian
You had more beard when I last saw you, but you
favour is well approved by your tongue. What's th
10 news in Rome? I have a note from the Volscian sta
to find you out there. You have well saved me a day
journey.

Nicanor
There hath been in Rome strange insurrections, th
people against the senators, patricians, and noble

Adrian
15 Hath been?—is it ended then? Our state thinks no
so. They are in a most warlike preparation, and hop
to come upon them in the heat of their division.

Nicanor
The main blaze of it is past, but a small thing woul
make it flame again, for the nobles receive so to hea
20 the banishment of that worthy Coriolanus that the
are in a ripe aptness to take all power from th
people, and to pluck from them their tribunes fo
ever. This lies glowing, I can tell you, and is almos
mature for the violent breaking out.

Adrian
25 Coriolanus banished?

Nicanor
Banished, sir.

Adrian
You will be welcome with this intelligence, Nicanor

Nicanor

The day serves well for them now. I have heard it
said the fittest time to corrupt a man's wife is when
30 she's fallen out with her husband. Your noble Tullus
Aufidius will appear well in these wars, his great
opposer Coriolanus being now in no request of his
country.

Adrian

He cannot choose. I am most fortunate thus
35 accidentally to encounter you. You have ended my
business, and I will merrily accompany you home.

Nicanor

I shall between this and supper tell you most strange
things from Rome, all tending to the good of their
adversaries. Have you an army ready, say you?

Adrian

40 A most royal one: the centurions and their charges
distinctly billeted already in th'entertainment, and to
be on foot at an hour's warning.

Nicanor

I am joyful to hear of their readiness, and am the
man, I think, that shall set them in present action.
45 So, sir, heartily well met, and most glad of your
company.

Adrian

You take my part from me, sir. I have the most cause
to be glad of yours.

Nicanor

Well, let us go together.

[*Exeunt*

---

28 *them*: i.e. the Volscians.

34 *He . . . choose*: he's bound to.

37 *this*: this time, now.

40 *charges*: centuries (= the 100 soldiers
under the command of each centurion).
41 *distinctly . . . in th'entertainment*:
separately entered into the pay-roll.

44 *present*: immediate.

Coriolanus encounters a Volscian citizen and
meditates on fortune.

Scene 4

Antium: *outside* Aufidius' *house. Enter*
Coriolanus *in mean apparel, disguised and
muffled*

Coriolanus

A goodly city is this Antium. City,
'Tis I that made thy widows. Many an heir
Of these fair edifices fore my wars
Have I heard groan and drop. Then know me not,

3 *fore my wars*: in the face of my
onslaughts.

5 Lest that thy wives with spits and boys with stones
In puny battle slay me.

Enter a Citizen

6 *Save you*: the gods save you.

                              Save you, sir.
          Citizen
And you.
          Coriolanus
Direct me, if it be your will,

9 *lies*: dwells.

Where great Aufidius lies. Is he in Antium?
          Citizen
10 He is, and feasts the nobles of the state
At his house this night.
          Coriolanus
                    Which is his house, beseech you
          Citizen
This here before you.
          Coriolanus
                    Thank you, sir. Farewell.
                              [*Exit* Citizen

14 *double*: separate (and also 'deceitful').

O world, thy slippery turns! Friends now fast sworn
Whose double bosoms seem to wear one heart,

16 *still*: always.

15 Whose hours, whose bed, whose meal and exercise
Are still together, who twin as 'twere in love

18 *dissension of a doit*: squabble about a
trifle.

Unseparable, shall within this hour,
On a dissension of a doit, break out

19 *So*: in the same way.
fellest: most deadly.
20 *broke their sleep*: i.e. kept them awake.

To bitterest enmity. So fellest foes,
20 Whose passions and whose plots have broke their
     sleep
To take the one the other, by some chance,
Some trick not worth an egg, shall grow dear friends

23 *interjoin their issues*: throw in their lots
together, allow their children to
intermarry.

And interjoin their issues. So with me.
My birthplace hate I, and my love's upon

26 *give me way*: let me have my way.

25 This enemy town. I'll enter. If he slay me,
He does fair justice; if he give me way,
I'll do his country service.
                              [*Exit*

Scene 5

Antium: Aufidius' *house. Music plays.*
Enter a Servingman

First Servingman
Wine, wine, wine! What service is here? I think our
fellows are asleep.   [*Exit*

Enter Second Servingman

Second Servingman
Where's Cotus? My master calls for him. Cotus!
                                                       [*Exit*

Enter Coriolanus, *as before*

Coriolanus
A goodly house. The feast smells well, but I
5 Appear not like a guest.

Enter the First Servingman

First Servingman
What would you have, friend? Whence are you
Here's no place for you. Pray go to the door.
                                                    [*Ex*

Coriolanus
I have deserv'd no better entertainment
In being Coriolanus.

Enter Second Servingman

Second Servingman
10 Whence are you, sir? Has the porter his eyes in h
head, that he gives entrance to such companion:
Pray get you out.
Coriolanus
Away!
Second Servingman
Away? Get you away.
Coriolanus
15 Now thou'rt troublesome.
Second Servingman
Are you so brave? I'll have you talked with anon.

Enter Third Servingman. *The* First *meets
him*

Third Servingman
What fellow's this?
First Servingman
A strange one as ever I looked on. I cannot get hir
out o'th' house. Prithee, call my master to him.

He retires

Third Servingman
20 What have you to do here, fellow? Pray you, avoi
the house.
Coriolanus
Let me but stand. I will not hurt your hearth.
Third Servingman
What are you?
Coriolanus
A gentleman.

8   *entertainment*: reception.

11   *companions*: fellows, rascals.

16   *brave*: insolent.
16s.d.   *The First meets him*: Having left the
stage at line 7, the Servingman now,
presumably, enters from a different
door.

19s.d.   *He retires*: The direction, and that at
line 53, allows the servant[s] to withdraw
from the immediate action without
leaving the stage.
20   *avoid*: clear out of.

Third Servingman

25 A marvellous poor one.

Coriolanus

True, so I am.

Third Servingman

Pray you, poor gentleman, take up some other station. Here's no place for you. Pray you, avoid. Come.

Coriolanus

30 Follow your function. Go and batten on cold bits.

He pushes him away from him

Third Servingman

What, you will not?—Prithee tell my master what a strange guest he has here.

Second Servingman

And I shall.   [*Exit*

Third Servingman

Where dwell'st thou?

Coriolanus

35 Under the canopy.

Third Servingman

Under the canopy?

Coriolanus

Ay.

Third Servingman

Where's that?

Coriolanus

I'th' city of kites and crows.

Third Servingman

40 I'th' city of kites and crows? What an ass it is! Then thou dwell'st with daws too?

Coriolanus

No, I serve not thy master.

Third Servingman

How, sir! Do you meddle with my master?

Coriolanus

Ay, 'tis an honester service than to meddle with thy

45 mistress. Thou prat'st and prat'st. Serve with thy trencher. Hence!

He beats him away.

[*Exit* Third Servingman

---

28 *station*: standing-place, *and also*, status; Coriolanus is too poor to call himself a 'gentleman'.

30 *Follow your function*: get on with your work.
batten: gorge yourself.

35 *Under the canopy*: beneath the sky (*and also*, under the canopy over the stage).

39 *kites and crows*: i.e. scavenging birds, carrion eaters.

41 *daws*: jackdaws (proverbially thought to be foolish birds); Coriolanus refers to the servant and not (as the servant supposes) to Aufidius.

43 *meddle with*: have anything to do with; Coriolanus takes up the sense = 'have sexual intercourse with'.

46 *trencher*: serving dish.

Enter Aufidius *with the* Second Servingman

Aufidius

Where is this fellow?

Second Servingman

Here, sir. I'd have beaten him like a dog but fo
disturbing the lords within.

He retires

Aufidius

50 Whence com'st thou? What wouldst thou? Thy
    name?

Why speak'st not? Speak, man. What's thy name?

Coriolanus

[*Unmuffling*]   If, Tullus

Not yet thou know'st me, and seeing me dost not

Think me for the man I am, necessity

Commands me name myself.

Aufidius

What is thy name?

Coriolanus

55 A name unmusical to the Volscians' ears

And harsh in sound to thine.

Aufidius

Say, what's thy name?

Thou hast a grim appearance, and thy face

Bears a command in't. Though thy tackle's torn,

Thou show'st a noble vessel. What's thy name?

Coriolanus

60 Prepare thy brow to frown. Know'st thou me yet?

Aufidius

I know thee not. Thy name?

Coriolanus

My name is Caius Martius, who hath done

To thee particularly, and to all the Volsces,

Great hurt and mischief. Thereto witness may

65 My surname Coriolanus. The painful service,

The extreme dangers, and the drops of blood

Shed for my thankless country, are requited

But with that surname—a good memory

And witness of the malice and displeasure

70 Which thou shouldst bear me. Only that name
    remains.

51s.d. *Unmuffling*: 'Then Martius unmuffled
himself'; the speech that follows is very
close to its source in Plutarch (see
'Source, Date, and Text', p. xxix).

51 *Tullus*: This is Aufidius' personal name
(*praenomen*), only to be used by
intimates.

58 *tackle*: rigging of a ship—i.e. Martius'
clothing.

68 *memory*: memento, souvenir.

The cruelty and envy of the people,
Permitted by our dastard nobles, who
Have all forsook me, hath devour'd the rest,
And suffer'd me by th' voice of slaves to be
75 Whoop'd out of Rome. Now this extremity
Hath brought me to thy hearth. Not out of hope—
Mistake me not—to save my life, for if
I had fear'd death, of all the men i'th' world
I would have 'voided thee, but in mere spite
80 To be full quit of those my banishers
Stand I before thee here. Then if thou hast
A heart of wreak in thee, that wilt revenge
Thine own particular wrongs and stop those maims
Of shame seen through thy country, speed thee
    straight,
85 And make my misery serve thy turn. So use it
That my revengeful services may prove
As benefits to thee; for I will fight
Against my canker'd country with the spleen
Of all the under-fiends. But if so be
90 Thou dar'st not this, and that to prove more fortunes
Thou'rt tir'd, then, in a word, I also am
Longer to live most weary, and present
My throat to thee and to thy ancient malice,
Which not to cut would show thee but a fool,
95 Since I have ever follow'd thee with hate,
Drawn tuns of blood out of thy country's breast,
And cannot live but to thy shame unless
It be to do thee service.
  Aufidius
              O Martius, Martius!
Each word thou hast spoke hath weeded from my
    heart
100 A root of ancient envy. If Jupiter
Should from yon cloud speak divine things
And say ' 'Tis true', I'd not believe them more
Than thee, all-noble Martius. Let me twine
Mine arms about that body where-against
105 My grained ash an hundred times hath broke,
And scarr'd the moon with splinters. [*He embraces
    Coriolanus*] Here I clip
The anvil of my sword, and do contest
As hotly and as nobly with thy love

As ever in ambitious strength I did
110 Contend against thy valour. Know thou first,
I lov'd the maid I married; never man
Sigh'd truer breath. But that I see thee here,
Thou noble thing, more dances my rapt heart
Than when I first my wedded mistress saw
115 Bestride my threshold. Why, thou Mars, I tell thee
We have a power on foot, and I had purpose
Once more to hew thy target from thy brawn,
Or lose mine arm for't. Thou hast beat me out
Twelve several times, and I have nightly since
120 Dreamt of encounters 'twixt thyself and me—
We have been down together in my sleep,
Unbuckling helms, fisting each other's throat—
And wak'd half dead with nothing. Worthy Martius
Had we no other quarrel else to Rome but that
125 Thou art thence banish'd, we would muster all
From twelve to seventy, and, pouring war
Into the bowels of ungrateful Rome,
Like a bold flood o'erbear't. O, come, go in,
And take our friendly senators by th' hands
130 Who now are here taking their leaves of me,
Who am prepar'd against your territories,
Though not for Rome itself.

Coriolanus
                                You bless me, gods.

Aufidius
Therefore, most absolute sir, if thou wilt have
The leading of thine own revenges, take
135 Th'one half of my commission and set down—
As best thou art experienc'd, since thou know'st
Thy country's strength and weakness—thine own
    ways:
Whether to knock against the gates of Rome,
Or rudely visit them in parts remote
140 To fright them ere destroy. But come in.
Let me commend thee first to those that shall
Say yea to thy desires. A thousand welcomes!
And more a friend than ere an enemy;
Yet, Martius, that was much. Your hand. Most
    welcome!   [*Exeunt* Coriolanus *and* Aufidius

113 *dances*: makes dance.
     rapt: enraptured.

115 *Bestride*: step across.
     thou Mars: Aufidius plays with the names
     'Martius' and 'Mars' (the Roman god of
     war).
116 *power*: army.
117 *target*: shield or buckler worn on the
     arm.
     brawn: i.e. brawny, muscular arm.

118 *out*: outright.
119 *several*: different.
121 *down together*: i.e. wrestling hand-to-
     hand on the ground.
127 *bowels*: i.e. the innermost part.
131 *prepar'd*: ready to fight.

133 *absolute*: consummate, perfect.

135 *commission*: warrant and forces for
     fighting.
     set down: determine, make arrangement.

144s.d *come forward*: They had retired to the back of the stage (line 19) to watch this encounter.

147 *gave*: warned.

150 *set up*: set spinning.

163, 164 *him*: In neither of these cases is it clear whether Coriolanus or Aufidius is intended; the comic confusion was probably intended by Shakespeare.

The two Servingmen *come forward*

First Servingman
145 Here's a strange alteration!
Second Servingman
By my hand, I had thought to have strucken him with a cudgel, and yet my mind gave me his clothes made a false report of him.
First Servingman
What an arm he has! He turned me about with his
150 finger and his thumb as one would set up a top.
Second Servingman
Nay, I knew by his face that there was something in him. He had, sir, a kind of face, methought—I cannot tell how to term it.
First Servingman
He had so, looking, as it were—would I were hanged
155 but I thought there was more in him than I could think.
Second Servingman
So did I, I'll be sworn. He is simply the rarest man i'th' world.
First Servingman
I think he is; but a greater soldier than he, you wot
160 one.
Second Servingman
Who? My master?
First Servingman
Nay, it's no matter for that.
Second Servingman
Worth six on him.
First Servingman
Nay, not so, neither; but I take him to be the greater
165 soldier.
Second Servingman
Faith, look you, one cannot tell how to say that. For the defence of a town our general is excellent.
First Servingman
Ay, and for an assault too.

Enter the Third Servingman

Third Servingman
O, slaves, I can tell you news—news, you rascals!

First and Second Servingmen

170 What, what, what? Let's partake.

Third Servingman

171 *lief*: gladly, willingly.

I would not be a Roman of all nations. I had as lief be a condemned man.

First and Second Servingmen

Wherefore? Wherefore?

Third Servingman

174 *thwack*: clobber, thrash.

Why, here's he that was wont to thwack our general,

175 Caius Martius.

First Servingman

Why do you say 'thwack our general'?

Third Servingman

I do not say 'thwack our general'; but he was alway good enough for him.

Second Servingman

Come, we are fellows and friends. He was ever too

180 hard for him. I have heard him say so himself.

First Servingman

181 *directly*: speaking plainly.

He was too hard for him directly. To say the truth on't, before Corioles he scotched him and notched

183 *carbonado*: piece of grilled fish or meat.

him like a carbonado.

Second Servingman

184 *An*: if.

An he had been cannibally given, he might have

185 broiled and eaten him too.

First Servingman

187 *so made on*: made so much of.
188 *upper end*: i.e. next to Aufidius.
190 *bald*: bareheaded.
191 *sanctifies . . . hand*: considers himself blessed with the touch of Coriolanus' hand.
192 *turns . . . eye*: i.e. rolls his eyes in an expression of adoring agreement.

But more of thy news.

Third Servingman

Why, he is so made on here within as if he were son and heir to Mars; set at upper end o'th' table, no question asked him by any of the senators but they

190 stand bald before him. Our general himself makes a mistress of him, sanctifies himself with's hand, and turns up the white o'th' eye to his discourse. But the

193 *cut i'th' middle*: i.e. his power is split in half.

bottom of the news is, our general is cut i'th' middle, and but one half of what he was yesterday, for the

195 other has half by the entreaty and grant of the whole

196 *sowl*: drag out.

table. He'll go, he says, and sowl the porter of Rome gates by th'ears. He will mow all down before him,

198 *polled*: cut down, cleared.

and leave his passage polled.

Second Servingman

And he's as like to do't as any man I can imagine.

Third Servingman

200 Do't? He will do't; for look you, sir, he has as many
friends as enemies; which friends, sir, as it were
durst not—look you, sir—show themselves, as we
term it, his friends whilst he's in dejectitude.

First Servingman

'Dejectitude'? What's that?

Third Servingman

205 But when they shall see, sir, his crest up again and
the man in blood, they will out of their burrows like
conies after rain, and revel all with him.

First Servingman

But when goes this forward?

Third Servingman

Tomorrow, today, presently. You shall have the drum
210 struck up this afternoon. 'Tis as it were a parcel of
their feast, and to be executed ere they wipe their
lips.

Second Servingman

Why, then we shall have a stirring world again. This
peace is nothing but to rust iron, increase tailors,
215 and breed ballad-makers.

First Servingman

Let me have war, say I. It exceeds peace as far as day
does night. It's sprightly walking, audible and full of
vent. Peace is a very apoplexy, lethargy; mulled,
deaf, sleepy, insensible; a getter of more bastard
220 children than war's a destroyer of men.

Second Servingman

'Tis so, and as war in some sort may be said to be a
ravisher, so it cannot be denied but peace is a great
maker of cuckolds.

First Servingman

Ay, and it makes men hate one another.

Third Servingman

225 Reason: because they then less need one another.
The wars for my money! I hope to see Romans as
cheap as Volscians. [*A sound within*] They are rising,
they are rising.

First and **Second Servingmen**

In, in, in, in.

[*Exeunt*

---

205 *crest up*: i.e. like a fighting cock.

206 *in blood*: in full vigour and cry (a hunting term).

207 *conies*: rabbits.

208 *goes this forward*: is this happening.

209 *presently*: now.

210 *parcel*: part.

215 *ballad-makers*: Ballads were the popular medium for the transmission of news.

217–18 *It's sprightly . . . vent*: The image is of a hound ready for the hunt and giving tongue as it scents the quarry.

218 *mulled*: stupefied.

227 *rising*: i.e. from the dining table.

Act 4   Scene 6

Rome is peaceful—but there is a new threat
from the Volscians.

7 *pest'ring*: obstructing, crowding.

9 *functions*: proper occupations.

10 *stood to't*: held out, were resolute about
the business.

Scene 6

*Rome: the Market-place. Enter the two
tribunes,* Sicinius *and* Brutus

Sicinius
We hear not of him, neither need we fear him.
His remedies are tame, the present peace
And quietness of the people, which before
Were in wild hurry. Here do we make his friends
5 Blush that the world goes well, who rather had,
Though they themselves did suffer by't, behold
Dissentious numbers pest'ring streets than see
Our tradesmen singing in their shops and going
About their functions friendly.
Brutus
10 We stood to't in good time.

Enter Menenius

                                    Is this Menenius?
Sicinius
'Tis he, 'tis he. O, he is grown most kind of late.
[*To* Menenius] Hail, sir.
Menenius
Hail to you both.
Sicinius
Your Coriolanus is not now much miss'd
15 But with his friends. The commonwealth doth stand
And so would do were he more angry at it.
Menenius
All's well, and might have been much better if
He could have temporiz'd.
Sicinius
Where is he, hear you?
Menenius
20 Nay, I hear nothing.
His mother and his wife hear nothing from him.

Enter three or four Citizens

All the Citizens
[*To the* Tribunes] The gods preserve you both.
Sicinius
                                    Good e'en, our neighbours.

22 *e'en*: evening (an expression used any
time after noon).

Brutus
Good e'en to you all, good e'en to you all.
First Citizen
Ourselves, our wives and children, on our knees
25 Are bound to pray for you both.
Sicinius
                                    Live and thrive.
Brutus
Farewell, kind neighbours.
We wish'd Coriolanus had lov'd you as we did.
All the Citizens
Now the gods keep you!
Sicinius and **Brutus**
                              Farewell, farewell.
                                        [*Exeunt* Citizens

Sicinius
This is a happier and more comely time
30 Than when these fellows ran about the streets
Crying confusion.
Brutus
                              Caius Martius was
A worthy officer i'th' war, but insolent,
O'ercome with pride, ambitious past all thinking,
Self-loving—
Sicinius
                              And affecting one sole throne
35 Without assistance.
Menenius
                              I think not so.
Sicinius
We should by this, to all our lamentation,
If he had gone forth consul found it so.
Brutus
The gods have well prevented it, and Rome
Sits safe and still without him.

Enter an Aedile

Aedile
                                        Worthy tribunes,
40 There is a slave whom we have put in prison
Reports the Volsces, with two several powers,
Are enter'd in the Roman territories,

34 *affecting . . . throne*: wanting to rule
alone.
35 *assistance*: partners, associates.

37 *found*: i.e. have found.

41 *several*: separate.

And with the deepest malice of the war
Destroy what lies before 'em.
Menenius
                                    'Tis Aufidius,
45 Who, hearing of our Martius' banishment,
Thrusts forth his horns again into the world,
Which were inshell'd when Martius stood for Rome
And durst not once peep out.
Sicinius
                        Come, what talk you of Martius?
Brutus
[*To the* Aedile] Go see this rumourer whipp'd. It
    cannot be
50 The Volsces dare break with us.
Menenius
                                    Cannot be?
We have record that very well it can,
And three examples of the like hath been
Within my age. But reason with the fellow,
Before you punish him, where he heard this,
55 Lest you shall chance to whip your information
And beat the messenger who bids beware
Of what is to be dreaded.
Sicinius
                                    Tell not me.
I know this cannot be.
Brutus
                        Not possible.

Enter a Messenger

Messenger
The nobles in great earnestness are going
60 All to the Senate-house. Some news is coming
That turns their countenances.
Sicinius
                                    'Tis this slave—
[*To the* Aedile] Go whip him fore the people's
    eyes!—his raising,
Nothing but his report.
Messenger
                        Yes, worthy sir,
The slave's report is seconded, and more
65 More fearful, is deliver'd.

47 *inshell'd*: withdrawn (like a snail) into his
shell.

51 *record*: The stress is on the second
syllable.

53 *reason*: have a talk.

60 *coming*: i.e. coming by instalments.

62 *raising*: rumour-raising.

Sicinius

                    What more fearful?

Messenger

It is spoke freely out of many mouths—

How probable I do not know—that Martius,

Join'd with Aufidius, leads a power 'gainst Rome,

And vows revenge as spacious as between

70   The young'st and oldest thing.

Sicinius

                   This is most likely!

Brutus

Rais'd only that the weaker sort may wish

Good Martius home again.

Sicinius

The very trick on't.

Menenius

This is unlikely.

75   He and Aufidius can no more atone

Than violent'st contrariety.

Enter a Second Messenger

Second Messenger

You are sent for to the Senate.

A fearful army, led by Caius Martius

Associated with Aufidius, rages

80   Upon our territories, and have already

O'erborne their way, consum'd with fire and took

What lay before them.

Enter Cominius

Cominius

[*To the* Tribunes] O, you have made good work!

Menenius

What news, what news?

Cominius

85   You have holp to ravish your own daughters and

To melt the city leads upon your pates,

To see your wives dishonour'd to your noses—

Menenius

What's the news? What's the news?

Cominius

Your temples burn'd in their cement, and

---

69   *as spacious as between*: wide and all-inclusive as the gulf between.

73   *trick*: style, manner.

75   *atone*: come together.

85   *holp*: helped.

86   *leads*: leaded roofs.

89   *in their cement*: to their foundations.

90 *franchises*: freedoms.
    whereon you stood: which you insisted
    on, on which your authority was
    founded.
91 *auger's bore*: drill-hole.

100 *apron-men*: tradesmen.
101 *voice of occupation*: working-class vote.

104 *Hercules . . . fruit*: The eleventh labour
    of Hercules (see *4, 1, 18*note) was to
    pluck the golden apples of the
    Hesperides.

109 *who resists*: whoever resists.

111 *constant*: loyal.

117 *For*: as for.
118 *charg'd*: would charge—i.e. would plead.

90 Your franchises, whereon you stood, confin'd
    Into an auger's bore.
        Menenius
                            Pray now, your news?
    [*To the* Tribunes] You have made fair work, I fear
        me. [*To* Cominius] Pray, your news.
    If Martius should be join'd wi'th' Volscians—
        Cominius
    If? He is their god. He leads them like a thing
95 Made by some other deity than nature,
    That shapes man better, and they follow him
    Against us brats with no less confidence
    Than boys pursuing summer butterflies,
    Or butchers killing flies.
        Menenius
    [*To the* Tribunes]   You have made good work,
100 You and your apron-men, you that stood so much
    Upon the voice of occupation and
    The breath of garlic-eaters!
        Cominius
    He'll shake your Rome about your ears.
        Menenius
    As Hercules did shake down mellow fruit.
105 You have made fair work!
        Brutus
    But is this true, sir?
        Cominius
    Ay, and you'll look pale
    Before you find it other. All the regions
    Do smilingly revolt, and who resists
110 Are mock'd for valiant ignorance,
    And perish constant fools. Who is't can blame him?
    Your enemies and his find something in him.
        Menenius
    We are all undone unless
    The noble man have mercy.
        Cominius
                            Who shall ask it?
115 The tribunes cannot do't for shame; the people
    Deserve such pity of him as the wolf
    Does of the shepherds. For his best friends, if they
    Should say 'Be good to Rome', they charg'd him
        even

20 *show'd*: would behave.

23 *made fair hands*: i.e. you have made a fine mess.

32 *roar*: i.e. roar for mercy.

33 *second . . . men*: i.e. second to Coriolanus in renown.
obeys his points: obeys his every command.

42 *coxcombs*: numbskulls (literally, the caps worn by professional jesters).

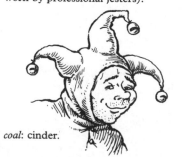

45 *coal*: cinder.

As those should do that had deserv'd his hate,
120 And therein show'd like enemies.
    Menenius
                    'Tis true.
If he were putting to my house the brand
That should consume it, I have not the face
To say 'Beseech you, cease'. [*To the* Tribunes] You
   have made fair hands,
You and your crafts! You have crafted fair!
    Cominius
                   You have brought
125 A trembling upon Rome such as was never
S'incapable of help.
    Sicinius and **Brutus**
Say not we brought it.
    Menenius
How? Was't we?
We lov'd him, but like beasts and cowardly nobles
130 Gave way unto your clusters, who did hoot
Him out o'th' city.
    Cominius
           But I fear
They'll roar him in again. Tullus Aufidius,
The second name of men, obeys his points
As if he were his officer. Desperation
135 Is all the policy, strength, and defence
That Rome can make against them.

        Enter a troop of Citizens

    Menenius
              Here come the clusters.
[*To the* Citizens] And is Aufidius with him? You are
   they
That made the air unwholesome when you cast
Your stinking greasy caps in hooting at
140 Coriolanus' exile. Now he's coming,
And not a hair upon a soldier's head
Which will not prove a whip. As many coxcombs
As you threw caps up will he tumble down,
And pay you for your voices. 'Tis no matter.
145 If he could burn us all into one coal,
We have deserv'd it.

All the Citizens
Faith, we hear fearful news.
     First Citizen
For mine own part,
When I said 'banish him' I said 'twas pity.
     Second Citizen
150 And so did I.
     Third Citizen
And so did I, and to say the truth so did very many
of us. That we did, we did for the best, and though
we willingly consented to his banishment, yet it was
against our will.
     Cominius
155 You're goodly things, you voices.
     Menenius
                          You have made good work,
You and your cry! Shall's to the Capitol?
     Cominius
O, ay, what else?
                       [*Exeunt* Menenius *and* Cominius
     Sicinius
Go, masters, get you home. Be not dismay'd;
These are a side that would be glad to have
160 This true which they so seem to fear. Go home,
And show no sign of fear.
     First Citizen
The gods be good to us! Come, masters, let's home.
I ever said we were i'th' wrong when we banished
him.
     Second Citizen
165 So did we all. But come, let's home.
                             [*Exeunt* Citizens
     Brutus
I do not like this news.
     Sicinius
Nor I.
     Brutus
Let's to the Capitol. Would half my wealth
Would buy this for a lie.
     Sicinius
                  Pray let's go.
                                 [*Exeunt*

156   *cry*: pack of hounds.

159   *side*: faction.

168   *Would*: I wish.

ufidius is jealous.

5 *darken'd*: eclipsed.
  action: campaign.
6 *your own*: your own men (*perhaps also* 'your own action in sharing the command with Coriolanus').

11 *no changeling*: i.e. is nothing different from what it was.

13 *for your particular*: as far as you are concerned.

22 *husbandry for*: management of.

28 *sits down*: lays siege to them.
29–30 *nobility . . . love him*: Shakespeare seems to distinguish between the 'young nobility' who (according to Plutarch) were always loyal to Coriolanus, and the old 'senators and patricians'.

Scene 7

Antium: enter Aufidius *with his* Lieutenant

Aufidius
Do they still fly to th' Roman?
Lieutenant
I do not know what witchcraft's in him, but
Your soldiers use him as the grace fore meat,
Their talk at table, and their thanks at end,
5 And you are darken'd in this action, sir,
Even by your own.
Aufidius
                I cannot help it now,
Unless by using means I lame the foot
Of our design. He bears himself more proudlier,
Even to my person, than I thought he would
10 When first I did embrace him. Yet his nature
In that's no changeling, and I must excuse
What cannot be amended.
Lieutenant
                Yet I wish, sir—
I mean for your particular—you had not
Join'd in commission with him, but either
15 Have borne the action of yourself or else
To him had left it solely.
Aufidius
I understand thee well, and be thou sure,
When he shall come to his account, he knows not
What I can urge against him. Although it seems—
20 And so he thinks, and is no less apparent
To th'vulgar eye—that he bears all things fairly
And shows good husbandry for the Volscian state,
Fights dragon-like, and does achieve as soon
As draw his sword, yet he hath left undone
25 That which shall break his neck or hazard mine
Whene'er we come to our account.
Lieutenant
Sir, I beseech you, think you he'll carry Rome?
Aufidius
All places yields to him ere he sits down,
And the nobility of Rome are his;
30 The senators and patricians love him too.
The tribunes are no soldiers, and their people

34 *osprey*: fish-hawk; it was fancied that
fish recognized the princely nature of
the osprey by turning over on their
backs in surrender.

37 *even*: equably.
38 *out of . . . fortune*: arising from regular
success.
39 *happy*: fortunate, lucky.
41 *whether nature*: whether it is his nature.
42 *Not . . . thing*: i.e. to be always the
same.
43 *casque to th' cushion*: i.e. battlefield to
senate house; 'casque' = helmet.
44 *austerity and garb*: austere demeanour.
45–7 *but one . . . free him*: any one of
these—and he has something of them
all—but I wouldn't accuse him of all;
Aufidius' perplexity is reflected in his
syntax.
46 *spices*: traces.
47 *free*: absolute.
48 *merit*: i.e. his valour.
49 *choke . . . utt'rance*: 'silence [any
criticism] before it is spoken'; 'silence
itself [the merit] in its self-conceit'.
50 *Lie . . . time*: depend on how they are
interpreted at any time (i.e. are not
absolute in themselves).
51 *unto . . . commendable*: most
praiseworthy in itself.
52–3 *Hath not . . . done*: has no more
certain way of destroying itself than by
extolling itself.
52 *evident*: inevitable, certain.
chair: rostrum.

Will he as rash in the repeal as hasty
To expel him thence. I think he'll be to Rome
As is the osprey to the fish, who takes it
35   By sovereignty of nature. First he was
A noble servant to them, but he could not
Carry his honours even. Whether 'twas pride,
Which out of daily fortune ever taints
The happy man; whether defect of judgement,
40   To fail in the disposing of those chances
Which he was lord of; or whether nature,
Not to be other than one thing, not moving
From th' casque to th' cushion, but commanding
     peace
Even with the same austerity and garb
45   As he controll'd the war; but one of these—
As he hath spices of them all—not all,
For I dare so far free him—made him fear'd,
So hated, and so banish'd. But he has a merit
To choke it in the utt'rance. So our virtues
50   Lie in th'interpretation of the time,
And power, unto itself most commendable,
Hath not a tomb so evident as a chair
T'extol what it hath done.
One fire drives out one fire, one nail one nail;
55   Rights by rights falter, strengths by strengths do fail
Come, let's away. When, Caius, Rome is thine,
Thou art poor'st of all; then shortly art thou mine.
                                                        [*Exeunt*

Act 5

Act 5   Scene 1

The Roman dilemma: how to appeal to
Martius. Eventually Menenius is persuaded
to go to the enemy.

1–2 *he . . . general*: i.e. Cominius.
3 *most dear particular*: close personal
affection.

Scene 1

Rome: *enter* Menenius, Cominius,
Sicinius, *and* Brutus, *the two tribunes, with
others*

Menenius
No, I'll not go! You hear what he hath said
Which was sometime his general, who lov'd him
In a most dear particular. He call'd me father,

But what o' that? [*To the* Tribunes] Go, you that
                banish'd him;
5   A mile before his tent fall down, and knee
    The way into his mercy.—Nay, if he coy'd
    To hear Cominius speak, I'll keep at home.
        Cominius
    He would not seem to know me.
        Menenius
    [*To the* Tribunes]   Do you hear?
        Cominius
    Yet one time he did call me by my name.
10 I urg'd our old acquaintance and the drops
    That we have bled together. 'Coriolanus'
    He would not answer to, forbade all names;
    He was a kind of nothing, titleless,
    Till he had forg'd himself a name o'th' fire
15 Of burning Rome.
        Menenius
    [*To the* Tribunes] Why, so: you have made good
                work!
    A pair of tribunes that have wrack'd fair Rome
    To make coals cheap—a noble memory!
        Cominius
    I minded him how royal 'twas to pardon
    When it was less expected. He replied
20 It was a bare petition of a state
    To one whom they had punish'd.
        Menenius
                                          Very well.
    Could he say less?
        Cominius
    I offer'd to awaken his regard
    For's private friends. His answer to me was
25 He could not stay to pick them in a pile
    Of noisome, musty chaff. He said 'twas folly,
    For one poor grain or two, to leave unburnt
    And still to nose th'offence.
        Menenius
                          For one poor grain or two!
    I am one of those; his mother, wife, his child,
30 And this brave fellow too: we are the grains.
    [*To the* Tribunes] You are the musty chaff, and you
                are smelt

5   *knee*: i.e. in the manner of pilgrims
    approaching a shrine.
6   *coy'd*: showed reluctance.

8   *would not seem*: affected not to.

16 *wrack'd*: ruined.
17 *coals*: i.e. charcoal.
    memory: reputation.

19 *When . . . expected*: the less it was
    expected.
20 *bare*: barefaced, beggarly.

23 *offer'd*: ventured, tried.

25–8 *a pile . . . offence*: The 'corn' metaphor
    here recalls the demands of the citizens
    in *Act 1*, Scene 1.

28 *nose th' offence*: smell the offensive
    matter.

Above the moon. We must be burnt for you.

Sicinius
Nay, pray be patient. If you refuse your aid
In this so-never-needed help, yet do not
35 Upbraid's with our distress. But sure, if you
Would be your country's pleader, your good tongue,
More than the instant army we can make,
Might stop our countryman.

Menenius
                                    No, I'll not meddle.

Sicinius
Pray you go to him.

Menenius
                    What should I do?

Brutus
40 Only make trial what your love can do
For Rome towards Martius.

Menenius
Well, and say that Martius return me,
As Cominius is return'd, unheard—what then?
But as a discontented friend, grief-shot
45 With his unkindness? Say't be so?

Sicinius
                                    Yet your good will
Must have that thanks from Rome after the measure
As you intended well.

Menenius
                    I'll undertake't.
I think he'll hear me. Yet to bite his lip
And hum at good Cominius much unhearts me.
50 He was not taken well, he had not din'd.
The veins unfill'd, our blood is cold, and then
We pout upon the morning, are unapt
To give or to forgive; but when we have stuff'd
These pipes and these conveyances of our blood
55 With wine and feeding, we have suppler souls
Than in our priest-like fasts. Therefore I'll watch him
Till he be dieted to my request,
And then I'll set upon him.

Brutus
You know the very road into his kindness,
60 And cannot lose your way.

---

34 *In this . . . help*: at this time when help was never more needed.

37 *instant . . . make*: the sort of army that we raise at such short notice.

44 *But as*: merely as.
discontented: unsatisfied.
grief-shot: grief-stricken.

50 *taken well*: approached at the right time.

54 *These pipes*: i.e. the digestive tract.
conveyances: channels, veins.
55 *suppler*: more amenable.

57 *dieted . . . request*: conditioned, by feeding, to agree to my request.

60 *prove*: try.

62 *my success*: what success I have had.

64 *Red*: i.e. with anger.
    his injury: his sense of injury.

67–9 *What . . . oath*: i.e. Martius sent after
      Cominius the details, bound with an
      oath, of what he would and would not
      concede.
70–1 *vain—Unless*: The broken half line is
      enough to express complete despair—
      from which Cominius plucks fresh hope
      with his next thought.

Menenius
                                    Good faith, I'll prove him
Speed how it will, I shall ere long have knowledge
Of my success.   [*Exi*
      Cominius
                  He'll never hear him.
      Sicinius
                                        Not?
      Cominius
I tell you he does sit in gold, his eye
Red as 'twould burn Rome, and his injury
65 The jailer to his pity. I kneel'd before him;
'Twas very faintly he said 'Rise', dismiss'd me
Thus, with his speechless hand. What he would do,
He sent in writing after me, what he would not:
Bound with an oath to hold to his conditions.
70 So that all hope is vain—
Unless his noble mother and his wife,
Who, as I hear, mean to solicit him
For mercy to his country—therefore let's hence,
And with our fair entreaties haste them on.
                                    [*Exeunt*

Act 5   Scene 2

The confidence of Menenius is rebuffed
when he encounters Martius.

Scene 2

      The Volscian Camp: *enter* Menenius *to the*
      Watch *or* guard

      First Watchman
Stay. Whence are you?
      Second Watchman
Stand, and go back.
      Menenius
You guard like men; 'tis well. But by your leave,
I am an officer of state, and come
5 To speak with Coriolanus.
      First Watchman
                              From whence?
      Menenius
From Rome.

First Watchman

           You may not pass, you must return.
Our general will no more hear from thence.

Second Watchman

You'll see your Rome embrac'd with fire before
You'll speak with Coriolanus.

Menenius

                Good my friends,
10 If you have heard your general talk of Rome
And of his friends there, it is lots to blanks
My name hath touch'd your ears. It is Menenius.

First Watchman

Be it so; go back. The virtue of your name
Is not here passable.

Menenius

              I tell thee, fellow,
15 Thy general is my lover. I have been
The book of his good acts, whence men have read
His fame unparallel'd, haply amplified;
For I have ever varnished my friends,
Of whom he's chief, with all the size that verity
20 Would without lapsing suffer. Nay, sometimes,
Like to a bowl upon a subtle ground,
I have tumbled past the throw, and in his praise
Have almost stamp'd the leasing. Therefore, fellow,
I must have leave to pass.

First Watchman

25 Faith, sir, if you had told as many lies in his behalf as
you have uttered words in your own, you should not
pass here, no, though it were as virtuous to lie as to
live chastely. Therefore go back.

Menenius

Prithee, fellow, remember my name is Menenius,
30 always factionary on the party of your general.

Second Watchman

Howsoever you have been his liar, as you say you
have, I am one that, telling true under him, must say
you cannot pass. Therefore go back.

Menenius

Has he dined, canst thou tell? For I would not speak
35 with him till after dinner.

First Watchman

You are a Roman, are you?

---

11 *lots to blanks*: a certainty (all the winning tickets in the lottery against the blank tickets).

14 *passable*: current, acceptable as a password.

15 *lover*: dear friend.

18 *varnished*: varnishèd.

19 *size*: Menenius puns on two senses of the word, 'height of praise' and 'substance used to stiffen cloth or fix colours on canvas'.

20 *lapsing*: slipping into exaggeration.

21–2 *Like . . . throw*: Menenius takes his imagery from the game of bowls (which provided Shakespeare with some of his favourite metaphors).

21 *subtle*: deceiving—i.e. not level.

22 *tumbled . . . throw*: overshot the mark.

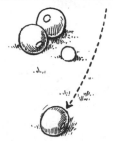

23 *stamp'd the leasing*: given currency to a falsehood (a metaphor from coining—or from legal documents).

30 *factionary on*: active in support of, partisan for.

31 *Howsoever*: notwithstanding.
his liar: one who tells lies about him.

Menenius

I am as thy general is.

First Watchman

Then you should hate Rome as he does. Can you
when you have pushed out your gates the ver
40 defender of them, and in a violent popular ignoranc
given your enemy your shield, think to front h
revenges with the easy groans of old women, th
virginal palms of your daughters, or with the palsie
intercession of such a decayed dotant as you seem t
45 be? Can you think to blow out the intended fire you
city is ready to flame in with such weak breath as this
No, you are deceived; therefore back to Rome, an
prepare for your execution. You are condemned, ou
general has sworn you out of reprieve and pardon.

Menenius

50 Sirrah, if thy captain knew I were here, he would us
me with estimation.

First Watchman

Come, my captain knows you not.

Menenius

I mean thy general.

First Watchman

My general cares not for you. Back, I say, go, lest
55 let forth your half-pint of blood. Back! That's the
utmost of your having. Back!

Menenius

Nay, but fellow, fellow—

Enter Coriolanus *with* Aufidius

Coriolanus

What's the matter?

Menenius

[*To* First Watchman] Now, you companion, I'll say
60 an errand for you. You shall know now that I am ir
estimation. You shall perceive that a jack guardan
cannot office me from my son Coriolanus. Guess bu
by my entertainment with him if thou stand'st no
i'th' state of hanging, or of some death more long ir
65 spectatorship and crueller in suffering. Behold now
presently, and swoon for what's to come upon
thee. [*To* Coriolanus] The glorious gods sit in hourly
synod about thy particular prosperity, and love thee

41 *front*: confront, oppose.

43 *virginal . . . daughters*: the hands of your
virgin daughters (held out, palms up, in
supplication).
44 *dotant*: dotard.

51 *estimation*: respect.

56 *utmost . . . having*: all you'll get, as far
as you can go.

59 *companion*: fellow (a term of abuse).
59–60 *I'll . . . you*: I'll show you how to
make a report.
61 *jack guardant*: jack-in-office, jumped-up
watchman (*guardant* is a term from
heraldry = protecting, guarding).
62 *office me from*: use his authority to keep
me from.
Guess: judge.
63 *entertainment with*: reception by.
64 *state*: risk.
65 *spectatorship*: to behold.
66 *presently*: immediately.
67 *sit*: i.e. may they sit.

71 *water*: i.e. tears.
    hardly moved: with difficulty persuaded.

75 *petitionary*: imploring.

77 *block*: blockage *and* blockhead.

81–2 *I owe . . . properly*: i.e. I am responsible
    for my revenge.
82–3 *my remission . . . breasts*: my power to
    grant remission belongs to the Volscians.
83–5 *That we . . . how much*: i.e. 'ingratitude
    and forgetfulness shall poison our
    friendship before pity can remind me of
    what it used to be'.
87 *for*: because.
    thee: Martius attempts to soften his
    rejection by this intimate form of
    address.

96 *shent*: scolded, rebuked.

no worse than thy old father Menenius does! O, my
70 son, my son, thou art preparing fire for us. Look
thee, here's water to quench it. I was hardly moved
to come to thee, but being assured none but myself
could move thee, I have been blown out of our gates
with sighs, and conjure thee to pardon Rome and thy
75 petitionary countrymen. The good gods assuage thy
wrath and turn the dregs of it upon this varlet here,
this, who like a block hath denied my access to thee!

Coriolanus
Away!

Menenius
How? Away?

Coriolanus
80 Wife, mother, child, I know not. My affairs
Are servanted to others. Though I owe
My revenge properly, my remission lies
In Volscian breasts. That we have been familiar,
Ingrate forgetfulness shall poison rather
85 Than pity note how much. Therefore be gone.
Mine ears against your suits are stronger than
Your gates against my force. Yet, for I lov'd thee,

He gives him a letter

Take this along. I writ it for thy sake,
And would have sent it. Another word, Menenius,
90 I will not hear thee speak.—This man, Aufidius,
Was my belov'd in Rome; yet thou behold'st.

Aufidius
You keep a constant temper.

[*Exeunt* Coriolanus *and* Aufidius

The Guard *and* Menenius *remain*

First Watchman
Now, sir, is your name Menenius?

Second Watchman
'Tis a spell, you see, of much power. You know the
95 way home again.

First Watchman
Do you hear how we are shent for keeping your
greatness back?

Second Watchman
What cause do you think I have to swoon?

Menenius
I neither care for th' world nor your general. For
100 such things as you, I can scarce think there's any
you're so slight. He that hath a will to die by himsel
fears it not from another. Let your general do hi:
worst. For you, be that you are long, and your misery
increase with your age. I say to you as I was said to,
105 'Away!'   [*Exi*

First Watchman
A noble fellow, I warrant him.

Second Watchman
The worthy fellow is our general. He's the rock, the
oak, not to be wind-shaken.   [*Exeun*

101 *die by himself*: by his own hand.

103 *long*: for a long time.

Act 5   Scene 3

The third embassy: Volumnia pleads with her
son—and prevails.

os.d. *chair of state*: Plutarch describes
Coriolanus 'in his chair of state, with all
the honours of a general'.

3 *plainly*: straightforwardly, openly.

Scene 3

The Volscian camp: enter Coriolanus *and*
Aufidius *with Volscian* soldiers. Coriolanus
sits in a chair of state

Coriolanus
We will before the walls of Rome tomorrow
Set down our host. My partner in this action,
You must report to th' Volscian lords how plainly
I have borne this business.

4 *their ends*: i.e. the purposes of the Volscian lords.

11 *godded me*: made a god of me.
latest refuge: last resort.
12 *for . . . love*: because of my former love for him.
13–16 *once more . . . more*: Coriolanus has conceded to Menenius (who had expected more) only a renewal of the terms offered to Cominius and already rejected by the Romans who cannot (as a point of honour) accept them now.

20–37 *Shall I . . . kin*: Coriolanus speaks in semi-soliloquy, heard only by the audience.

22 *mould*: body, earth.

24 *out*: get away.
affection: emotion.
25 *bond . . . nature*: natural ties of duty and affection.
26 *obstinate*: obdurate, inflexible.

30 *Olympus*: The mountain which, in Greek mythology, was the home of the gods.

32 *aspect*: The stress is on the second syllable.

Aufidius

Only their ends
5 You have respected, stopp'd your ears against
The general suit of Rome, never admitted
A private whisper, no, not with such friends
That thought them sure of you.

Coriolanus

This last old man,
Whom with a crack'd heart I have sent to Rome,
10 Lov'd me above the measure of a father,
Nay, godded me indeed. Their latest refuge
Was to send him, for whose old love I have—
Though I show'd sourly to him—once more offer'd
The first conditions, which they did refuse
15 And cannot now accept, to grace him only
That thought he could do more. A very little
I have yielded to. Fresh embassies and suits,
Nor from the state nor private friends, hereafter
Will I lend ear to. [*Shout within*] Ha, what shout is
this?
20 Shall I be tempted to infringe my vow
In the same time 'tis made? I will not.

Enter Virgilia, Volumnia, Valeria, Young
Martius, *with* attendants

My wife comes foremost; then the honour'd mould
Wherein this trunk was fram'd, and in her hand
The grandchild to her blood. But out, affection!
25 All bond and privilege of nature break;
Let it be virtuous to be obstinate.

Virgilia *curtsies*

What is that curtsy worth? Or those doves' eyes
Which can make gods forsworn? I melt, and am not
Of stronger earth than others.

Volumnia *bows*

My mother bows,
30 As if Olympus to a molehill should
In supplication nod; and my young boy
Hath an aspect of intercession which
Great nature cries 'Deny not'. Let the Volsces
Plough Rome and harrow Italy! I'll never

35 *gosling*: Martius (*1*, 5, 5) referred to the
plebeians as having 'souls of geese'.
to: as to.

36 *author of himself*: self-begotten (like a
god).

38 *These . . . Rome*: Coriolanus refers to
the change in his disposition—but
Virgilia takes his words literally.

39 *delivers*: presents.

41 *out*: A theatrical term for an actor
forgetting his lines.

43 *tyranny*: cruelty, violence.

44 *For that*: i.e. because I have asked you
to forgive me.

46 *jealous . . . heaven*: i.e. Juno, the Roman
goddess who protected marriage and
avenged infidelity.

48 *virgin'd it*: The expression (= been
chaste) is a Shakespearean coinage.

51 *more impression show*: make a deeper
impression on the earth.

52 *blest*: Volumnia is sarcastic: she has not
given a mother's blessing but
acknowledges Martius' good fortune.

54 *unproperly*: against propriety, unfittingly.

55 *mistaken*: having been mistaken.

57 *corrected*: Coriolanus accepts his
mother's rebuke.

---

35 Be such a gosling to obey instinct, but stand
As if a man were author of himself
And knew no other kin.
        Virgilia
                                My lord and husband.
        Coriolanus
These eyes are not the same I wore in Rome.
        Virgilia
The sorrow that delivers us thus chang'd
40 Makes you think so.
        Coriolanus
                        Like a dull actor now
I have forgot my part, and I am out
Even to a full disgrace. [*Rising*] Best of my flesh,
Forgive my tyranny, but do not say
For that 'Forgive our Romans'.

            Virgilia *kisses him*

                                    O, a kiss
45 Long as my exile, sweet as my revenge!
Now, by the jealous queen of heaven, that kiss
I carried from thee, dear, and my true lip
Hath virgin'd it e'er since. You gods, I prate,
And the most noble mother of the world
50 Leave unsaluted! Sink, my knee, i'th' earth;

            He kneels

Of thy deep duty more impression show
Than that of common sons.
        Volumnia
                            O, stand up blest,
Whilst with no softer cushion than the flint
I kneel before thee, and unproperly
55 Show duty as mistaken all this while
Between the child and parent.

            She kneels

        Coriolanus
                                What's this?
Your knees to me? To your corrected son?

He rises

58 *hungry*: The adjective is more usually
   applied to the sea.
59 *Fillip*: strike against.

Then let the pebbles on the hungry beach
Fillip the stars; then let the mutinous winds
60 Strike the proud cedars 'gainst the fiery sun,
Murd'ring impossibility to make
What cannot be slight work.

61 *Murd'ring impossibility*: i.e. destroying
   the laws of nature by which some things
   are impossibilities.

He raises her

Volumnia
                              Thou art my warrior,
I holp to frame thee. Do you know this lady?
   Coriolanus
The noble sister of Publicola,

63 *this lady*: In Plutarch's account it was
   Valeria who instigated this female
   embassy, having been inspired 'by some
   god' to take hold of 'a noble device'.
65-7 *The moon . . . Valeria*: This surprising
   lyrical outburst has no counterpart in
   Shakespeare's source.
65 *moon*: The moon was associated with
   the virgin goddess Diana.
66 *candied*: crystallized.
68-70 *a poor . . . yourself*: 'a little abstract of
   you which the fullness of time may
   amplify into your likeness'.

65 The moon of Rome, chaste as the icicle
That's candied by the frost from purest snow
And hangs on Dian's temple—dear Valeria!
   Volumnia
[*Showing* Young Martius] This is a poor epitome of
   yours
Which by th'interpretation of full time
70 May show like all yourself.
   Coriolanus
[*To* Young Martius]   The god of soldiers,
With the consent of supreme Jove, inform
Thy thoughts with nobleness, that thou mayst prove
To shame unvulnerable, and stick i'th' wars
Like a great sea-mark, standing every flaw
75 And saving those that eye thee!
   Volumnia
Your knee, sirrah.

70 *god of soldiers*: i.e. Mars.
71 *inform*: fashion, give form to.

73 *To shame unvulnerable*: incapable of
   dishonour.
   stick: stand out firmly.
74 *sea-mark*: beacon (such as those used by
   sailors for steering a course).
   standing: withstanding.
   flaw: gust of wind.
75 *those . . . thee*: those who look to you.

Young Martius *kneels*

Coriolanus
That's my brave boy.
   Volumnia
Even he, your wife, this lady, and myself
Are suitors to you.
   Coriolanus
                    I beseech you, peace!
80 Or if you'd ask, remember this before:
The things I have forsworn to grant may never
Be held by you denials. Do not bid me

81 *forsworn to*: already sworn not to.
82 *Be held . . . denials*: 'be taken personally
   by you', 'be thought of as denials of
   your requests'.

83 *capitulate*: come to terms with.

84 *mechanics*: common workmen.

> Dismiss my soldiers, or capitulate
> Again with Rome's mechanics. Tell me not
> 85 Wherein I seem unnatural. Desire not
> T'allay my rages and revenges with
> Your colder reasons.

Volumnia

> O, no more, no more!
> You have said you will not grant us anything—
> For we have nothing else to ask but that
> 90 Which you deny already. Yet we will ask,
> That, if you fail in our request, the blame
> May hang upon your hardness. Therefore hear us.

Coriolanus

> Aufidius and you Volsces, mark, for we'll
> Hear naught from Rome in private. [*Sitting*] Your
> request?

94 *Hear . . . private*: At this point Coriolanus probably sits in his chair of state.

95–126 *Should we . . . this world*: Volumnia's great speech is a close rendering of Shakespeare's source (see 'Plutarch', p. 145).

96 *bewray*: reveal, declare.

97 *exile*: The stress is on the second syllable.

Volumnia

> 95 Should we be silent and not speak, our raiment
> And state of bodies would bewray what life
> We have led since thy exile. Think with thyself
> How more unfortunate than all living women
> Are we come hither, since that thy sight, which
> should
> 100 Make our eyes flow with joy, hearts dance with
> comforts,
> Constrains them weep and shake with fear and
> sorrow,
> Making the mother, wife, and child to see
> The son, the husband, and the father tearing
> His country's bowels out; and to poor we

105 *capital*: deadly.

> 105 Thine enmity's most capital. Thou barr'st us
> Our prayers to the gods, which is a comfort
> That all but we enjoy. For how can we,
> Alas, how can we for our country pray,
> Whereto we are bound, together with thy victory,
> 110 Whereto we are bound? Alack, or we must lose
> The country, our dear nurse, or else thy person,
> Our comfort in the country. We must find

113 *evident*: certain, inevitable.

> An evident calamity, though we had
> Our wish which side should win. For either thou
> 115 Must as a foreign recreant be led

115 *foreign recreant*: treacherous deserter to a foreign power.

> With manacles thorough our streets, or else
> Triumphantly tread on thy country's ruin,

118   *bear the palm*: be crowned victor.

120   *purpose*: intend.
121   *determine*: come to an end (and decide things for me).

And bear the palm for having bravely shed
Thy wife and children's blood. For myself, son,
120 I purpose not to wait on fortune till
These wars determine. If I cannot persuade thee
Rather to show a noble grace to both parts
Than seek the end of one, thou shalt no sooner
March to assault thy country than to tread—
125 Trust to't, thou shalt not—on thy mother's womb
That brought thee to this world.

Virgilia
                                        Ay, and mine,
That brought you forth this boy to keep your name
Living to time.

Young Martius
                          A shall not tread on me.
I'll run away till I am bigger, but then I'll fight.

128   *A*: he.

130–1 *Not . . . see*: i.e. 'if I am not to show a woman's tenderness (and weep), I must not look upon their faces'.

Coriolanus
130 Not of a woman's tenderness to be
Requires nor child nor woman's face to see.
I have sat too long.

                    He rises

Volumnia
                          Nay, go not from us thus.
If it were so that our request did tend
To save the Romans, thereby to destroy
135 The Volsces whom you serve, you might condemn us
As poisonous of your honour. No, our suit
Is that you reconcile them: while the Volsces

137   *while*: so that at the same time.

May say 'This mercy we have show'd', the Romans
'This we receiv'd', and each in either side
140 Give the all-hail to thee and cry 'Be blest
For making up this peace!'—Thou know'st, great
          son,
The end of war's uncertain; but this certain,
That if thou conquer Rome, the benefit
Which thou shalt thereby reap is such a name

142   *but this*: only this is.
146   *thus writ*: will thus be written.
149   *Speak to me*: Volumnia will now try to put the words into her son's mouth.
150–4 *Thou hast . . . oak*: 'You have been putting on these high and mighty airs only so that you can behave like the gods, frightening human beings with your thunder yet striking nothing but trees with your lightning'.
150   *affected*: assumed.

145 Whose repetition will be dogg'd with curses,
Whose chronicle thus writ: 'The man was noble,
But with his last attempt he wip'd it out,
Destroy'd his country, and his name remains
To th'ensuing age abhorr'd.'—Speak to me, son!
150 Thou hast affected the fine strains of honour,

152 *cheeks o'th' air*: Winds are depicted in early maps as being blown from the cheeks of the god Aeolus.

153 *charge*: load.
     sulphur: i.e. lightning.
     bolt: thunderbolt.

154 *rive*: split.

156 *Still*: always.

160 *bound to*: indebted to *and* emotionally dependent on.

161 *Like . . . stocks*: i.e. despised and disregarded.

163 *fond of*: wishing for, desirous of.

166 *so*: i.e. 'unjust'.

167 *honest*: truthful.

168 *thou restrain'st*: you withhold.

171 *surname 'Coriolanus'*: The addition was intended to signify 'conqueror of Corioles', but now Volumnia understands it as 'man of Corioles'.
     'longs: belongs.

172 *an end*: let's make an end.

176 *for fellowship*: as one of us.

177 *reason*: argue.

181 *dispatch*: dismissal.

185–6 *The gods . . . at*: The idea of the gods looking down from heaven and mocking human endeavour is a commonplace of classical and Renaissance literature.

To imitate the graces of the gods,
To tear with thunder the wide cheeks o'th' air,
And yet to charge thy sulphur with a bolt
That should but rive an oak.—Why dost not speak?
155 Think'st thou it honourable for a noble man
Still to remember wrongs? Daughter, speak you,
He cares not for your weeping. Speak thou, boy,
Perhaps thy childishness will move him more
Than can our reasons. There's no man in the world
160 More bound to's mother, yet here he lets me prate
Like one i'th' stocks. Thou hast never in thy life
Show'd thy dear mother any courtesy,
When she, poor hen, fond of no second brood,
Has cluck'd thee to the wars and safely home,
165 Loaden with honour. Say my request's unjust,
And spurn me back. But if it be not so,
Thou art not honest, and the gods will plague thee
That thou restrain'st from me the duty which
To a mother's part belongs.—He turns away!
170 Down, ladies; let us shame him with our knees.
To his surname 'Coriolanus' 'longs more pride
Than pity to our prayers. Down: an end!
This is the last. [*The* ladies *and* Young Martius
     kneel] So, we will home to Rome
And die among our neighbours.—Nay, behold's.
175 This boy, that cannot tell what he would have,
But kneels and holds up hands for fellowship,
Does reason our petition with more strength
Than thou hast to deny't.—Come, let us go.

          They rise

This fellow had a Volscian to his mother;
180 His wife is in Corioles, and his child
Like him by chance.—Yet give us our dispatch.
I am hush'd until our city be afire,
And then I'll speak a little.

          He holds her by the hand, silent

Coriolanus
[*Weeping*]   O mother, mother!
What have you done? Behold, the heavens do ope,
185 The gods look down, and this unnatural scene
They laugh at. O my mother, mother, O!

You have won a happy victory to Rome;
But for your son, believe it, O believe it,
Most dangerously you have with him prevail'd,
190 If not most mortal to him. But let it come.—
Aufidius, though I cannot make true wars,
I'll frame convenient peace. Now, good Aufidius,
Were you in my stead would you have heard
A mother less, or granted less, Aufidius?

Aufidius

195 I was mov'd withal.

    Coriolanus

                  I dare be sworn you were.
And, sir, it is no little thing to make
Mine eyes to sweat compassion. But, good sir,
What peace you'll make, advise me. For my part,
I'll not to Rome; I'll back with you, and pray you
200 Stand to me in this cause.—O mother! Wife!

He speaks to them apart

Aufidius

[*Aside*] I am glad thou hast set thy mercy and thy
    honour
At difference in thee. Out of that I'll work
Myself a former fortune.

    Coriolanus

[*To* Volumnia *and* Virgilia] Aye, by and by.
But we will drink together, and you shall bear
205 A better witness back than words, which we
On like conditions will have counter-seal'd.
Come, enter with us. Ladies, you deserve
To have a temple built you. All the swords
In Italy, and her confederate arms,
210 Could not have made this peace.

                              [*Exeunt*

---

90 *mortal*: fatally.
But . . . come: Coriolanus accepts his
fate.
91 *true wars*: wars in accordance with the
original undertaking.
92 *convenient*: i.e. one which brings benefit
to both parties.

95 *withal*: by it.

97 *sweat compassion*: 'nature so wrought
with him that the tears fell from his
eyes' (Plutarch).

200 *Stand to*: stand by.

202–3 *I'll work . . . fortune*: I'll contrive to
win back my former fortunes.

205 *better witness*: i.e. a written document of
formal treaty.
206 *On . . . counter-seal'd*: Coriolanus
promises to have this renewal of the
treaty ratified by the Roman Senate
(see 5, 6, 81–4).
207–8 *Ladies . . . you*: Plutarch tells how a
'Temple of Fortune of the Women' was
erected in Rome by a grateful Senate.

Act 5   Scene 4

Menenius is worried and Sicinius is
frightened—but there is good news.

1 *quoin*: cornerstone.

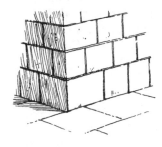

7 *stay upon*: wait for.
9 *condition*: character, disposition.

10 *differency*: difference.

16 *than . . . horse*: i.e. remembers his dam.

18 *engine*: i.e. engine of war.
19 *corslet*: steel body-armour.
20 *his hum . . . battery*: i.e. 'his slightest
   expression of anger or contempt has the
   force of a military assault'.
21 *state*: chair of state, throne.
   as a thing . . . Alexander: like a statue of
   Alexander the Great.
23 *wants*: lacks.

26 *in the character*: as he is, to the life.

29 *'long of you*: on your account, your fault.

Scene 4

Rome: *enter* Menenius *and* Sicinius

Menenius
See you yon quoin o'th' Capitol, yon cornerstone?
Sicinius
Why, what of that?
Menenius
If it be possible for you to displace it with your little
finger, there is some hope the ladies of Rome
5 especially his mother, may prevail with him. But
say there is no hope in't, our throats are sentenced
and stay upon execution.
Sicinius
Is't possible that so short a time can alter the
condition of a man?
Menenius
10 There is difference between a grub and a butterfly
yet your butterfly was a grub. This Martius is grown
from man to dragon. He has wings, he's more than a
creeping thing.
Sicinius
He loved his mother dearly.
Menenius
15 So did he me, and he no more remembers his
mother now than an eight-year-old horse. The
tartness of his face sours ripe grapes. When he walks
he moves like an engine, and the ground shrinks
before his treading. He is able to pierce a corslet with
20 his eye, talks like a knell, and his hum is a battery. He
sits in his state as a thing made for Alexander. What
he bids be done is finished with his bidding. He
wants nothing of a god but eternity and a heaven to
throne in.
Sicinius
25 Yes: mercy, if you report him truly.
Menenius
I paint him in the character. Mark what mercy his
mother shall bring from him. There is no more
mercy in him than there is milk in a male tiger. That
shall our poor city find; and all this is 'long of you.
Sicinius
30 The gods be good unto us!

36 *hale*: haul, drag.
38 *death by inches*: long drawn-out death by torture.
40 *are dislodg'd*: have left their military positions.
42 *expulsion of the Tarquins*: The last of the Tarquins was driven out of Rome in about 510 BC (see *1, 3, 14*note).
46 *blown*: swollen, wind-blown.

47s.d. *hautboys*: oboes.

48 *sackbuts*: brass instruments rather like trombones.

psalteries: stringed instruments.

49 *Tabors*: small drums, often accompanied by pipes played by the same performer.

Menenius
No, in such a case the gods will not be good unto us.
When we banished him we respected not them, and,
he returning to break our necks, they respect not us.

Enter a Messenger

Messenger
[*To* Sicinius] Sir, if you'd save your life, fly to your
house.
35 The plebeians have got your fellow tribune
And hale him up and down, all swearing if
The Roman ladies bring not comfort home
They'll give him death by inches.

Enter another Messenger

Sicinius
                                    What's the news?
Second Messenger
Good news, good news. The ladies have prevail'd,
40 The Volscians are dislodg'd, and Martius gone.
A merrier day did never yet greet Rome,
No, not th'expulsion of the Tarquins.
Sicinius
                                         Friend,
Art thou certain this is true? Is't most certain?
Second Messenger
As certain as I know the sun is fire.
45 Where have you lurk'd that you make doubt of it?
Ne'er through an arch so hurried the blown tide
As the recomforted through th' gates.

Trumpets, hautboys, drums beat, all together

                                        Why, hark you,
The trumpets, sackbuts, psalteries, and fifes,
Tabors and cymbals, and the shouting Romans
50 Make the sun dance.

A shout within

                        Hark you!
Menenius
                                This is good news.
I will go meet the ladies. This Volumnia
Is worth of consuls, senators, patricians,

A city full; of tribunes such as you,
A sea and land full. You have pray'd well today.
55 This morning for ten thousand of your throats
I'd not have given a doit.

56 *doit*: worthless coin.

Sound still with the shouts

                        Hark how they joy!
Sicinius
[*To* Second Messenger] First, the gods bless you for
    your tidings; next,
Accept my thankfulness.
Second Messenger
                        Sir, we have all
Great cause to give great thanks.
Sicinius
                                They are near the city
Second Messenger
60 Almost at point to enter.
Sicinius
                        We'll meet them,
And help the joy.
                                        [*Exeunt*

Act 5   Scene 5

The ladies return to Rome.

os.d. *passing . . . stage*: This direction
usually indicates a movement from the
yard up to and across the stage
platform, and down into the yard again.

3 *triumphant fires*: These were a common
feature of Elizabethan (not Roman)
celebrations.

5 *Repeal*: recall.

6s.d. *flourish*: fanfare.

Scene 5

> *Rome: a triumphant procession. Enter two*
> Senators *with the ladies,* Volumnia,
> Virgilia, *and* Valeria, *passing over the stage,*
> *with other* Lords

A Senator

Behold our patroness, the life of Rome!
Call all your tribes together, praise the gods,
And make triumphant fires. Strew flowers before
   them.
Unshout the noise that banish'd Martius,
5 Repeal him with the welcome of his mother.
Cry 'Welcome, ladies, welcome!'

All

                Welcome, ladies, welcome!

> *A flourish with drums and trumpets.*

                       [*Exeunt*

Act 5   Scene 6

The revenge is planned. Coriolanus returns in triumph, but the victor becomes the victim when he is denounced as a traitor.

5 *Him*: he whom.
6 *ports*: gates.

10 *by . . . empoison'd*: destroyed by his own generosity.

13 *parties*: supporters.
14 *Of*: from.

17 *difference*: rivalry.

19 *pretext*: The stress is on the second syllable.
   admits: is capable of.
20 *construction*: interpretation.
21 *so heighten'd*: raised thus to a position of power.
22 *plants*: i.e. those on whom he had conferred honours.

Scene 6

Antium: enter Tullus Aufidius *with* Attendants

Aufidius
Go tell the lords o'th' city I am here.
Deliver them this paper. Having read it,
Bid them repair to th' market-place, where I,
Even in theirs and in the commons' ears,
5 Will vouch the truth of it. Him I accuse
The city ports by this hath enter'd, and
Intends t'appear before the people, hoping
To purge himself with words. Dispatch.
                    [*Exeunt* Attendants

Enter three or four Conspirators *of* Aufidius' *faction*

                              Most welcome.
First Conspirator
How is it with our general?
Aufidius
                              Even so
10 As with a man by his own alms impoison'd,
And with his charity slain.
Second Conspirator
                              Most noble sir,
If you do hold the same intent wherein
You wish'd us parties, we'll deliver you
Of your great danger.
Aufidius
                         Sir, I cannot tell.
15 We must proceed as we do find the people.
Third Conspirator
The people will remain uncertain whilst
'Twixt you there's difference, but the fall of either
Makes the survivor heir of all.
Aufidius
                              I know it,
And my pretext to strike at him admits
20 A good construction. I rais'd him, and I pawn'd
Mine honour for his truth; who being so heighten'd,
He water'd his new plants with dews of flattery,
Seducing so my friends; and to this end

He bow'd his nature, never known before
25 But to be rough, unswayable, and free.
          Third Conspirator
Sir, his stoutness
When he did stand for consul, which he lost
By lack of stooping—
          Aufidius
                    That I would have spoke of.
Being banish'd for't, he came unto my hearth,
30 Presented to my knife his throat. I took him,
Made him joint-servant with me, gave him way
In all his own desires; nay, let him choose
Out of my files, his projects to accomplish,
My best and freshest men; serv'd his designments
35 In mine own person, holp to reap the fame
Which he did end all his, and took some pride
To do myself this wrong, till at the last
I seem'd his follower, not partner, and
He wag'd me with his countenance as if
40 I had been mercenary.
          First Conspirator
                    So he did, my lord;
The army marvell'd at it; and in the last,
When he had carried Rome and that we look'd
For no less spoil than glory—
          Aufidius
                    There was it,
For which my sinews shall be stretch'd upon him.
45 At a few drops of women's rheum, which are
As cheap as lies, he sold the blood and labour
Of our great action; therefore shall he die,
And I'll renew me in his fall.

          Drums and trumpets sound, with great
          shouts of the people

                    But hark.
          First Conspirator
Your native town you enter'd like a post,
50 And had no welcomes home; but he returns
Splitting the air with noise.

25 *free*: uncontrollable.

26 *stoutness*: obstinacy.

28 *That . . . of*: I was coming to that.

31 *joint-servant*: equal partner in serving the state.

33 *files*: ranks.

34 *designments*: designs, purposes.

35-6 *holp . . . all his*: helped him to gather in the success which he finally claimed as his own.

39-40 *wag'd . . . mercenary*: i.e. 'patronized me with his approval as if I had been no more than a hired fighter'.

41 *in the last*: at the last.

42 *had carried*: had conquered.

43 *There was it*: that was the thing.

45 *rheum*: water drops, tears.

49 *your native town*: i.e. Antium.
post: messenger.

Second Conspirator

                                          And patient fools,
Whose children he hath slain, their base throats tear
With giving him glory.

Third Conspirator

                              Therefore, at your vantage,
Ere he express himself or move the people
With what he would say, let him feel your sword,
Which we will second. When he lies along,
After your way his tale pronounc'd shall bury
His reasons with his body.

Aufidius

                              Say no more:
Here come the lords.

Enter the Lords *of the city*

All the Lords

You are most welcome home.

Aufidius

I have not deserv'd it.
But, worthy lords, have you with heed perus'd
What I have written to you?

All the Lords

                              We have.

First Lord

                              And grieve to hear't
What faults he made before the last, I think
Might have found easy fines. But there to end
Where he was to begin, and give away
The benefit of our levies, answering us
With our own charge, making a treaty where
There was a yielding—this admits no excuse.

Aufidius

He approaches. You shall hear him.

Enter Coriolanus *marching with drum and*
colours, the Commoners *being with him*

Coriolanus

Hail, lords! I am return'd your soldier,
No more infected with my country's love
Than when I parted hence, but still subsisting
Under your great command. You are to know
That prosperously I have attempted, and

---

53 *at your vantage*: seizing your opportunity.

56 *along*: prostrate.
57 *After . . . pronounc'd*: his own story told in your way.
58 *His reasons*: his explanations.

65 *easy fines*: light penalties.

67 *benefit . . . levies*: profit from having already recruited soldiers.
67–8 *answering . . . charge*: making his account to us only with a return of expenses.
70s.d. *colours*: banners.

72 *infected with*: under the influence of.
73 *hence*: i.e. from Antium.
    subsisting: remaining.
75 *prosperously . . . attempted*: my endeavours have been successful.

With bloody passage led your wars even to
The gates of Rome. Our spoils we have brought
   home

78 *more than . . . part*: outweigh by more than a third.

Doth more than counterpoise a full third part
The charges of the action. We have made peace

80 *Antiates*: people of Antium.

80 With no less honour to the Antiates
Than shame to th' Romans. And we here deliver,
Subscrib'd by th' consuls and patricians,
Together with the seal o'th' Senate, what

84 *compounded*: agreed.

We have compounded on.

He offers the Lords *a scroll*

Aufidius
                                        Read it not, noble lords,

85 *in . . . degree*: of the most extreme kind; Martius has now betrayed the Volscians as well as the Romans.

85 But tell the traitor in the highest degree
He hath abus'd your powers.
   Coriolanus
Traitor? How now?
   Aufidius
Ay, traitor, Martius.
   Coriolanus
Martius?
   Aufidius

90 Ay, Martius, Caius Martius. Dost thou think
I'll grace thee with that robbery, thy stol'n name
'Coriolanus', in Corioles?

92 *'Coriolanus' . . . Corioles*: The pronunciation 'Cor-eye-olanus' (necessary to scan the line correctly) would emphasize Aufidius' contempt; the usual pronunciation, with short 'i', would enforce his point about the impropriety of the addition.

You lords and heads o'th' state, perfidiously
He has betray'd your business, and given up,

95 For certain drops of salt, your city, Rome—
I say your city—to his wife and mother,
Breaking his oath and resolution like
A twist of rotten silk, never admitting

98–9 *never . . . war*: never consulting other officers.
99 *nurse's*: i.e. Volumnia's.

Counsel o'th' war. But at his nurse's tears

101 *men of heart*: brave men.

100 He whin'd and roar'd away your victory,
That pages blush'd at him, and men of heart
Look'd wond'ring each at others.
   Coriolanus
                                        Hear'st thou, Mars?
   Aufidius
Name not the god, thou boy of tears.
   Coriolanus
                                        Ha?

Aufidius

No more.

Coriolanus

Measureless liar, thou hast made my heart

105 105 Too great for what contains it. 'Boy'? O slave!—
Pardon me, lords, 'tis the first time that ever
I was forc'd to scold. Your judgements, my grave
          lords,
108 Must give this cur the lie, and his own notion—
Who wears my stripes impress'd upon him, that
110 110 Must bear my beating to his grave—shall join
To thrust the lie unto him.

First Lord

Peace both, and hear me speak

Coriolanus

Cut me to pieces, Volsces. Men and lads,
113 Stain all your edges on me. 'Boy'! False hound,
114 If you have writ your annals true, 'tis there
115 115 That, like an eagle in a dovecote, I
Flutter'd your Volscians in Corioles.
Alone I did it, boy!

Aufidius

Why, noble lords,
Will you be put in mind of his blind fortune,
Which was your shame, by this unholy braggart,
120 120 Fore your own eyes and ears?

All the Conspirators

Let him die for't!

All the People

Tear him to pieces!—Do it presently!—He killed my
son!—My daughter!—He killed my cousin Marcus!—
He killed my father!

Second Lord

Peace, ho! No outrage: peace!
125 125 The man is noble, and his fame folds in
This orb o'th' earth. His last offences to us
Shall have judicious hearing. Stand, Aufidius,
And trouble not the peace.

Coriolanus

[*Drawing his sword*]   O that I had him,
With six Aufidiuses, or more, his tribe,
130 130 To use my lawful sword.

Glosses (left margin):

105 *what contains it*: i.e. his chest.

108 *notion*: understanding.

113 *Stain*: discolour, dishonour.
   edges: swords.
114 *'tis there*: it is recorded there.

118 *blind fortune*: sheer good luck.
121 *presently*: immediately.

125–6 *folds . . . earth*: envelopes the whole world.
127 *judicious hearing*: a proper trial by law.
   Stand: hold off.

129 *his tribe*: his kindred.
130 *lawful*: i.e. as on the battlefield.

Aufidius

        Insolent villain!

All the Conspirators

Kill, kill, kill, kill, kill him!

> *Two* Conspirators *draw and kill* Martius,
> *who falls.* Aufidius *stands on him*

Lords

        Hold, hold, hold, hold!

Aufidius

My noble masters, hear me speak.

First Lord

          O Tullus!

Second Lord

Thou hast done a deed whereat valour will weep.

Third Lord

Tread not upon him. Masters all, be quiet!

135 Put up your swords.

Aufidius

My lords, when you shall know—as in this rage
Provok'd by him you cannot—the great danger
Which this man's life did owe you, you'll rejoice
That he is thus cut off. Please it your honours.

140 To call me to your Senate, I'll deliver
Myself your loyal servant, or endure
Your heaviest censure.

First Lord

       Bear from hence his body,
And mourn you for him. Let him be regarded
As the most noble corpse that ever herald

145 Did follow to his urn.

Second Lord

        His own impatience
Takes from Aufidius a great part of blame.
Let's make the best of it.

Aufidius

      My rage is gone,
And I am struck with sorrow. Take him up.
Help three o'the' chiefest soldiers; I'll be one.

150 Beat thou the drum, that it speak mournfully.
Trail your steel pikes. Though in this city he

---

131 *Kill . . . kill*: The battle cry for complete massacre.

138 *owe you*: hold in store for you.

140 *deliver*: show, prove.

144–5 *herald . . . urn*: 'men came out of all parts to honour his body, and did honourably bury him, setting out his tomb with great store of armour and spoils as the tomb of a worthy person and great captain' (Plutarch); in grand English funerals a herald would follow the procession, reciting the titles and achievements of the deceased.

145 *urn*: sepulchre.
 impatience: rage, anger.

149 *I'll be one*: Aufidius honours Martius by making the fourth bearer.

151 *Trail . . . pikes*: It was a usual English practice at military funerals for pikes to be trailed, head down, behind the bearers.

Hath widow'd and unchilded many a one,
Which to this hour bewail the injury,
Yet he shall have a noble memory. Assist.
                    [*Exeunt bearing the body of* Martius

A dead march is sounded

Plutarch

'The Life of Martius Coriolanus'
Parallel Lives of the Greeks and Romans translated by
Sir Thomas North (1575, 3rd edition 1603)

Act 1, Scene 1: sedition in the city

. . . it fortuned there grew sedition in the city because the Senate
did favour the rich against the people, who did complain of the sore
oppression of usurers, of whom they borrowed money. For those
that had little were yet spoiled of that little they had by their
creditors (for lack of ability to pay the usury) . . . [Eventually the
people] fell then even to flat rebellion and mutiny, and to stir up
dangerous tumults within the city . . . The Senate met many days
in consultation about it; but in the end they concluded nothing.
The poor common people, seeing no redress, gathered themselves
one day together and [left the city] . . . The Senate, being afeared
of their departure, did send unto them certain of the pleasantest
old men and the most acceptable to the people . . . Of these
Menenius Agrippa was he who was sent for chief man of the
message from the Senate. He, after many good persuasions and
gentle requests made to the people on behalf of the Senate, knit up
his oration in the end with a notable tale [i.e. the fable of the belly].
These persuasions pacified the people, conditionally that the
Senate would grant there should be yearly chosen five magistrates
which they now call *Tribuni plebii* [tribunes of the people], whose
office should be to defend the poor people from violence and
oppression. So Junius Brutus and Sicinius Velutus were the first
Tribunes of the People that were chosen, who had only been the
causers and procurers of this sedition . . .

[Some years later, after the battle of Corioles] the flatterers of
the people began to stir up sedition again [and] did ground this
second insurrection against the nobility and patricians upon the
people's misery and misfortune that could not but fall out . . .
because the most part of the arable land within the territory of
Rome was become heathy and barren for lack of ploughing, for that
they had no time nor mean to cause corn to be brought them out
of other countries to sow, by reason of their wars which made the

extreme dearth they had among them. Now those busy prattler
that sought the people's good will by such flattering words
perceiving great scarcity of corn to be within the city, and, thoug
there had been plenty enough, yet the common people had n
money to buy in, they spread abroad false tales and rumour
against the nobility: that they, in revenge of the people, ha
practised and procured the extreme dearth among them.

Act 1, Scene 1: he did it to please his mother

. . . And as for other [men], the only respect that made them valian
was they hoped to have honour. But touching Martius, the onl
thing that made him to love honour was the joy he saw his mothe
did take of him. For he thought nothing made him so happy an
honourable as that his mother might hear everybody praise an
commend him; that she might always see him return with a crow
upon his head . . . But Martius thinking all due to his mother tha
had also been due to his father if he had lived, did not only conten
himself to rejoice and honour her, but at her desire took a wife als
. . . and yet never left his mother's house therefore.

Act 2, Scene 2: brow-bound with oak

Caius Martius . . . being left an orphan by his father, was brough
up under his mother, a widow . . . Martius, being more inclined t
the wars than any other gentleman of his time, began from hi
childhood to give himself to handle weapons and daily did exercis
himself therein; and outward he esteemed armour to no purpos
unless one were naturally armed within . . . The first time he wen
to the wars, being but a stripling . . ., Martius valiantly fought i
the sight of the Dictator and, a Roman soldier being thrown to th
ground even hard by him, Martius straight bestrid him and sle
the enemy with his own hands . . . After the battle was won, th
Dictator did not forget so noble an act and therefore he crowne
Martius with a garland of oaken boughs . . .

Act 2, Scene 2: the election

For the custom of Rome was, at that time, that such as did sue fo
any office should for certain days before be in the market-place
only with a poor gown on their backs and without any coa

underneath, to pray the citizens to remember them at the day of election; which was thus devised either to move the people the more by requesting them in such mean apparel, or else because they might show them their wounds they had gotten in the wars in the service of the commonwealth, as manifest marks and testimony of their valiantness.

Act 5, Scene 3: Volumnia pleads with her son

'If we held our peace, my son, and determined not to speak, the state of our poor bodies and present sight of our raiment would easily bewray to thee what life we have led at home, since thy exile and abode abroad. But think now with thyself how much more unfortunately than all the women living we are come hither, considering that the sight which should be most pleasant to all other to behold, spiteful fortune hath made most fearful to us; making myself to see my son, and my daughter here her husband, besieging the walls of his native country; so as that which is the only comfort to all other in their adversity and misery, to pray unto the gods and to call to them for aid, is the only thing which plungeth us into most deep perplexity. For we cannot, alas, together pray both for victory for our country and for safety of thy life also. But a world of grievous curses, yea, more than any mortal enemy can heap upon us, are forcibly wrapped up in our prayers. For the bitter sop of most hard choice is offered thy wife and children, to forgo the one of the two: either to lose the person of thyself or the nurse of their native country. For myself, my son, I am determined not to tarry till fortune in my lifetime do make an end of this war. For if I cannot persuade thee, rather to do good unto both parties than to overthrow and destroy the one, preferring love and nature before the malice and calamity of wars—thou shalt see, my son, and trust unto it, thou shalt no sooner march forward to assault thy country but thy foot shall tread upon thy mother's womb, that brought thee first into this world.'

What the Critics have said

William Hazlitt

'The cause of the people is indeed but little calculated as a subject for poetry . . . The language of poetry naturally falls in with the language of power . . . There is nothing heroical in a multitude of miserable rogues not wishing to be starved, or complaining that they are like to be so: but when a single man comes forward to brave their cries and to make them submit to the last indignities, from mere pride and self-will, our admiration of his prowess is immediately converted into contempt for their pusillanimity. The insolence of power is stronger than the plea of necessity.'

from *Characters of Shakespeare's Plays* (1817)

A. C. Swinburne

'I cannot but think that enough at least of time has been spent if not wasted by able and even by eminent men on examination of *Coriolanus* with regard to its political aspect or bearing upon social questions. It is from first to last, for all its turmoil of battle and clamour of contentious factions, rather a private and domestic than a public or historical tragedy . . . The subject of the whole play is not the exile's revolt, the rebel's repentance, or the traitor's reward, but above all it is the son's tragedy.'

from *A Study of Shakespeare* (1880)

A. C. Bradley

'He is very eloquent, but his only free eloquence is that of vituperation and scorn. It is sometimes more than eloquence, it is splendid poetry; but it is never such magical poetry as we hear in the four greatest tragedies. Then, too, it lies in his nature that his deepest and most sacred feeling, that for his mother, is almost dumb. It governs his life and leads him uncomplaining towards death, but it cannot speak. And, finally, his inward conflicts are veiled from us. The change that came when he found himself alone and homeless in exile is not exhibited . . . In the most famous scene, when his fate is being decided, only one short sentence reveals the gradual loosening of purpose during his mother's speech. The actor's face and hands must show it, not the hero's voice; and his submission is announced in a few quiet words, deeply moving and impressive, but destitute of the effect we know elsewhere of a lightning-flash that rends the darkness and discloses every cranny of the speaker's soul. All this we can see to be perfectly right, but it does set limits to the flight of Shakespeare's imagination.'

from '*Coriolanus*', Second Annual Shakespeare Lecture, *Proceedings of the British Academy* (1912)

O. J. Campbell

'Instead of enlisting our sympathy for Coriolanus, he deliberately alienates it. Indeed he makes the figure partly an object of scorn. Instead of ennobling Coriolanus through his fall, he mocks and ridicules him to the end [and] fills the tragedy so full of the spirit of derision that the play can be understood only if it be recognized as perhaps the most successful of Shakespeare's satiric plays . . . As a political *exemplum* the play presents a case of violent political disorder and reveals its causes. The trouble lies in the fact that no civil group performs its prescribed duties properly. As a result the divinely revealed pattern for the state is disrupted and society reels towards primal chaos. This lesson could not be clearly taught in the terms of tragedy. With its interest concentrated upon the tragic career of Coriolanus the man, an audience might easily ignore the political significance of the play. But the satiric form gave Shakespeare an opportunity to treat derisively both the crowd and Coriolanus, between whose 'endless jars' the commonwealth was sorely wounded.'

from 'Coriolanus', in *Shakespeare's Satire* (1943)

A. P. Rossiter

So our virtues
Lie in th' interpretation of the time.

'Now that, in one and a half lines, gives the essence of the play. Run over the whole action, act by act, and each is seen as an "estimation" or valuation of Martius: enemy of the people—demigod of war—popular hero home in triumph—consul-elect—and then (through his assertion of what he always *had* asserted) public enemy and banished man, "a lonely dragon" (*IV*. i. 30). Throughout all this, he himself is almost an absolute *constant*.'

from 'Coriolanus' in *Angel with Horns* (1961)

G. K. Hunter

'Coriolanus, like Timon and Macbeth, searches for an *absolu*
mode of behaviour, and like them he finds it; but the finding it
the destruction of humanity in him, as it was in them. And as fa
as it concerns personality, the process is as irreversible fo
Coriolanus as for Timon or Macbeth; he can, however, avoid tha
final stage, where the absoluteness of the individual is only to b
guaranteed by the destruction of his society. He is unable to sustai
the absoluteness of "Wife, mother, child, I know not"; but I do no
think we should see the collapse before Volumnia as a grea
triumph of human love. The play's judgement on that beast
machine nature of "absolute" man stands unchanged. Only deat
can chillingly enough satisfy the hunger for absoluteness; and th
final scene in Corioli, with its ironic repetition of the political an
personal pattern already set in Rome, makes it clear that nothing i
Coriolanus has altered or can alter. Greatness is seen as a doubtfu
and destructive blessing; love is powerless to change it.'

from 'The Last Tragic Heroes', in *The Later Shakespear*
eds. J. R. Brown and Bernard Harris (196(

Classwork and Examinations

The plays of Shakespeare are studied all over the world, and this classroom edition is being used in many different countries. Teaching methods vary from school to school and there are many different ways of examining a student's work. Some teachers and examiners expect detailed knowledge of Shakespeare's text; others ask for imaginative involvement with his characters and their situations; and there are some teachers who want their students, by means of 'workshop' activities, to share in the theatrical experience of directing and performing a play. Most people use a variety of methods. This section of the book offers a few suggestions for approaches to *Coriolanus* which could be used in schools and colleges to help with students' understanding and *enjoyment* of the play.

    A Discussion
    B Character Study
    C Activities
    D Context Questions
    E Comprehension and Appreciation Questions
    F Essays
    G Projects

A   Discussion

Talking about the play—about the issues it raises and the characters who are involved—is one of the most rewarding and pleasurable ways of studying Shakespeare. It makes sense to discuss each scene as it is read, sharing impressions—and perhaps correcting misapprehensions. It can be useful to compare aspects of this play with other fictions—plays, novels, films—or with modern life. A large class can divide into small groups, each with a leader, who can discuss different aspects of a single topic and then report back to the main assembly.

Suggestions

A1 What is the ideal government? Do you favour monarchy, democracy, a republic, or . . . ?

A2 Are you convinced by the argument of Menenius' fable of th
belly (*1*, 1, 88–147)? Can you suggest a better working model for th
government of a nation or state?

A3 'the drama begins in a way that makes us ask at once whethe
its author puts himself on the commoners' or the patricians' side
(Willard Farnham, 1950). What would be *your* answer?

A4 William Hazlitt said that we tend to identify ourselves with
Coriolanus 'because our vanity or some other feeling makes u
disposed to place ourselves in the situation of the strongest party'
Do you agree?

A5 Coriolanus would like his army to consist only of those wh
'think brave death outweighs bad life, And that his country's deare
than himself' (*1*, 7, 72–3). Would you enlist? Would you fight fo
your country?

A6 Policy and strategy:

> If it be honour in your wars to seem
> The same you are not, which for your best ends
> You adopt your policy, how is it less or worse
> That it shall hold companionship in peace
> With honour, as in war, since that to both
> It stands in like request?   (*3*, 2, 48–53)

How would you answer Volumnia? Does the end justify the means

A7 With so few virtues and so many faults, can Coriolanus really
be considered a tragic hero?

A8 Could you stage this play in modern dress (or anything other
than Elizabethan/Roman)? What might be gained—or lost?

B   Character Study

Shakespeare is famous for his creation of characters who seem like
real people. We can judge their actions and we can try to
comprehend their thoughts and feelings—just as we criticize and
try to understand the people we know. As the play progresses, we
learn to like or dislike, love or hate, them—just as though they lived
in *our* world.

Characters can be studied *from the outside*, by observing what
they do and listening sensitively to what they say. This is the
scholar's method: the scholar—or any reader—has access to the

entire play, and can see the function of every character within the whole scheme of that play.

Another approach works *from the inside*, taking a single character and looking at the action and the other characters from his/her point of view. This is the way an actor prepares for performance, creating a personality who can have only a partial notion of what is going on, and it asks for a student's inventive imagination and creative writing. The two methods—both useful in different ways—are really complementary to each other, and for both of them it can be very helpful to re-frame the character's speeches *in your own words*, using the vocabulary and idiom of everyday parlance.

Suggestions

a) from 'outside' the character

B1 What impressions of Caius Martius do you take away from the first scene of *Coriolanus*? Are these modified by the subsequent action of the play?

B2 The 'many-headed multitude': comment on Shakespeare's presentation of the Roman citizens as individuals and as 'rabble'.

B3 Was the citizen correct who described Menenius Agrippa as 'one that hath always loved the people' (*1*, 1, 45–6)?

B4 Compare Martius, Cominius, and Lartius as soldiers and leaders of men.

B5 'His bloody brow? O Jupiter, no blood' (*1*, 3, 39): compare Virgilia and Volumnia in their love for Coriolanus.

B6 Describe the character and function of Valeria.

B7
> Know, good mother,
> I had rather be their servant in my way
> Than sway with them in theirs.

How does this remark affect your opinion of Caius Martius?

B8 Consider the opinions of the Capitol officers (*Act 2*, Scene 2). What is their contribution to the play?

b) from 'inside' the character.

B9 'What Rome needs now is . . . ' Write a manifesto for any one of the following:

a) Coriolanus
b) a Citizen
c) a Senator
d) Brutus/Sicinius.

B10 'How to bring up your boy': Volumnia gives Virgilia a lesson in child-rearing.

B11 After the victory over the Volsces, there are the letters: in *Act 2*, Scene 1 Volumnia has received one, Virgilia another, there's one at home for Menenius, and the senate has letters from the general. Perhaps even a common soldier has also managed to write a few lines to his family and friends. Compose some of these letters.

B12 Virgilia, described by Coriolanus as his 'gracious silence', has few words to speak—but perhaps she confides her thoughts and feelings in

i) her diary
ii) her letters to Coriolanus at the battlefront
iii) correspondence with her girlfriend
iv) poetry.

Compose any of these.

B13 Menenius, with a view to publication, writes his version of the events in Rome:

'UNADULTERATED! MEMOIRS OF A HUMOROUS
    PATRICIAN'
('one that loves a cup of hot wine with not a drop of allaying
    Tiber in't'.)

B14   It is held
That valour is the chiefest virtue, and
Most dignifies the haver.

In modern English, but in the manner of Cominius, write an encomium for Coriolanus or some other heroic character, past or present.

B15 'Our fight for democracy': Brutus and Sicinius write a history of early Rome.

B16 *He holds her by the hand, silent.* In the character of any one of those present (*Act 5*, Scene 3), articulate your thoughts in this timeless moment.

B17 'I Did It My Way': notes for an autobiography by Caius Martius Coriolanus (with introduction and final chapter written by *either* Volumnia *or* Tullus Aufidius).

B18 When their procession passes over the stage (*Act 5*, Scene 5), none of the Roman ladies has a single word to say: in the character of any one of them, express your thoughts and feelings at this time.

B19 'I am struck with sorrow' (5, 6, 148): Aufidius looks back on his relationship with his greatest rival.

B20 'he shall have a noble memory' (5, 6, 154): as any one of the characters in the play, write an obituary for Coriolanus.

C Activities

These can involve two or more students, preferably working *away from* the desk or study-table. They can help students to develop a sense of drama and the dramatic aspects of Shakespeare's play—which was written to be *performed*, not read!

C1 Act the play—or at least part of it! Read aloud the scenes of argument and debate, taking sides with the different factions. Express the thoughts of the characters in your own words.

C2 Experiment with different methods of staging the battle scenes between the Romans and the Volsces (*Act 1*, Scenes 4–10).

C3 'Foolhardiness!' (1, 5, 17). Create a scene in which the soldiers discuss their leader and their exploits when they were fighting—and looting—at Corioles.

C4 It can be both instructive and entertaining to transpose events and characters into the twentieth century, giving them the treatment they would receive today—full media coverage, with considerable debate about the principles and personalities involved and much speculation about the political manoeuvrings behind the scenes; research into the background, private as well as public; interviews with anybody of any importance—and even, sometimes, with those of no importance. As though they were happening in the modern world, present

   i) The hero's return (*Act 2*, Scenes 1 and 2)
   ii) Election special! Martius for Consul (*Act 2*, Scene 3)
  iii) Guilty or not guilty? The trial of Caius Martius (*Act 3*)
  iv) Changing sides: Volsces welcome Coriolanus (*Act 4*)
   v) Summit conference: a peace treaty (*Act 5*)

C5 Caius Martius has somehow attracted a large female following
in Rome:

  All tongues speak of him . . . Your prattling nurse
  Into a rapture lets her baby cry
  While she chats him; the kitchen malkin pins
  Her richest lockram 'bout her reechy neck,
  Clamb'ring the walls to eye him.   (2, 1, 204–9)

Devise one of these all-girl gossipings.

C6 'Do you two know how you are censured here in the city—
mean of us o'th' right-hand file?' (2, 1, 19–21). Invent a scene for
gathering of patricians—perhaps in one of their clubs—who discuss
the modern trend towards the democratization of Rome.

C7 The tribunes end most scenes with their comments: present
some of these endings, using modern English and the idioms of
today.

D Context Questions

In written examinations, these questions present you with short
passages from the play and ask you to explain them. They are
intended to test your knowledge of the play and your
understanding of its words. Usually you have to make a choice of
passages: there may be five on the paper, and you are asked to
choose three. Be very sure that you know exactly how many
passages you must choose. Study the ones offered to you, and
select those you feel most certain of. Make your answers accurate
and concise—don't waste time writing more than the examiner is
asking for.

D1 All tongues speak of him, and the blear'd sights
  Are spectacled to see him. Your prattling nurse
  Into a rapture lets her baby cry
  While she chats him; the kitchen malkin pins
  Her richest lockram 'bout her reechy neck
  Clamb'ring the walls to eye him.

(i) Two men are talking to each other: who are they?
(ii) What is the occasion they describe?
(iii) What is a 'kitchen malkin'?
(iv) What honour has been awarded to the man they refer to as 'him'?

D2   From face to foot
He was a thing of blood, whose every motion
Was tim'd with dying cries. Alone he enter'd
The mortal gate of th' city, which he painted
With shunless destiny, aidless came off,
And with a sudden reinforcement struck
——like a planet.

(i) Who is speaking and where does he make this speech?
(ii) What city does he refer to, and what has happened to it?
(iii) What is the occasion for this speech?
(iv) What happens next?

D3   You should have said
That as his worthy deeds did claim no less
Than what he stood for, so his gracious nature
Would think upon you for your voices and
Translate his malice towards you into love,
Standing your friendly lord.

(i) What is the position of the speaker?
(ii) Who is he talking about, and what has this man just done?
(iii) What has the man 'stood for', and has he received it?
(iv) Who are the listeners, and why are their 'voices' important?

D4   In that day's feats,
When he might act the woman in the scene,
He prov'd best man i'th' field, and for his meed
Was brow-bound with the oak.

(i) Who is the speaker, who is listening, and who is spoken of?
(ii) When was 'that day' and what was especially remarkable about the 'best man i'th' field'?
(iii) What battle has this man just fought, what name has been given to him?
(iv) What must he do next, and what does he hope to gain thereby?

E   Comprehension and Appreciation Questions

These also present passages from the play and ask questions about them; again you often have a choice of passages, but the extracts are much longer than those presented as context questions. A detailed knowledge of the language of the play is required here, and you must be able to express unusual or archaic phrases in your own words; you may also be expected to comment critically on the dramatic techniques of the passage and the poetic effectiveness of Shakespeare's language.

E1   **Menenius**

There was a time when all the body's members,
Rebell'd against the belly, thus accus'd it:
That only like a gulf it did remain
I'th' midst o'th' body, idle and unactive,
Still cupboarding the viand, never bearing   5
Like labour with the rest; where th'other instruments
Did see and hear, devise, instruct, walk, feel,
And, mutually participate, did minister
Unto the appetite and affection common
Of the whole body. The belly answer'd—   10

   First Citizen

Well, sir, what answer made the belly?

   Menenius

Sir, I shall tell you. With a kind of smile,
Which ne'er came from the lungs, but even thus—
For, look you, I may make the belly smile
As well as speak—it tauntingly replied   15
To th' discontented members, the mutinous parts
That envied his receipt; even so most fitly
As you malign our senators for that
They are not such as you.

   First Citizen

                        Your belly's answer—what?
The kingly, crowned head, the vigilant eye,   20
The counsellor heart, the arm our soldier,
Our steed the leg, the tongue our trumpeter,
With other muniments and petty helps
In this our fabric, if that they—

   Menenius

                        What then?

'Fore me, this fellow speaks! What then, what then?   25
   First Citizen
Should by the cormorant belly be restrain'd,
Who is the sink o'th' body—
   Menenius
                                Well, what then?
   First Citizen
The former agents, if they did complain,
What could the belly answer?
   Menenius
                            I will tell you,
If you'll bestow a small—of what you have little—   30
Patience a while, you'st hear the belly's answer.

(i) What is the meaning of '*gulf*' (line 3); '*receipt*' (line 17);
'*muniments*' (line 23); '*'Fore me*' (line 25); '*cormorant*'
(line 26)?

(ii) Express in your own words the meaning of lines 5–6, 'Still
cupboarding the viand . . . the rest'; lines 6–10, 'th' other
instruments . . . whole body'.

(iii) Comment on the dramatic qualities of this passage.

(iv) Discuss the image of the belly and its relevance to other
'body' imagery in the play.

E2   **Herald**
Know, Rome, that all alone Martius did fight
Within Corioles' gates, where he hath won
With fame a name to 'Martius Caius'; these
In honour follows 'Coriolanus'.
Welcome to Rome, renowned Coriolanus!   5

     A flourish sounds

   All
Welcome to Rome, renowned Coriolanus!
   Coriolanus
No more of this, it does offend my heart.
Pray now, no more.
   Cominius
                    Look, sir, your mother.
   Coriolanus
[*To* Volumnia] You have, I know, petition'd all the gods
For my prosperity!

He kneels

Volumnia
                         Nay, my good soldier, up,   10
My gentle Martius, worthy Caius,
And, by deed-achieving honour newly nam'd—
What is it?—'Coriolanus' must I call thee?

He rises

But O, thy wife!
          Coriolanus
                    My gracious silence, hail.
Wouldst thou have laugh'd had I come coffin'd home,   15
That weep'st to see me triumph? Ah, my dear,
Such eyes the widows in Corioles wear,
And mothers that lack sons.
          Menenius
                                        Now the gods crown thee!
          Coriolanus
And live you yet? [*To* Valeria] O my sweet lady, pardon.
          Volumnia
I know not where to turn. O, welcome home!   20
And welcome, general, and you're welcome all.
          Menenius
A hundred thousand welcomes! I could weep
And I could laugh, I am light and heavy. Welcome!
A curse begin at very root on's heart
That is not glad to see thee. You are three   25
That Rome should dote on. Yet, by the faith of men,
We have some old crab-trees here at home that will not
Be grafted to your relish. Yet welcome, warriors!
We call a nettle but a nettle, and
The faults of fools but folly.   30
          Cominius
Ever right.
          Coriolanus
Menenius, ever, ever.
          Herald
Give way there, and go on.

(i) What is the meaning of '*deed-achieving honour*' (line 12);
    '*coffin'd*' (line 15); '*heavy*' (line 23)?
(ii) Express in your own words the meaning of lines 27–8,
     'We have . . . relish'; lines 29–30, 'We call . . . folly'.

   (iii) What qualities of the different characters are shown in this passage?

   (iv) Comment on Shakespeare's dramatic verse as it is used in this passage.

F   Essays

These will usually give you a specific topic to discuss, or perhaps a question that must be answered, in writing, *with a reasoned argument*. They *never* want you to tell the story of the play—so don't! Your examiner—or teacher—has read the play, and does not need to be reminded of it. Relevant quotations will always help you to make your points more strongly.

F1 'The subject of *Coriolanus* is the ruin of a noble life through the sin of pride' (Edward Dowden, 1875). Is the play no more than this?

F2 'the drama begins in a way that makes us ask at once whether its author puts himself on the commoners' or the patricians' side' (Willard Farnham, 1950). What would be *your* answer?

F3 Is Menenius a diplomat or merely a hypocrite?

F4 'a brace of unmeriting, proud, violent, testy magistrates'. Do the tribunes deserve no further commendation?

F5 Has Menenius any grounds for saying of Coriolanus 'His nature is too noble for the world' (3, 1, 257)?

F6 'Could you not have told him As you were lesson'd' (2, 3, 173–4): comment on the tribunes' arts of persuasion.

F7 'Coriolanus has no *vision*: even the tribunes' delight in the peaceful city, although flawed by their spite, is beyond his appreciation.' Is this true?

F8 'Coriolanus represents the values that Rome holds most dear—and this is why he must die!' How just is this observation?

F9 'Perhaps, after all, Volumnia is the best politician!' Do you agree?

F10   Mine emulation
Hath not that honour in't it had.   (1, 11, 12–13)

This realization, early in the play, helped Aufidius to win through to the end: compare Aufidius the survivor with Coriolanus, the victim of his own honour.

G   Projects

In some schools, students are required to do more 'free-ranging' work, which takes them outside the text—but which should always be relevant to the play. Such Projects may demand skills other than reading and writing: design and artwork, for instance, may be involved. Sometimes a 'portfolio' of work is assembled over a considerable period of time; and this can be offered to the examiner for assessment.

The availability of resources will, obviously, do much to determine the nature of the Projects; but this is something that only the local teachers will understand. However, there is always help to be found in libraries, museums, and art galleries.

Suggested Subjects

G1 The city of Rome.
G2 Staging the play: set designs for *Coriolanus*.
G3 Costume designs for *Coriolanus*.
G4 The Roman matriarchs.
G5 The gods of Rome.
G6 Roman weaponry.

Background

England c. 1608

When Shakespeare was writing *Coriolanus*, many people still believed that the sun went round the earth. They were taught that this was a divinely ordered scheme of things, and that—in England—God had instituted a Church and ordained a Monarchy for the right government of the land and the populace.

'The past is a foreign country; they do things differently there.'

L. P. Hartley

Government

For most of Shakespeare's life, the reigning monarch of England was Queen Elizabeth I: when she died, she was succeeded by King James I. He was also king of Scotland (James VI), and the two kingdoms were united in 1603 by his accession to the English throne. With his counsellors and ministers, James governed the nation (population less than six million) from London, although fewer than half a million people inhabited the capital city. In the rest of the country, law and order were maintained by the land-owners and enforced by their deputies. The average man had no vote, and his wife had no rights at all.

Religion

At this time, England was a Christian country. All children were baptized, soon after they were born, into the Church of England; they were taught the essentials of the Christian faith, and instructed in their duty to God and to humankind. Marriages were performed, and funerals conducted, only by the licensed clergy and in accordance with the Church's rites and ceremonies. Attendance at divine service was compulsory; absences (without good—medical—reason) could be punished by fines. By such means, the authorities were able to keep some check on the populace—recording births, marriages, and deaths; being alert to any religious nonconformity, which could be politically dangerous; and ensuring a minimum of orthodox instruction through the official 'Homilies' which were regularly preached from the pulpits of all parish churches throughout the realm.

Following Henry VIII's break away from the Church of Rome, all people in England were able to hear the church services *in their own language*. The Book of Common Prayer was used in every church, and an English translation of the Bible was read aloud in public. The Christian religion had never been so well taught before!

Education

School education reinforced the Church's teaching. From the age of four, boys might attend the 'petty school' (French *'petite école'*) to learn the rudiments of reading and writing along with a few prayers; some schools also included work with numbers. At the age of seven, the boy was ready for the grammar school (if his father was willing and able to pay the fees).

Here, a thorough grounding in Latin grammar was followed by translation work and the study of Roman authors, paying attention as much to style as to matter. The arts of fine writing were thus inculcated from early youth. A very few students proceeded to university; these were either clever scholarship boys, or else the sons of noblemen. Girls stayed at home, and acquired domestic and social skills—cooking, sewing, perhaps even music. The lucky ones might learn to read and write.

Language

At the start of the sixteenth century the English had a very poor opinion of their own language: there was little serious writing in English, and hardly any literature. Latin was the language of international scholarship, and Englishmen admired the eloquence of the Romans. They made many translations, and in this way they extended the resources of their own language, increasing its vocabulary and stretching its grammatical structures. French, Italian, and Spanish works were also translated and, for the first time, there were English versions of the Bible. By the end of the century, English was a language to be proud of: it was rich in synonyms, capable of infinite variety and subtlety, and ready for all kinds of word-play—especially the *puns*, for which Elizabethan English is renowned.

Drama

The great art-form of the Elizabethan and Jacobean age was its drama. The Elizabethans inherited a tradition of play-acting from the Middle Ages, and they reinforced this by reading and translating the Roman playwrights. At the beginning of the sixteenth century plays were performed by groups of actors, all-male companies (boys acted the female roles) who travelled from town to town, setting up their stages in open places (such as inn-yards) or, with the permission of the owner, in the hall of some noble house. The touring companies continued in the provinces into the seventeenth century; but in London, in 1576, a new building was erected for the performance of plays. This was the Theatre, the first purpose-built playhouse in England. Other playhouses followed, (including the Globe, where most of Shakespeare's plays were performed), and the English drama reached new heights of eloquence.

There were those who disapproved, of course. The theatres, which brought large crowds together, could encourage the spread of disease—and dangerous ideas. During the summer, when the plague was at its worst, the playhouses were closed. A constant censorship was imposed, more or less severe at different times. The Puritan faction tried to close down the theatres, but—partly because there was royal favour for the drama, and partly because the buildings were outside the city limits—they did not succeed until 1642.

Theatre

From contemporary comments and sketches—most particularly a drawing by a Dutch visitor, Johannes de Witt—it is possible to form some idea of the typical Elizabethan playhouse for which most of Shakespeare's plays were written. Hexagonal in shape, it had three roofed galleries encircling an open courtyard. The plain, high stage projected into the yard, where it was surrounded by the audience of standing 'groundlings'. At the back were two doors for the actors' entrances and exits; and above these doors was a balcony—useful for a musicians' gallery or for the acting of scenes '*above*'. Over the stage was a thatched roof, supported on two pillars, forming a canopy—which seems to have been painted with the sun, moon, and stars for the 'heavens'.

Underneath was space (concealed by curtaining) which could be used by characters ascending and descending through a trapdoor in the stage. Costumes and properties were kept backstage, the 'tiring house'. The actors dressed lavishly, often wearing the secondhand clothes bestowed by rich patrons. Stage properties were important for defining a location, but the dramatist's own words were needed to explain the time of day, since all performances took place in the early afternoon.

A replica of Shakespeare's own theatre, the Globe, has been built in London, and stands in Southwark, almost exactly on the Bankside site of the original.

Further Reading

Editions:

Excellent introductions to *Coriolanus* are to be found in:

Brockbank, Philip (ed.), *Coriolanus* (Arden Shakespeare, London, 1976).
Hibbard, G. R. (ed.), *Coriolanus* (New Penguin Shakespeare, Harmondsworth, 1967).
Parker, R. B. (ed.), *Coriolanus* (Oxford Shakespeare, 1994).

Critical Works:

Adelman, Janet, *Suffocating Mothers: Fantasies of Maternal Origin in Shakespeare's Plays, 'Hamlet' to 'The Tempest'* (1992).
Barton, Anne, 'Livy, Machiavelli, and Shakespeare's *Coriolanus*', *Shakespeare Survey 38* (1985), 115–29.
Brockman, B. A. (ed.), *Shakespeare's 'Coriolanus': a Casebook* (Macmillan, 1977).
Brower, Reuben A., *Hero & Saint: Shakespeare and the Graeco-Roman Heroic Tradition* (Oxford, 1971).
Charney, M., *Shakespeare's Roman Plays: The Function of Imagery in the Drama* (1961).
Daniell, D., *'Coriolanus' in Europe* (1980).
Granville-Barker, Harley, *Prefaces to Shakespeare*, 5th series (London, 1947).
Leggatt, A., *Shakespeare's Political Drama: The History Plays and the Roman Plays* (London, 1988).
Palmer, J., *Political Characters of Shakespeare* (1945).
Patterson, A., *Shakespeare and the Popular Voice* (1989).
Spencer, T. J. B. (ed.), *Shakespeare's Plutarch* (1964).
Traversi, Derek, *Shakespeare: The Roman Plays* (London, 1963).

Sources:

Bullough, Geoffrey (ed.), *Narrative and Dramatic Sources Shakespeare*, vol. v (London, 1964).
Muir, Kenneth, *The Sources of Shakespeare's Plays* (London, 1977).

Additional background reading:

Bate, Jonathan, *The Genius of Shakespeare* (Picador [Macmillan 1997).
Blake, N. F., *Shakespeare's Language: an Introduction*, (London, 1983
Muir, K., and Schoenbaum, S., *A New Companion to Shakespea Studies*, (Cambridge, 1971).
Schoenbaum, S., *William Shakespeare: A Documentary Life*, (Oxfor 1975).
Thomson, Peter, *Shakespeare's Theatre*, (London, 1983).

William Shakespeare, 1564–1616

Elizabeth I was Queen of England when Shakespeare was born in 1564. He was the son of a tradesman who made and sold gloves in the small town of Stratford-upon-Avon, and he was educated at the grammar school in that town. Shakespeare did not go to university when he left school, but worked, perhaps, in his father's business. When he was eighteen he married Anne Hathaway, who became the mother of his daughter, Susanna, in 1583, and of twins in 1585.

There is nothing exciting, or even unusual, in this story; and from 1585 until 1592 there are no documents that can tell us anything at all about Shakespeare. But we have learned that in 1592 he was known in London, and that he had become both an actor and a playwright.

We do not know when Shakespeare wrote his first play, and indeed we are not sure of the order in which he wrote his works. If you look on page 169 at the list of his writings and their approximate dates, you will see how he started by writing plays on subjects taken from the history of England. No doubt this was partly because he was always an intensely patriotic man—but he was also a very shrewd business-man. He could see that the theatre audiences enjoyed being shown their own history, and it was certain that he would make a profit from this kind of drama.

The plays in the next group are mainly comedies, with romantic love-stories of young people who fall in love with one another, and at the end of the play marry and live happily ever after.

At the end of the sixteenth century the happiness disappears, and Shakespeare's plays become melancholy, bitter, and tragic. This change may have been caused by some sadness in the writer's life (one of his twins died in 1596). Shakespeare, however, was not the only writer whose works at this time were very serious. The whole of England was facing a crisis. Queen Elizabeth I was growing old. She was greatly loved, and the people were sad to think she must soon die; they were also afraid, for the queen had never married, and so there was no child to succeed her.

When James I came to the throne in 1603, Shakespeare continued to write serious drama—the great tragedies and the plays based on Roman history (such as *Coriolanus*) for which he is most famous. Finally, before he retired from the theatre, he wrote another set of comedies. These all have the same theme: they tell of happiness which is lost, and then found again.

Shakespeare returned from London to Stratford, his home town. He was rich and successful, and he owned one of the biggest houses in the town. He died in 1616.

Shakespeare also wrote two long poems, and a collection of sonnets. The sonnets describe two love-affairs, but we do not know who the lovers were. Although there are many public documents concerned with his career as a writer and a business-man, Shakespeare has hidden his personal life from us. A nineteenth-century poet, Matthew Arnold, addressed Shakespeare in a poem, and wrote 'We ask and ask—Thou smilest, and art still'.

There is not even a trustworthy portrait of the world's greatest dramatist.

Approximate order of composition of Shakespeare's works

Period	Comedies	History plays	Tragedies	Poems
I	Comedy of Errors	Henry VI, part 1	Titus Andronicus	
	Taming of the Shrew	Henry VI, part 2		
	Two Gentlemen of Verona	Henry VI, part 3		
1594		Richard III		Venus and Adonis
	Love's Labour's Lost	King John		Rape of Lucrece
II	Midsummer Night's Dream	Richard II	Romeo and Juliet	Sonnets
	Merchant of Venice	Henry IV, part 1		
1599	Merry Wives of Windsor	Henry IV, part 2		
	Much Ado About Nothing			
	As You Like It	Henry V		
III	Twelfth Night		Julius Caesar	
	Troilus and Cressida		Hamlet	
1608	Measure for Measure		Othello	
	All's Well That Ends Well		Timon of Athens	
			King Lear	
			Macbeth	
			Antony and Cleopatra	
			Coriolanus	
IV	Pericles			
	Cymbeline			
1613	The Winter's Tale	Henry VIII		
	The Tempest